'So, they suppose frankly. 'They are shocks them that w married.'

'I'm here becaus here with you beca him!' Charlotte pro

'You don't need Lucien,' Marc said quietly. 'Not any more.' He ran his fingers lightly down her cheek and rested them on the pulse that beat nervously in her throat. Then they continued their downward journey across her neck and shoulder, tracing the soft contour of her breast. His touch, sensitive and warm through the thin cotton of the nightgown, aroused strange stirrings within her. He was aware of that too, and smiled slightly.

'Forget him, Charlotte,' he whispered. 'He's a ghost in the past. We all have such ghosts in our pasts. Leave them there, where they belong.'

Ann Hulme was born in Portsmouth and educated at the Royal Holloway College—part of the University of London—where she took a degree in French. She has travelled extensively, and it was the fascination of the various countries in which she made her home—France, Germany, Czechoslovakia, Yugoslavia and Zambia—which made her begin to write. She now lives in Bicester, Oxfordshire, with her husband and two sons.

A Woman of the Regiment is her sixth Masquerade Historical Romance.

A WOMAN OF
THE REGIMENT

ANN HULME

MILLS & BOON LIMITED
15–16 BROOK'S MEWS
LONDON W1A 1DR

First published in Great Britain 1985
by Mills & Boon Limited

© Ann Hulme 1985

Australian copyright 1985
Philippine copyright 1985
This edition 1985
ISBN 0 263 75105 8

Set in 10 on 10½pt. Linotron Times
04–0785–70,600

Photoset by Rowland Phototypesetting Ltd
Bury St Edmunds, Suffolk
Made and printed in Great Britain by
Cox & Wyman Ltd, Reading

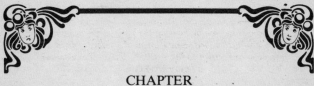

CHAPTER
ONE

'IT's NOT that I don't want us to be married, but we can't
be married *now*!'

The young man turned from the window and gestured
widely with his arm to accompany his words, as if to
sweep away Charlotte's protestations. The pale Decem-
ber light from the open window fell on the blue and red
of his jacket, which marked its owner as an artilleryman,
and sparkled on the gold of the epaulettes. It struck
echoing golden streaks in his cropped fair hair, and
emphasised his youthful, attractive features, which were
marred only by a weak and slightly petulant mouth.

The pretty, slender girl with the abundant ash-blonde
curls sighed, but an obstinate expression had crossed her
face, which he could not fail to notice, and a slightly
apprehensive look entered his own eyes.

'Come, cousin Charlotte, be reasonable,' he pleaded.

'But you promised,' Charlotte burst out, gold flecks
sparkling dangerously in her grey-green eyes. 'You always said, Lucien, we should be married, and last time
you were here you said that for sure we should be
married the next time you came!'

'The last time I was here was more than two years ago,
Charlotte,' he returned patiently, 'and a great deal has
happened since then. Dearest cousin, France is at war!'

Charlotte looked despondently at her adored older
cousin. As a little boy, he had spoken of nothing else but
his ambition to be a soldier, always including the promise, 'But I'll come back and marry you, Charlotte, I
swear, my word of honour as a Saint-Laurent!'

And here he was, resplendent in his artillery uniform,

still promising to marry her—some day. But she was growing tired of promises. She was eighteen, and he visited them so rarely nowadays that there was no telling when he would come again. She was afraid to let him go, haunted by a fear that some malevolent fate would prevent his return.

'I only want us to be together, Lucien,' she protested, leaning her head against his chest. The ornate braiding was rough to the touch. 'When you are away, I imagine such disasters. I couldn't bear it if anything happened to you. When Papa's friends call here, they reminisce about the army and I can hardly bear to listen to some of the tales they tell.'

Lucien's demeanour had gained in confidence as his cousin's spirits visibly sank. He tipped up her chin with his index finger and said complacently, 'What's going to happen to *me*? I've a lucky star. Bullets fly all around me, and none of them comes near! Besides, I can take care of myself pretty well.' Satisfaction echoed in his voice.

'It is so much harder for me,' Charlotte said in frustration, 'because I am left behind, not *knowing*. I wish I could go with you.'

He laughed. 'You were always a tomboy. But you wouldn't like it in reality, believe me! Besides, my uncle needs you here.' His tone grew sober.

She nodded. 'Papa is dying. He knows it, I know it, and you know it. But no one speaks of it. When he is gone—and I must face the fact that he will be gone soon—then I shall have nothing and no one but you, Lucien.'

He was silent for a moment, then said awkwardly, 'You know I *am* devoted to you, Charlotte.'

'Yes, I know,' Charlotte answered simply. She was devoted to him, so it followed he must be to her. But he was clearly troubled. 'What is it?' she asked.

'Nothing.' He bit his lip. 'Charlotte, you mustn't worry about me. Think now only about your father. We'll trounce the Austrians, and I'll be back before you hardly know I've gone!' He smiled at her, but the smile was not reflected in his eyes.

'And we shall be married? Truly, Lucien?' Charlotte persisted.

The young man hesitated almost imperceptibly, then said hastily, 'Yes, of course!'

'I wish you would let me tell Papa about us,' Charlotte told him wistfully. 'I know it would make him so happy. He's so fond of you, Lucien, and you are also Mama's nephew. You know how much *family* matters to Papa. Why won't you let me tell him? I *know* he would approve our marriage.'

'No!' His tone was almost sharp, and Charlotte looked up questioningly. 'Trust me, Charlotte,' he added cajolingly. 'Please, I beg you.'

'But of course I trust you.'

'Then listen to me, my dear. Listen carefully.' He put his arm about her shoulders and led her to the sofa, where they sat down, and he leaned towards her earnestly. 'You know how much I admire my uncle . . . and how much I want to marry you. But your father is very sick, Charlotte. How could we trouble him now with such an important decision? It would be quite wrong. He would start to be fussing about the details, lawyers and contracts and dowry, and a dozen other things! You know what a stickler he is for "doing things correctly"!'

'Yes, I do,' Charlotte admitted reluctantly. 'But supposing we married very quietly, without all that, and told him afterwards? He'd be a little angry, but I'm sure he'd understand.'

'Well, I don't think he would,' Lucien said sullenly. 'These old fellows can be damn difficult. He's been grumbling at me since yesterday because of—of something which isn't at all important. Look, Charlotte, how could we possibly get married, just for me to leave immediately, and be gone for maybe months!'

'It's better than not being married at all,' argued Charlotte.

'We can't get *married*, Charlotte!' For a moment he almost sounded angry. 'I keep trying to explain it to you, and you just won't understand!' Seeing her look at him in amazement, he went on hastily in his former coaxing tone, 'Be reasonable, Charlotte. You do see I'm right, don't you?'

'You *do* love me, Lucien?' Charlotte asked, her eyes fixed frankly on his face.

'Of course I do! I swear I do! You know I love you! When this present campaign is over, I'll come back and we'll sort out everything.'

He looked at her anxiously, and Charlotte, feeling that she would believe anything Lucien told her, because he was so sincere and so open, nodded.

He smiled, betraying his relief. 'In the meantime, pretty cousin, I leave my poor soldier's heart in your keeping, knowing that you will treat it well.' He kissed her fingers elegantly. 'And you'll say nothing to my uncle, eh? This shall be our secret, between the two of us. Let me hear you promise?'

'I love you, Lucien,' Charlotte said quietly. 'I'll wait for you—for years, if need be. And if ever I heard that you were a prisoner, or wounded, I'd come to that place, wherever it was. I'd climb mountains and ford rivers to find you!'

The young man was silent, and looked away from her enthusiastic face with its frame of blonde curls. 'There *is* no one like you, Charlotte, for me,' he muttered awkwardly, a deep flush darkening his face. 'There never has been anyone like you. I wish . . .' He broke off, and leaning urgently towards her, burst out, 'I swear it, Charlotte, I do mean it! Whatever—Whatever happens, remember that!'

'How can I forget?' Charlotte demanded, scrubbing away the tears which obstinately spilled down her cheeks, despite her efforts to contain them. 'I shall pray for you every single night, Lucien, and wait for your letters.'

'I shall write, never fear!' he promised optimistically,

squeezing her hand reassuringly. 'I'll tell you everything I do. But now, dearest cousin, I really must be off. It would never do if the regiment were to move out without *me*!'

He kissed her hastily. His sword lay propped against a chair, and he seized it and buckled it on with rapid efficiency. 'A smile!' he commanded, looking up. 'I want a smile from you as I leave. I want no sad faces at the window.'

'I promise,' Charlotte said, thinking, 'If I could only follow . . .'

She listened to the urgent tap of his heels descending the main staircase, and the jingle of his spurs. Then, pushing the window open wide, she leaned out across the wrought-iron *garde-fou*. Below her, in the courtyard, guarded by bare winter trees, the groom held Lucien's horse. She saw the young officer come out of the house with a quick, confident step and swing himself into the saddle. He glanced up and saw her at the window, and, smiling, saluted her, a dashing figure in a fine uniform imprinting his image on her memory. Even from that distance his debonair charm was obvious. He looked a personification of youth and vitality and adventure, riding with all the confidence of his years towards a future of combat and glory.

Charlotte felt a pang of something almost akin to resentment, or perhaps even jealousy. He had scarcely expressed regret at their parting, and looked almost eager to be away now, to rejoin the life he had chosen. Even, perhaps, to be free of her clinging embraces and protestations of love.

'What foolishness!' Charlotte told herself sternly. 'Do you expect him to strike his brow like the hero of a three-volume novel? He is a soldier, and knows his duty, and you, my girl, are a soldier's daughter, and ought to know yours!'

She waved her hand enthusiastically and forced herself to smile down brightly at him.

The gates were dragged open and Lucien rode

through, out into the narrow street and, with a last carefree salute of his hand, was lost from her view.

The girl at the window sighed and went back slowly into the room, trying to recall how it had been moments before, when he had still been there, with her. He had stood here, just here, where the carpet showed a faint indentation from his heels pressing on the pile. But no more than a ghost remained behind. The reality had gone. Charlotte sat down and leaned back, closing her eyes, letting her mind drift back over their brief time together.

She had always lived in Châlons-sur-Marne. All her life had been spent here, in this large, old, rambling comfortable house, with its Renaissance gables and huge stone fireplaces. The ancient wood panelling on the stairwell, blackened with age, creaked and groaned at night, as if the portraits of long-dead Lacostes which lined the walls whispered to each other from their dusty frames.

They were military men. Every son of the Lacoste family had entered the army and the service of the king of France. But now everything was different. It was the winter of 1799. France was a republic. The young Napoleon Bonaparte, the nation's hero, was about to have himself elected First Consul, the master of France's fortunes. The army forged in revolution and civil conflict had come quickly of age, and already won its own battle-honours. For France was at war. She fought the British and, in Italy, the Austrians.

It was to fight these last that a new Army of Reserve was hastily being raised, and a part of it had been garrisoned here at Châlons. It had brought Lucien back to them, seconded from his own regiment to this new force.

The last male of the Lacoste line was Charlotte's father, a retired colonel of Royalist allegiance who had languished in the prisons of the Terror, and now lay bedridden upstairs, a prisoner again, but in his own house. A courtesy the Republic had graciously accorded him, as he himself wryly expressed it.

Charlotte was an only child and, growing up motherless, might have been lonely. But the little girl had been petted and indulged by the servants, and spoiled by a doting father. His friends, elderly gentlemen of military mien, had always treated her as a favourite niece, praising everything she did and said. So Charlotte had grown up, but just as her body told her she was no longer a child, so she had become aware of an inner restlessness, an emptiness, which only a different kind of loving could assuage.

There had never been a moment's doubt who should be the object of this passion. It had always been Lucien. Lucien would come back and marry her, as he had promised. She had waited with growing impatience. She had never even considered the possibility of another person taking a part in her life. In any case she knew nobody else, certainly no men, except those kindly elderly gentlemen who pinched her cheek and said, 'Upon my word, my dear, I wish I were forty years younger!'

Once she had overheard a snatch of conversation between one of these and her father.

'Your daughter grows a beauty, Charles. You will have to watch out. France today is full of rogues!'

'I know it,' her father had said with a sigh. 'But I fear Charlotte doesn't. She has the innocence of a child, trusting everyone!'

Charlotte had longed to rush in and tell them it didn't matter, that they shouldn't worry, because she was going to marry Lucien and he would take care of her.

A dull thud above Charlotte's head roused her. Others followed in rapid succession. Colonel Lacoste was summoning his daughter to his bedside.

'Well?' he demanded as she entered. 'Has young Saint-Laurent gone?' He released the walking-stick with which he had hammered on the parquet.

'Yes, Papa.' Charlotte went to perch on the end of his bed.

'Let us hope he distinguishes himself!' he said gruffly. 'He will have his opportunity to do so very soon—if General Bonaparte, as our illustrious First Consul, has anything to do with it! Pah! Glory-seekers, all of them—rabble! One hopes Saint-Laurent remembers that he at least is a gentleman, and does not sully an ancient name!'

'I only hope he comes to no harm!' Charlotte whispered to herself.

Colonel Lacoste's hearing was sharp. He eyed his daughter thoughtfully from the pillows, and then sighed. 'You are very like your Mama, dear child.'

Charlotte's gaze wandered to the portrait of her mother, which hung by the bed. She supposed she did look like that, allowing for the changing fashions. Charlotte's ash-blonde hair tumbled in loose curls, whereas her mother's had been pomaded and powdered in the style of long-lost days. The young woman in the portrait wore a stiffly corseted gown, and Charlotte the loose, high-waisted draperies which reflected the new liberty in every facet of life in France. A liberty which had turned to a nightmare during the years of the Terror.

'My one wish,' Colonel Lacoste now said sadly, 'is that I could have seen you married. But I fear, my dear, I shall not be spared to see you a bride.' He glanced at her. 'You will be left quite alone, Charlotte, when I am gone.'

'You must not worry about me, Papa,' Charlotte reassured him, a lump in her throat.

'Of course I must worry about you!' he retorted testily. 'I would have liked to have seen you at least engaged, before I died. Indeed, now that Saint-Laurent has left us, I will confess to you that at one time I entertained a hope that you would make a match of it with your cousin.'

Charlotte looked up, her heart leaping painfully in her breast. Remembering Lucien's strictures, she stammered, 'If that—if that were so—if I were to marry

Lucien, you would be pleased, Papa? You would approve?'

'Ah!' he snorted. 'I said "at one time"! I did not say I wished it now.'

'But—why?' Charlotte faltered, feeling a cold dismay creeping over her. 'What has changed your mind? Is it because he has to go away?'

Her father shifted on the pillows as if he were uncomfortable, and automatically Charlotte reached out to help him.

He looked up at her as she bent over him. 'You are young, Charlotte,' he said gently. 'The accursed Revolution and all the sorry events which followed have meant that you have not had the kind of life your dear late mother and I would have anticipated. No parties, no balls, no young friends of your own kind . . . You've sat here at home and fretted over me. It was wrong, wrong . . .'

'It could not be helped, Papa, I want to look after you. Besides, what need should I have of parties and silly girl-friends with no thoughts in their heads but which dress to wear?'

He chuckled and patted her hand. 'Well, perhaps some things have been for the better! Nevertheless, it is not what I wished for you.' He grew serious again. 'Saint-Laurent is a fine enough young fellow. I don't doubt women find him handsome, charming . . .'

Charlotte flushed.

'But a young man needs time to sow his wild oats, settle himself. I have had reports from military acquaintances about my nephew. Well, their import need not concern you, Charlotte, but the boy has been wild. Gaming debts! I spoke to him of them while he was here, and he assured me—gave me his word, which I am obliged to take—that all his debts had been settled. But how? That's what I want to know! He has no money of his own. It was all lost, thanks to the Jacobins. I pressed him for details, but he would not tell me. He was evasive. Frankly, he had a guilty look about him, which I can hardly say I liked! I am the boy's godfather, as well as his uncle by marriage. He should have been open with me. He has kept bad company, these ruffianly Republican officers who have sprung from God knows where! I fear it has harmed him.'

'But, Papa, you are unjust!' Charlotte cried out, despite herself, unable to bear hearing the man she loved criticised. 'Forgive me, I must object. If Lucien were here to defend himself, I would say nothing. But he isn't, and I must speak for him!'

'Must you, indeed, mademoiselle? And why, pray, should *you* be his advocate?' Her father's eyes bored into hers with a look which had once reduced many a bold recruit to ashen-faced confusion.

Charlotte drew a deep breath, and in a voice which trembled despite her resolve, said, 'Papa, I must tell you that Lucien and I *do* hope to be married some day.'

'*What?*' Colonel Lacoste struggled to a sitting position. 'What's this? Saint-Laurent said nothing to *me* of this!'

'No, Papa, we did not wish to worry you, you see. Lucien is very fond of you, Papa, and respects you very much. He felt that as he had to leave, and there was no time to arrange matters, we should not tell you yet.'

The colonel's expression had grown choleric. 'He should have spoken to me! He had no right to speak to you of marriage without my permission, and *you*, Charlotte, had no right to engage your affections, even with Saint-Laurent, without consulting me first!'

Seeing that her father was becoming quite agitated, Charlotte hastened to soothe him. 'Lucien acted for the best, Papa! You should know he would not do otherwise.'

'And since when do young people know what is best, know it better than their elders, who have experience of this world? It is all the result of the Revolution! Every man, and every young girl, too, it seems, may think for himself and needs no advice from those older and wiser!'

'Papa, you exaggerate! Of course we respect you! But we would never have dreamed you would object! Lucien's family is as good as ours; he is Mama's own nephew! I know he has no money, but no one now has money! He has his army pay.'

'His army pay! Dear heaven! The girl imagines they may live on *that*, and what little I may leave!'

'Papa, you must not distress yourself so!' Charlotte insisted. 'You must rest. Let me pour out a little of your medicine.'

'Filthy stuff!' muttered her father. But he seemed tired now, and fell back on the pillows, his energy spent. 'Should have spoken to me,' he mumbled fitfully. 'Not right. Not the proper thing.'

Charlotte sat with him for a little while, until she saw that he had fallen asleep, and then softly left the room.

The days passed, unbearable to Charlotte impatiently awaiting the promised letter. Colonel Lacoste's strength failed him. Already people spoke in whispers and drew the curtains, as if the cold hand of death already lay upon the house. But from Lucien came not even a scribbled note to say he was well. Charlotte's impatience turned first to annoyance, but then she became desperately worried at the lack of news.

She was sure in her heart that something had happened to him. Something dreadful which prevented his writing. He had been arrested, perhaps. Things were much quieter now in France. The arbitrary arrests and disappearances of the Terror had ceased, but were not forgotten. Or possibly he had met with some accident, or some fever had struck him down. Soldiers died like flies in camp from every kind of fever, from cholera to the measles—Charlotte knew that much. Her father had once told her how, very often, a general might lose more men through such sicknesses than in battle.

At the end of January 1800, Colonel Lacoste died. They had not spoken of Lucien again. Her father's mind had wandered at the end, and she had not wished to raise a question which could only distress him, and which could no longer be discussed with him.

It rained on the day of the funeral. Charlotte came home, damp and cold, to an empty, shuttered house and a wretched, desolate and lonely existence, without her father, and still without news from Lucien.

January passed into February, and February into March. Charlotte could bear it no longer. In April, Pascal the coachman was ordered to harness the horses to the creaking old-fashioned carriage, and set off on a journey to take his young mistress to Paris, to the Ministry of War.

There Charlotte underwent one brief, humiliating, and frustrating interview. She would never forget the official who received her, a tall, thin, pallid fellow with the mark of consumption on his sickly features.

'You are a member of Captain Saint-Laurent's *immediate* family, Citizeness Lacoste?' he asked, seated amid his stacks of files. A fly, awakened by the first pale sun of early spring, buzzed fitfully on top of one yellowed folder. He swatted it dispassionately.

'Not exactly, but I am his cous—' she began, but was not allowed to finish.

'Either you are, or you are not!' the official interrupted testily. He brushed the fly's squashed remains on to the unswept floor. 'In any case, you cannot expect the Ministry of War to reveal the movements of its troops to young women who simply walk in off the street and, with smiles and fluttering eyelashes, persuade the clerks to allow them *this* far!'

'I did no such thing! How dare you?' Charlotte cried angrily. 'I explained my situation . . .'

'Your situation is no concern of the Ministry of War, Citizeness!' the official snapped.

He paused, overcome by a paroxysm of coughing which set bright spots of red glowing on his pale cheekbones, and spat into a soiled linen handkerchief.

'You are wasting my time, young woman! What is more, your behaviour is thoroughly unpatriotic! France is at war! The British and the Austrians have infiltrated their spies into every corner of French society. How do I know you are what you say you are?'

'But this is nonsense,' she argued. 'You've seen my papers.'

'I have. And I know you to be the daughter of one Lacoste, formerly a colonel of the *maison du roi*, and no doubt having many links with Royalist emigrés in England and Austria!'

'But I haven't!' Charlotte protested. 'And my father is dead.'

'Because of that, and because of your extreme youth, Citizeness Lacoste,' the official said tersely, 'I propose to allow you to leave. I shall not pursue the matter further. Now kindly leave my office and don't bother me any more!' He took up his quill pen.

'But I only want . . .' she began again despairingly.

'This interview is at an end, Citizeness!' the man said curtly, and when she stood her ground obstinately, he threw down his pen with an expression of annoyance, got up from his desk, took Charlotte roughly by the elbow and bundled her unceremoniously through the door.

In the anteroom, another woman was waiting. She turned as Charlotte made her precipitous exit.

The official exclaimed, 'Ah!', and thrust Charlotte inelegantly aside in order to hasten towards the new arrival. 'My dear Madame Thierry! What a pleasure! Of course he will see *you*. Allow me to conduct you.'

He bowed obsequiously and led the way down a corridor. Before following him, the woman glanced idly at Charlotte. She was a very handsome woman of perhaps five and thirty, her beauty a little overblown now, a plumpness about the chin and a few faint lines marking the carefully-tended ivory skin. She had fine dark eyes which seemed to glitter as if they held secrets, and was dressed very fashionably. Her bonnet had a long, projecting brim, and her velvet pelisse was trimmed with fur. The fine eyes assessed Charlotte briefly

before their owner followed the clerk, moving with a
sinuous, inviting grace, swaying her hips.

'Well!' thought Charlotte rebelliously. 'So fluttering
one's eyelids does gain entry here!'

The woman had said something to the official, and his
grating voice drifted back down the corridor.

'Oh, nobody, *chère madame*. A little thing from the
provinces, asking after her lover. These girls besiege this
office. One would think we were in the business of
matchmaking!'

'You don't bring people together, you keep them
apart!' called Charlotte angrily, and the other two
turned and stared at her. The official looked outraged,
the woman amused. Charlotte stalked away with
dignity.

'A complete waste of time!' Charlotte told herself fiercely on her return to Châlons. 'If I'm to learn anything, I'll
have to seek out the information for myself. One cannot
rely on others.'

She seated herself at her father's old desk, and spread
her household accounts out carefully before her. She
and her father had lived frugally, occupying only a suite
of rooms in a house otherwise closed up and shuttered.
Of course, their income was no longer that which earlier
Lacostes would have considered adequate for a gentleman and his family. But Colonel Lacoste, mindful of his
failing health, had carefully set aside small sums
whenever possible to ensure his daughter's future. He
had left her in possession of a respectable income, and
if—Charlotte made rapid calculations on a scrap of
paper, blessing her unfeminine aptitude for arithmetic—
if she realised the few assets they had left, it would be
enough for what she planned. It was risky, of course.
Charlotte chewed the end of her pencil. Well, she would
certainly end up much the poorer, whatever the out-
come of her project. But it could be done, and that was
all that mattered.

She rang the bell, and when the servant appeared,

ordered that Pascal come up immediately. The coach-man entered the room in his stockinged feet, having left his boots outside the back door for fear of bringing stable-yard dirt into the house. He stood unhappily on the parquet, curling and uncurling his toes, and breathing noisily.

'Pascal,' Charlotte said firmly. 'We know the Army of Reserve is on its way to Italy, don't we?'

'Everyone knows that,' the man agreed, twisting his hat in his hands. He suddenly became aware of the grimy condition of his fingernails, and put his stubby hands quickly behind his back.

'A whole army can't move without people *knowing*. So to follow it ought not to be difficult?'

Pascal rolled a bloodshot eye suspiciously at his young employer. 'True enough, mam'zelle. Generally it strips the country bare, and leaves a load of unpaid bills behind it.'

'So that's settled,' she said serenely. 'That's what we'll do. You and I, Pascal, will follow the Army of Reserve and find out for ourselves what's happened to Captain Saint-Laurent.'

'And maybe that's not all we'd find!' Pascal objected. '*Mon Dieu*, mam'zelle, have you any idea what an army on the move is like? It's a rough life, and you'd very likely find yourself in some strange company. There's other things, too, mam'zelle, that I hardly like to speak to you of, you being a young lady and not knowing about such things. How can I put it? Some of those fellows— Well, they're not all gentlemen, not by a long way!' Pascal added with grim feeling. 'Not even the officers!'

'My mind is made up!' Charlotte told him. 'So make the carriage ready, Pascal. As for what you say, I should hope that any French officer would respect someone on such an errand as mine, and behave *honourably*.'

'Some of them,' Pascal retorted dourly, 'respect neither God, man nor hellfire. And this isn't the old army, the one your father served in and I did, too. These modern fellows, they're spawn of the Revolution.

Honour?' he snorted. 'They honour nothing, neither their own word, nor a woman's reputation!'

He broke off, conscious of having said too much and withdrew in red-faced embarrassment.

But Charlotte hardly heard him. She had sat down with pencil and paper to plan the greatest adventure of her life. Yet even she could not have guessed just how great an adventure it would prove, or what would lie at the end of it.

CHAPTER
TWO

LIKE THE flood-waters breaching a dike wall, the Army
of Reserve rolled inexorably down the length of France
in the early spring of 1800. Its progress, like the flood,
was disorderly and destructive, here clogged, here spill-
ing freely onwards, encumbered by a flotsam of followers. Women, wives and mistresses, *vivandières* and
bawds, together with their children, and the grooms and
servants of the officers, all scrambled pell-mell after the
trudging infantry, eddied and whirled around the hooves
of the horses, and narrowly failed to be sucked beneath
the wheels of the guns.

At the tail of this dishevelled and seemingly chaotic
horde, progressing with agonising slowness and a dogged
tenacity towards its Italian goal, came Charlotte, driven
by Pascal. At every halt, Charlotte sought out the senior
officer and repeated her query. Sometimes she was
received with kindliness, sometimes with hostility, often
with impatience and frequently with suspicion.

While she persevered, Pascal pursued the same quest
among the liquor-tents of the *vivandières* and (although
he took care not to tell his employer this), the business-
places of the bawds. But when the two of them com-
pared notes at the end of the day, the results were always
the same. Lucien Saint-Laurent proved as elusive as the
Philosopher's Stone.

Such a one had heard of him. Another had seen him,
for sure, a month earlier. Yet another declared he had
been re-posted to the army beyond the Rhine. At
length, when they had reached Lausanne, and Charlotte
was near despair, they were given a name.

'*Forestier* . . .' said their informant. 'He's an artillery-man, Captain Marc Forestier. He moved out from here to Villeneuve yesterday, and if you hurry, you'll catch up with him. He was always a good friend of Saint-Laurent, and will know for sure where he's to be found now. Ask in Villeneuve for him. They'll direct you to him.' The speaker seemed to hesitate before adding enigmatically, 'He's not a man anyone forgets in a hurry! Captain Forestier . . .'

So here they were in this little Swiss town where the advancing flood had come temporarily to rest, dammed for the moment by the great natural barrage of the Alps, rising ominous and forbidding above them with a terrifying beauty. It was May, too early for the mountain snows to have melted. Charlotte could see how the sun glittered up there on the cold blue ice of the glaciers, and how the cruel wind, on the slopes leading to the Great St Bernard Pass, snatched up handfuls of the crisp white blanket and hurled them up into the clear air, darkening it with sudden storms in the way the country people called 'Mother Frost shaking her feather-bed'.

Despite their informant's optimism, they searched until nightfall for Forestier, before someone pointed out to them an inn at the far end of the main street. Early dusk had necessitated the lighting of lanterns, and the little community hummed with activity. Charlotte and Pascal, sheltering beneath the steep overhanging eaves of an Alpine hut, took counsel together as they watched the stream of disorderly soldiery swarm up and down the street.

'I'll come with you, mam'zelle,' said Pascal gruffly, interposing his burly form between the slight figure of his companion and the passers-by. 'You can't go over there alone, not among all this riff-raff!' He grunted in disgust.

'You must stay here, Pascal,' Charlotte answered firmly. 'You must not leave the carriage unattended—We should return to find it stripped bare! It'll be all right. It shouldn't take me long to find the man, if he's there.'

A slight uncertainty accompanied these last few words, as weariness overtook her.

'Monsieur your father wouldn't have approved of this,' he growled obstinately. 'This is no place for a lady, and that's a fact. You don't even know what kind of fellow he is we're seeking. Very likely he's a ruffian like the rest. If you ask me, we've been brought on a fool's errand.'

'I don't ask you, Pascal!' Charlotte retorted sharply. 'So don't argue, and do as I say!'

She pulled the hood of her cloak over her head and set off purposefully, threading her way determinedly through the throng and watched unhappily by Pascal. On a patch of muddy ground she stumbled and slipped, and put out a hand to save herself by bracing her arm against one of the eight-pounders which had been drawn up and, covered by a tarpaulin, abandoned for the night by its attendant gunners. A little further down the street could be seen the lights of her destination, from which echoed raucous laughter and shouting. Charlotte bit her lip nervously. Then she pulled the woollen cloak more closely round her, and struggled on to reach the hostelry.

As she approached the door, it suddenly burst open and yet another group of unshaven gunners in ragged uniforms was deposited onto the muddy pavement. With them came the odours of tobacco-smoke and frying from within.

'Where to, then, my pretty?' demanded one with drunken gallantry, catching at Charlotte's arm as she rashly attempted to squeeze past him and through the doorway before it swung closed.

'Let go of me!' she retaliated fiercely, trying to wrench her arm free. The hood of her cloak fell back to reveal her ringlets clustered about her pale, heart-shaped face.

'Don't take fright, *ma petite*!' the man chuckled. 'See here, I've got money, too, you know. No need to seek your custom in there!'

He jerked his head towards the noisy inn behind them, and his companions laughed.

'You are insolent,' Charlotte's tone was icy, 'and you are badly mistaken. I'm looking for a Captain Forestier. My business is with him.'

'Oh, officers only, is it?' he retorted sarcastically.

'Let her go,' advised one of his companions. 'You can see she's different from the others. If she's the Captain's woman, he won't thank you for setting your sights on her. Let her go. She'll bring you trouble!'

Charlotte's admirer shrugged and, to her great relief, released his grip on her arm. 'Your Captain Forestier's in there; you'll find him over in the far corner, eating his dinner!' he informed her gruffly.

'Thank you,' said Charlotte stiffly.

The gunners stumbled away unsteadily through the slush, and she pushed open the inn door and entered the stuffy, noisy, overcrowded interior. It was almost impossible to make out individuals among the throng. Every nook and cranny seemed crammed with French uniforms, and a thick pall of smoke from clay-pipes and guttering candles hung over it all, stinging her eyes and making them water. There was an overpowering smell of wet clothing drying in the warmth, of beer, sweat, tobacco and unwashed human bodies. Through it all, the innkeeper and his minions struggled with tankards of beer and plates of sausage, each attempting to serve a dozen customers all at once, all of whom loudly demanded instant attention.

No one took any notice of Charlotte, who coughed helplessly as the thick atmosphere invaded her nose and lungs. After a few minutes she managed to regain some composure and become accustomed to the air. She was now also aware of the heat. At first it had seemed a pleasant contrast to the cold of the night air, but now it seemed asphyxiating. If she didn't move soon, she would faint, right here, on this spot. Not that anyone seemed likely to notice if she did.

She began to search the faces in the crowd. As she did

so, her father's words, condemning the army of the new French Republic, echoed in her ears again. He had been right, she thought bitterly. This was not an army—it was a motley band of brigands, a sea of lively, sharp, un-shaven faces, a mixture of uniforms, some newly issued, many darned and mended, some faded from dark blue to grey. Somewhere, among all these, was the man she sought, a man she had never met, whose very appear-ance was unknown to her.

'Captain Forestier?' she demanded of the nearest drinker to wear an artillery uniform, shaking his shoul-der and shouting her request into his ear above the surrounding din.

He gestured with his beer-mug towards a corner, and grunted something she did not catch. No matter. He had indicated the object of her search.

Determinedly Charlotte pushed, squeezed and wriggled her way across the room until she reached a primitive wooden table in one corner.

A man was seated there alone. He wore a dark blue coat with the red facings of an artillery officer, unbut-toned over untidy shirt linen. His bicorne hat lay on the table beside him, adorned with a grimy tricolour rosette and a spray of ostrich plumes, in the fashion beloved of officers who had sprung from the Revolution. He was busy eating, or rather devouring, an extraordinary mess of fried eggs and melted cheese. As he kept his head well down over his dinner, she could see only a mop of long, thick, unkempt black hair, sadly in need of a comb, curling over his coat-collar and falling about his face, and trimmed, it would seem, by the hand of a very amateur barber. She suspected he might even have cut it himself. His table-manners were atrocious. He ate very fast, with his elbows on the table, forking the food into his mouth and occasionally wiping the back of his hand across his lips in the absence of a table-napkin.

'Captain, indeed!' thought Charlotte scornfully in disgust. 'Before the Revolution, this lout would have counted himself lucky to achieve sergeant.'

She waited patiently, but if the solitary diner realised she was there, he showed no sign of it and continued to eat in his hurried way. She cleared her throat. 'Captain Forestier? Captain Marc Forestier?'

'What do you want?' he answered indistinctly through a mouthful of egg and cheese, and without looking up.

'I'd like a moment of your time, Captain,' she said with some asperity, adding, '*if* you can stop eating for so long!'

The man paused with a forkful of food half-way to his mouth, and glanced up sharply.

Disconcerted, Charlotte found herself shrewdly assessed by a pair of bright blue eyes fringed with long, dark lashes, all the more striking for being contrasted with a complexion which constant exposure to sun, wind and rain had tanned to the walnut hue of a gipsy's. The untidy locks of black hair framed a lean face, an aquiline nose and high cheekbones: in all, a visage better suited to some southern bandit than a serving officer. The more so because behind it lay something else, something which led a warning tocsin to sound in her brain.

Charlotte was young, but old enough to recall the Terror which had raged a mere seven years earlier in France. There had been men then with such faces . . . and instinct, rather than sight, discerned that behind the clear blue eyes and gipsy countenance lay a nature in which all the gentler traits had been ruthlessly suppressed, leaving only a man as efficient and dangerous as the guns under his command.

Beneath the piercing and unnerving scrutiny of that gaze, Charlotte, growing alarmed, faltered, 'I apologise for disturbing you, Captain, but I've come today from Lausanne, expressly to find you, and I've been seeking you here for more than two hours.'

'Have you?' was the insolent reply. 'Well, I'm a busy man, and though I appreciate the kind thought of whoever sent you to me, I fear I have no time for your charms just now. You'll have to peddle them elsewhere.'

Charlotte felt her cheeks burn. 'You mistake my

purpose, Captain. I am Charlotte Lacoste, the daughter of Colonel Lacoste.'

'I know of no Colonel Lacoste,' he said shortly, falling to his dinner again.

'My father had been several years on the retired list when he died,' she informed him. 'After a most distinguished career.'

'In the service of King Louis, I take it?' said the man sarcastically.

'Yes!' Charlotte snapped.

'And what would the daughter of this distinguished Royalist want with me?'

'I was told you might be able to help me.' As Charlotte spoke, she felt the futility of appealing for aid to a man like this. He did not even have the manners to get to his feet, and was probably a rabid Jacobin. Nevertheless, she persisted.

'I have had great difficulty in finding you, Captain,' she said, quietly but firmly. 'And although I take no pleasure in being in this company, I certainly do not intend to turn and walk away now, however discourteous you may choose to be. In my situation, I believe you would do as I am. I am seeking news of a Captain Saint-Laurent. It is of the greatest importance that I find him. I believe you are acquainted with him.'

The Captain seemed to hesitate, perhaps struck by her calm, resolute tone. 'I might be. What do you want with him?' He gestured with his knife at the bench on Charlotte's side of the table. 'Sit down.'

Charlotte sat, having struggled to pull out the wooden bench unaided. He might have noticed her efforts; he certainly made none of his own to help. Still, being invited to join him was a step in the right direction.

'I've been trying to contact Captain Saint-Laurent for the past four months,' she began in explanation. 'But all my letters have been unanswered. I appealed to the Ministry of War, but they told me they were not in the habit of passing details of military movements to civilians.'

The Captain chuckled. 'Don't let that worry you, my dear. They pass precious little information to those of us more closely concerned!' He glanced briefly at her. 'But you were unwise. They have spy mania in Paris. You might have been arrested.'

'I was desperate. I could get no news, and as my father died in January, and I found myself alone, I decided there was nothing for it but to come and look for Lucien—for Captain Saint-Laurent—myself.'

'Very intrepid,' commented her new acquaintance discouragingly. 'So you thought you'd follow the regiment, did you?' His sharp eyes flickered over her sardonically, a gleam of amusement in their depths. 'And what, may I be so bold to ask—if it's not indiscreet—is Lucien Saint-Laurent to you?'

'He is my fiancé,' she said proudly.

This news had a more dramatic effect on her companion than she could have anticipated. He put down his knife and fork, pushed away his plate and, for the first time in their conversation, brought his entire attention to bear on her. The blue eyes studied her with a new intensity, and a slightly puzzled frown briefly puckered his forehead. She could have sworn he looked almost startled.

Charlotte fidgeted nervously. The whole atmosphere between them had changed and was charged with a tingling awareness, as when lightning plays about a house.

'He is your *what*?' he demanded at last, incredulously.

'My fiancé. We're engaged to be married.' Charlotte felt a certain embarrassment at having to repeat herself, especially as he seemed disinclined to believe her.

'Does *he* know this?' enquired the man opposite her, with some curiosity in his voice.

'Of course he knows! What a ridiculous question!' she snapped, beginning to find it hard to control her irritation. But then the reality of her situation swept over her, and she added in a quieter, less assured, tone, in which a note of desperation threatened to break through, 'Only I do want to find him. Something may be terribly wrong, or why doesn't he answer my letters?'

A feeling of loneliness invaded her heart and she fought off dejection. It had seemed such a simple thing, when she had set out, to go and find Lucien herself. She had never imagined so many men, such chaos, the mass of inaccurate information which had sent her from pillar to post in vain searches. She had pinned such hopes on her meeting with this man, Forestier. Her informant in Lausanne had been so sure. But now, yet again, those hopes were to be cruelly dashed.

She became aware that Marc Forestier was still staring at her, studying her face thoughtfully. She lifted her chin and returned his gaze with as much assurance as she could muster in such difficult circumstances.

'You're a very pretty girl,' he said slowly, but in a tone of detached observation, rather than in any admiration. 'Such a white skin, like fine porcelain. The women who follow *us* are all as brown as berries.' He reached out and took hold of her hands by the fingertips before she had time to realise his intention. He turned them palm uppermost and contemplated the rose-pink flesh. 'And hands as soft as silk. A young lady,' he added drily. 'Your place is not here, mademoiselle. Go home. Go home now!'

Charlotte jerked her hands from his. 'No! I came to find Lucien!'

He leaned slightly forward and opened his mouth, but before he could speak they were interrupted by a sudden increase in the surrounding noise, and quarrelling voices burst on the ear from the next table.

Two gunners sat there with a young woman in a very low-cut gown and with heavily rouged lips. She now began to scream abuse at them, her voice rising to a shrill note, pouring out invective such as Charlotte had never heard before and more than half of which was, mercifully, unintelligible to her.

Her two male companions retaliated in good measure,

one of them with particular eloquence, and the rouged damsel abruptly broke off her own diatribe to seize a jug of beer from the table and tip it unceremoniously over the artilleryman's head.

Shouts of laughter and approval from the surrounding tables greeted this, but the gunner, streams of beer running down his neck and into his collar, was not prepared to see any humour in his situation, and with a bloodcurdling roar pushed aside the table and prepared for battle.

'One moment . . .' Forestier murmured to Charlotte.

He moved with quite astonishing speed, sliding out from behind the table and crossing the floor in the space of a second. He seized the gunner by his coat-collar and the rouged damsel by the arm, and propelled both forcibly ahead of him and out of the room. At the sight of an officer, the other gunner chose a discreet retreat, slipping away through the crowd, and with the departure of the combatants, the hubbub settled down and the drinkers returned to their own affairs. Forestier returned, pushing his way across the room, and resumed his seat, panting slightly from his exertions.

'One of my men,' he explained briefly. 'Best to intervene and prevent trouble in a crowded place like this, or every man will be fighting his neighbour before you know what's happening.' He rubbed a hand the colour of walnut across his perspiring forehead.

'Whatever was it all about?' gasped Charlotte, her ears still tingling from the colourful language employed by both parties to the dispute.

A faint smile touched the Captain's saturnine features. 'The girl asked too much,' he said. 'It was an argument over price.'

'Oh . . .' Charlotte avoided his eyes and stared down at the table.

'That shocks you, does it?' he observed mockingly. 'Mademoiselle Lacoste does not approve. My, my,' he added in a parody of a female falsetto. 'So such dreadful women really do exist!'

'I am not so naïve as to be quite ignorant!' she retorted in a muffled voice, flushing scarlet.

'Quite a woman of the world, eh?' he chuckled. 'Well, *ma belle*, such women do exist, and some of us are very grateful for the fact. But you? A little incident like that sets you blushing like a sunset. Do you imagine that you will be able to move freely about this company and not so much as another misplaced word will fall on your delicate ear? Let alone any worse fate befall you! Have you thought of *that*, eh? I see I set you blushing prettily again. Well, I make no apology for it. Remember, *you* chose to come in here and seek me out.'

'I can't imagine why!' Charlotte flung at him. 'You are the most ill-mannered wretch I have ever met, and you refuse to help me at all!'

'I've already helped you with the best advice at my disposal,' he said swiftly. 'Go home. Go somewhere where the company is more polite, better suited to your fragile sensibilities!'

'I am very far from being as feeble as you think me!' she returned. 'It will take more than a trivial incident to send me scurrying for home!'

He narrowed his eyes, and muttered, 'Humph!' Then, picking up his hat, he said unexpectedly, 'This is no place to discuss private affairs. We should go elsewhere. But mind! I'm busy. I've a limited amount of time to spend on you and your troubles. Tomorrow I take my guns across the Great St Bernard.' He gestured towards the door and all that lay beyond it, outside, beneath the hovering mountains, and smiled slightly. 'The local people think us lunatics.'

Charlotte recalled the sinister shapes which crouched like strange beasts, slumbering beneath the tarpaulins in the thick mud outside, and the awesome ascent to the great pass, still blocked by winter snow. Momentarily diverted from her own problems, she asked, 'How will you manage it?'

'Sledges,' Forestier said briefly. '*He* thought of it.'

'Who?' she asked, bewildered.

He looked faintly surprised at her lack of comprehension. 'Our First Consul,' he said. 'Bonaparte.'

For the first time a note of enthusiasm sounded in his voice, and she looked at him curiously. There was a faraway look in the blue eyes. Perhaps he contemplated his fearful task of hauling the guns in his charge across the precipitous snowy pass.

Then he gave himself a little shake. 'Come along!' he ordered her briskly. He pushed the table aside and stood up. He was very much taller and more solidly built than was apparent when he was seated, and his action in dealing with the near-by dispute had indicated all at once an authoritative, even impressive, figure.

'Where to?' Charlotte scrambled to her feet.

'I've a room here, upstairs.' Forestier pointed with his plumed hat towards the staircase leading to the inn's bedrooms. 'We can talk privately.'

'But *I* can't go upstairs with you . . .' she began in dismay, but he was already on his way, ignoring her.

At the foot of the stairs, he paused and glanced back to where she still stood irresolutely by the table. 'Well, are you coming or not?' he demanded impatiently.

'Yes—Yes!' Charlotte, realising that her one chance of obtaining the information she sought so desperately might be about to disappear for ever, hastened after him, and seizing her petticoats in both hands, stumbled up the rickety staircase behind him.

CHAPTER
THREE

IT WAS impossible for two parties to cross on the narrow stairs, and another officer, who evidently intended to come down, paused at the top to allow Forestier and Charlotte to pass him. He was a young man with a blond moustache and the air of one who enjoys life without troubling himself unduly about its profundities. Even on the darkened stairwell, Charlotte was aware of the twinkle in his eye as it lit on her, and the grin on his chubby face as he murmured something to Forestier in passing. The Captain only shrugged.

The room, at the end of a long narrow corridor, was in darkness, and he told her to wait while he lit a candle. As this of necessity took a few moments, she was left in the doorway, uneasily aware of how her visit to his room had already been interpreted by at least one observer—and would no doubt have been interpreted by any others who had seen them come up.

The candle stuttered and flickered into life, and a dull yellow glow bathed the little room. The wooden bed, bedecked with a fat, feather-filled quilt, stood against one wall. There was a small table and only one chair. Against a further wall there was, indeed, a threadbare sofa of unsteady appearance, but it was strewn with various items of linen. The Captain's box also stood open near by, surrounded by more of its contents, as though he had been rummaging for something.

It was an odd little scene, intimate and personal, and very human. It suggested that the occupant was the sort of man who, dedicated and scrupulous in the extreme in his work, was neglectful of what he would probably consider irritating domestic trifles. This vagabond military life no doubt suited him ideally. Life in one spot, with all its mundane involvements, would be unbearable to him. She was drawn from this brief rêverie by his voice.

'Here . . .' he said, pulling out the chair in lackadaisical gallantry and indicating it with a casual gesture.

Charlotte advanced cautiously and sat down. She had hoped that delicacy might inspire the Captain to leave the door at least ajar, but to her dismay he shut it firmly and turned the key in the lock.

'Why have you done that?' she whispered, her heart leaping up wildly in alarm.

'To avoid our being disturbed by any idiot who can't remember which is his room.' He glanced over his shoulder at her pale, set face. 'I thought you were intrepid,' he said. 'You look about to faint.'

'I'm not . . .' Charlotte mumbled huskily.

Strolling lazily to where she sat, he stood looking down at her. Despite herself, she cowered slightly in her chair. He gave a little snort; partly, it seemed, of amusement and partly of disgust. Silently, he held out the key towards her. Charlotte stared up at him uncomprehendingly.

'The key,' he said with patient emphasis, as if he spoke to one of impaired understanding. 'I give it into your keeping. After all, you might discover an urgent need to flee my improper advances.'

She flushed brick red, and snatched the key from him, holding on to it tightly.

He turned away and unbuckled his sword-belt, hanging it over the bedpost. Then he threw himself down casually onto the end of the bed, which creaked noisily, and leaned back to slouch against the wall, supporting himself on one elbow. The candle-flame barely illuminated thus far, and when a draught through some chink in the window-frame sent it leaping up and flickering wildly, it sent a weird shadow dancing over his face. This, together with his dark complexion and long hair, to say nothing of his untidy dress, enhanced his general appearance of a gipsy, at once handsome, clever and untrustworthy.

'A rogue and an adventurer,' her father would have judged him instantly.

Charlotte wondered what were his origins and where his birthplace had been. The Midi, perhaps, to judge by that Mediterranean complexion, but his voice lacked the distinctive accents of the South.

She turned the key nervously in her perspiring fingers. She had never been alone with a man in his room, and was dismayed at the ease with which she had been persuaded to accept such a situation in the company of one who appeared so eminently disreputable. The key gave her little confidence. In the event, she would be unlikely to have the time or opportunity to put it to use.

'Go on, then,' Forestier ordered suddenly, and she jumped at the sound of his voice. 'Let's hear your tale of woe.'

'Very well,' she said uncertainly, her eyes fixed on him. It occurred to her that with so much noise coming from downstairs, and outside in the street, no one would be likely to hear her, were she to be obliged to scream. She could only hope, rather desperately, that he would prove more of a gentleman than he looked. Miserably aware that he could read all these thoughts easily in her face, she saw him grin briefly. It has the effect of making him look even more of a brigand.

Charlotte began her story hesitantly. Then, as he only rarely interrupted, and to her great relief did not move, she gained courage and poured out everything. Indeed, once she began, it was difficult to stop.

'We live in Châlons-sur-Marne. My mother died when I was only a baby, and for that reason, I suppose, I was always especially close to Father. He was already on the retired list, as I told you, when the Revolution broke out. Despite that, they arrested him twice—an old man, and quite helpless, no possible threat to anyone, much less to *them*. The first time, in 1791, was for a few weeks.

He was released, and we believed that to be the end of
the matter. But in 1792 they came to arrest him again.
They did not dare to bring him to trial, because of his
distinguished record, so they left him to suffer wretchedly in prison, until that monster Robespierre fell from
power, and he was released with so many others.'

'To be replaced with fresh detainees,' the Captain
interpolated coldly. 'We have all of us spent our time in
the prisons of the French Republic, for one reason or
another. Even Bonaparte. Even myself.'

'Father was an old, sick man!' Charlotte cried.

'Since when does the guillotine trouble itself about
youth or age? We were all lucky to keep our heads
attached to our shoulders, your father as much as any
other. Better to rot for a few months than to mount the
scaffold.'

'Rot for a few months? My father's health was ruined
by it all. I'll never forgive them, never!' she flung at him
passionately.

There was no flicker of sympathy or understanding on
the dark, gipsy countenance. He cared neither for her
troubles nor for her father's. He was a man accustomed
to look out for himself, and, by his reasoning, those who
could not do the same must perish. Charlotte understood it well enough. She gathered her composure and
continued her story.

'Last year Father was very ill, at home. In fact, he was
dying. You can imagine what a blessing it was for us to
see my cousin, Lucien Saint-Laurent, arrive, quite unexpectedly, on our doorstep. He had been seconded from
his own regiment to this new Army of Reserve, which
lacked experienced officers. They were raising men for
the ranks at the time, and some of them were garrisoned
in the barracks at Châlons. My father was always very
proud that Lucien was a soldier, as he himself had been,
even though, I must admit, he had a very low opinion of
Republican officers generally.'

'So I imagine,' came in a sour tone from the bed.

'Oh, please don't think I mean to insult you in any

way, Captain Forestier,' she said hastily. 'I mean no
reflection on your abilities at all. I'm sure you're very
capable, even if you are—you are a little forthright in
your manner. But Father was very old fashioned and a
believer in tradition. *Family*, meant so much to him,
good family, I mean.'

The very faintest twitch animated the muscles of his
face, but he made no comment.

'So I hope you understand, and are not offended,'
Charlotte added.

'Believe me, *mignonne*, I am not in the least offended.
Your father's opinions are of not the slightest interest to
me. I don't doubt for a minute that, had it been in his
power, he would have had me struck permanently from
the list of commissions. But, I assure you, I shall lose no
sleep over it.'

'Very well,' Charlotte said uneasily. She paused, then
continued very quietly, 'I can't tell you what seeing
Lucien meant to me. I've always loved him. There is no
one like him, no one in the world. I truly believe I shall
be the happiest person on earth when we are married.'

Forestier grunted. 'You have an optimistic view of the
state of matrimony.' He looked up shrewdly. 'He is your
cousin, you say? Your father, then, knew of your attach-
ment to Saint-Laurent?'

'He knew, but not that we were to be married, at
least.' She stumbled over the words in her eagerness to
explain. 'Lucien said we should *not* tell Father, because
of his ill-health, but after he left us, I did tell him.'

'Really? Well, well . . . Your father was delighted, I
presume?'

'No,' Charlotte admitted flatly, 'I cannot honestly say
he was.'

'Did he say why?'

'I don't know why. Someone had written him a letter,
I believe, to say that Lucien had been gambling. But I
don't see why that should be so bad. After all, Lucien
assured Father that all his gaming debts had been paid,
so what more was there to worry about?'

Her interrogator chose not to answer this, but only scratched the bridge of his aquiline nose thoughtfully. Without warning, he asked, 'Did you and Saint-Laurent sign a marriage contract?'

'No,' she replied, a little taken aback at this very pertinent question. 'There wasn't time, in the circumstances and anyway, we had no need of lawyers to seal our faith in one another! I know Lucien to be a man of honour and of his word. That's why I know he would have written to me, if he could! But, since he left, I've not heard one word. Something's happened to prevent him, something terrible. That's why I'm here. I mean to find him. I stayed last night in Lausanne, where someone gave me your name. So today I came here, and have spent the better part of two whole hours seeking you.'

Recalling those two frustrating and exhausting hours, she added, 'I never knew such a muddle. There are men and horses and women and even little children, who have no place here at all. At every turn the way is blocked by carts and guns, and makeshift tents, where women sell some most peculiar-looking brandy that I swear they've distilled themselves. I was driven quite distracted. It's more like a fairground than an army camp.'

'You were lucky to find me,' was his comment. 'How have you travelled?'

'In my own carriage, driven by Pascal, our coachman.'

'Family retainer, eh?' Forestier stirred at last, sliding off the bed and standing up with an easy, almost feline, grace, which put her in mind of some supple and predatory great cat. 'How old are you?' he demanded brusquely.

'Twenty!' Charlotte replied quickly, adding, 'Though that is not a question you are entitled to ask!'

'Eighteen, I wager—nineteen, at the very most,' he countered, ignoring her reproof.

'Very well, eighteen, if you must know it!' She almost stamped her foot, but managed to avoid this display of feminine petulance. 'But I shall be nineteen in two months' time. So, you see, I am not a child.'

'I do not consider you one. For my own part, I've always considered women at their best between sixteen and twenty-two, and so, I should warn you, do the majority of men here. If you expect to be treated as a little girl, you are due a very unpleasant shock, *mignonne*. However, to be almost nineteen, and still unmarried, must be a worry for you. You are practically an old maid. No wonder you chase after poor Saint-Laurent with such tenacity.'

'I do not think I have to tolerate your oafish sense of humour, Captain.'

'I don't joke. Couldn't you find anyone else at home to marry you? Or was there no one else in Châlons good enough for the daughter of Colonel Lacoste? I suppose the wretched Saint-Laurent might make a general one day, especially if urged on by an ambitious wife. To say nothing of a Greek chorus of their combined relations to remind him of his obligations to the family name!'

'I love Lucien!' Charlotte burst out. 'How dare you jeer at our feelings for one another? You are ignorant and coarse. Even to speak of Love before you is to—to sully its name!'

'Oh, yes—Love,' he murmured with an insulting disdain. 'Always a complication, and women will make such a fuss about it.'

'I see it means nothing to you,' she retorted. 'I dare say you see women as nothing but a hindrance.'

'On the contrary, nobody appreciates a pretty girl more than I,' he informed her calmly. 'In the right place, of course.'

'Which is?' she demanded unwisely.

A gleam entered the blue eyes, and the walnut-tanned skin of his cheeks creased in a grin. 'Well, *there* is one very good place,' Forestier indicated the bed behind him.

Charlotte sprang to her feet. All that she had suffered, all the despair, worries, discomforts and disappointments she had endured so patiently over the past months surged up in her in one mighty wave of anger.

'How dare you speak to me in such a way?' A cold rage echoed in her voice, and though she trembled inwardly, her tone was quiet, even and controlled. 'France is ill served when she must promote to command men such as you! You are an ill-mannered ruffian without honour or decency. You have not the slightest respect for me, either as the fiancée of a brother officer, or as a woman alone and without help or protection. I cannot imagine that Lucien ever called you a friend. He is worth a dozen of you! Go outside among your guns!' She flung her hand towards the window. 'That is where you belong! You are about as capable of any civilised behaviour as they are!'

She had not paused to consider the danger to herself in speaking this way to such a man, or the circumstances in which they found themselves. She had not stopped to think how he might react. The words poured out in a spate of humiliation and fury. She stood before him defiantly, challenging him to reply. There was a brief silence, and then his words cut savagely into it, having almost the force of physical blows.

'This is an army on its way to war,' he snarled at her, an angry flush seeping across his high cheekbones beneath the tan. 'It is *not* civilised! It deals in pain and violence and death! You, Mademoiselle Lacoste, are an ignorant, silly chit, a little *Sainte Nitouche*—Saint Touch-Not! You enter this inn unaccompanied, the kind of place no respectable woman would wish to go near. You walk up to a perfect stranger and pepper him with your questions, which concern personally someone who is not only a brother officer, but a friend, and when you do not receive the answers to which you fancy yourself entitled, you produce a display of outraged self-righteousness! There is no reason why I, or any other, should help you. In fact, quite the opposite. I should be quite unjustified in discussing Lucien's recent movements with you!'

Charlotte's face burned. She could not deny that a

good deal of what he had said was correct. She had been so single-minded in her quest that she had not paused to consider how others might view it.

'I see. Then there is no way I may persuade you?'

Forestier's manner relaxed imperceptibly, and he said drily, 'I did not say I might not be persuaded, *mignonne*. A woman always has *one* strong bargaining counter at her disposal. Why don't you try and see what your charms may do?'

But that was too much. Ready though she had been to accept uncomfortable truths, if they were in part deserved, she was not ready to swallow such an obvious insult . . . nor the all too clear suggestion which lay behind it.

Though her heart had begun to throb painfully in instinctive alarm, she drew a deep breath, and said quietly and with great conviction, 'You are totally despicable . . .'

He gave her an odd, mirthless smile, reflected in a cold determination in his eyes, which was unbelievably frightening. 'Am I? Then let's see if I'm not right.' He moved slowly towards her. 'Tell me, Mademoiselle Lacoste, how deep does all that virtue run, all that loyalty? *Would* you be prepared to pay a price for what you want?'

Without further warning he cupped his long, strong fingers about her face so that she could not move, and stooping, crushed his mouth brutally against hers, without passion or emotion, almost as if, in some way, he wanted to hurt her.

Charlotte gasped and twisted her head away from the pressure of his lips. '*No!* I called you despicable, and I was right! If you want anything from me, you will have to take it by force!'

She knew as she spoke that she could not prevent his doing just that, if he chose, but as she struggled desperately to escape from his embrace, his grip slackened and he released her, suddenly thrusting her away from him.

'Pah!' he said in a disgusted voice. 'I can't be bothered with you!'

'You need not be!' she retaliated shakily, putting out a hand to ward off any further attack. 'I won't trouble you any further, Captain. I am only sorry I ever sought you out in the first place!'

She turned towards the door in a swirl of petticoats, and almost stumbled in her agitation. He put out his hand and caught her by the elbow to steady her, but she shook him away. 'The man I love may be dead. I have no news of him, and I have taken endless trouble to come here to seek news. I hope you sleep well, Captain.'

'Wait.' He spoke quite normally, much more quietly than before, and she glanced back at him.

He half-turned away from her, walking back into the room. 'As far as I know, he isn't dead, though his situation is hardly enviable. They sent him back to his own regiment. He's already in Italy, with the army of Masséna. They are pinned down at Genoa between the Austrian army and the British fleet. You won't find him here, nor can you reach him there.'

At last! At last she had some tangible information. She drew a deep breath, frantically considering its import, little caring what might have induced the Captain to part with it. 'What shall I do?' she asked, more of herself than of him.

'You can go home,' he said unkindly, 'where you should have stayed. I'm becoming rather tired of telling you this, especially as you should be intelligent enough to realise it yourself. An army on campaign is no place for fine young ladies.'

'Plenty of women follow the army,' she protested obstinately.

'You're not one of *them*.' His voice was gentler.

Charlotte flushed. 'Respectable women do so also—wives of the officers.'

'And mostly they fare very badly!' Forestier's voice echoed in the little room, almost savagely. Harshly, he added, 'I doubt your Lucien would care to know you here. Go and tell your coachman that in the morning he can set off to drive you home.'

'No,' she insisted. 'Not after coming so far. If Lucien is already in Italy, that's where I'll go.'

'And how do you propose to get there? First, you will fly over the mountains somehow. Travel unescorted through the Italian population, the male members of which will be delighted to see you. Cut your way single-handed through the Austrian forces. Ah, but no—I have it! You're going to take ship and sail down the coast, right through the middle of the British fleet!'

'I see indeed that you do not lack a sense of humour, Captain!' Charlotte said sharply. 'For your information, I shall travel as you intend to do, with the army.'

'Good grief!' he exploded, taking a rapid step towards her. 'Are you quite mad? How do you propose seriously to get a carriage across the Great St Bernard? You will block the path, get stuck in the drifts, probably overturn and be a thorough nuisance. You're to go back, and that's an order!'

'I'm not under your command, Captain!' she retorted icily, 'and quite able to make my own decisions.'

'Stupid little fool!' He sounded very angry.

'I think I have wit enough to get myself to Italy!' she snapped, her scorn flaring up again.

'Indeed? I doubt you had even had the wit, this evening, to secure yourself a bed for the night before spending so much time seeking me out.'

That was true. Charlotte said coldly, 'I am aware that it will be impossible to find a bed here at this hour. But please do not distress yourself on that account, Captain. I shall sleep in my carriage.'

'You'll freeze.' He gestured briefly towards his own bed. 'You can sleep there.'

'How dare you repeat your insulting . . .' she began angrily, but he silenced her.

'Spare me the fit of hysterics!' he said a little wearily. 'I'm offering you my bed because I shall have no use for it. I *don't* offer you my company in it, in the place of your missing lover. Come, you have my word on it—and my word is good! Another time, perhaps, we might make good the omission, but there are more important matters than you to occupy me just now. I have to supervise the dismounting of the guns in my charge, and the loading of them onto the sledges. It will take the best part of the night. The room is yours.'

'Thank you,' Charlotte said awkwardly. 'I'll go and tell Pascal. He'll be getting worried about me.'

'I'll tell him. Where is he?'

'Just at the end of the street.' She was grateful that she need not descend into the robust company of the room below. 'Turn to your right outside the inn.'

'I'll find him.' Deftly he twitched the key from her grasp, where she had clenched it so tightly that an impression of it lay in a red mark on her damp palm. He stared down at her for a moment, his expression thoughtful, as if he turned over something in his mind.

Holding up the glinting key, he exclaimed suddenly, 'I have the key, and I have you. Why should I go and find Pascal, eh? What if I should change my mind? You are too trusting, mademoiselle. You should have hung onto this key with every breath in your body.'

'I cannot defend myself against you,' she said quietly. 'But you gave me your word, and told me it was good. I accept it.'

'Take my advice, my dear Charlotte,' he returned even more softly, so that the words were scarcely more than a whisper. 'Trust no man, and take no man's word. I do not intend to break mine to you. But, always remember, I am a man and a soldier, and not a knight in shining armour.'

'I cannot believe I should ever think you that!' she retorted.

'Ah? And what of Saint-Laurent, eh? Is he the "perfect knight without reproach"?'

She could read the mockery in his eyes, and flushed deeply because she understood the real question which lay behind his words. 'Lucien is the finest person I ever met,' she told him with deep emotion. 'He respected me, because he loves me! That is why I love and respect him.'

Forestier fell silent, still looking down at her, the expression on his saturnine features a little moody. Then he shrugged and turned away, as if he wished to dismiss the whole matter from his mind. He strode towards the door, his spurs jingling, but when he had inserted the key in the lock, he paused, his hand on the catch, to glance back at her.

'Love is no excuse for being foolish,' he said brusquely. 'You can't cross into Italy with us. Nor is it possible for you even to travel in this company, unless you travel with some man in it. Mostly, though not always, the others respect another man's woman, but a pretty girl alone is the property of any man who cares to claim her. Just another woman of the regiment, do you understand me?'

'I understand you well enough.'

He still hesitated, his hand on the door-handle. His bronzed, handsome, yet disreputable and hard-bitten looks, his unruly mop of long black hair, and something in his stance and attitude gave him less the look of an officer of the Republic than of some *condottiere*, such as had roamed Renaissance Italy, part-mercenary, part-bandit, selling his skills as a warrior to the highest bidder, changing allegiance in order to survive, and always dangerous. Indeed, looking at him now, Charlotte could believe him capable of almost anything, and wondered that Lucien, or any man, could call such a person 'a friend'.

Her informant in Lausanne had said of Forestier, 'not a man anyone forgets in a hurry'.

'How many men,' thought Charlotte with a little shiver, 'have crossed Marc Forestier's path, and have good cause to remember him?'

And how many women . . . ? echoed an involuntary voice in her brain.

'Then I shall tell Pascal you'll set off home in the morning?' His voice broke into her rěverie.

'If you wish.' The controlled tone of her voice was the product of great effort, but the words rang confidently on her ear.

Forestier's sharp blue eyes, so strikingly fringed with dark lashes, ran over her face appraisingly. He gave a little grunt of satisfaction. 'That's a good girl. After all, who knows, a letter from your Lucien could be waiting for you at Châlons even now, eh?'

He gave her a brief nod of farewell, and let himself out.

As the latch clicked, Charlotte untied her cloak and dropped it onto the chair. 'I'm going to Italy,' she muttered rebelliously. 'And *you* won't stop me, you uncouth barbarian!'

She felt better for having restated her resolve to herself, and for the abusive words of her late companion which helped to release the pent-up tensions within her. Not that he had gone, she could feel herself begin to tremble, and although after a moment she was able to control this, she still felt strangely nervous, as though she trembled still inside.

'I am tired,' she thought.

She was glad of the bed. For all he had behaved so badly, Captain Forestier had made a kind enough gesture in relinquishing it to her. It was a pity that, on his departure, he should inadvertently have taken the key with him, and she could not relock the door. She would just have to hope no one tried to come in.

Charlotte crossed the room to close the wooden shutters. A train of pack-mules outside in the street was already laden with the wheels of the dismembered guns. The sight of these patient, long-suffering beasts with their grim burdens was a reminder of the purpose which lay behind all this noise and confusion. She slammed the shutters to block out the sight, and turned to survey with distaste the litter of clothing and personal belongings scattered about the room.

She picked up two cambric shirts from the floor, folded them tidily and put them back in the open box.

She was surprised to see that this contained a number of books, and picked up a few out of curiosity. Most were manuals of a military nature, but she was surprised to find among them a copy of Caesar's *Gallic Wars* in the original Latin. So he was not without education!

Even more curious now about the Captain, Charlotte, having glanced cautiously over her shoulder towards the door, took a further look in his box. In one corner, right at the bottom, lay a little velvet bag fastened with a draw-string. She pulled it open, and shook out the contents onto her lap. Two gold rings fell out, threaded together on a scrap of silk ribbon. One was large, a man's, and the other very much smaller. She slipped it on to her own finger, where it sat snugly. Both rings appeared new, or at least were very little worn. She wondered to whom they had belonged.

With a puzzled frown, she replaced the bag and its contents where she had found it, beneath a pile of clothing, and as she did so, her ear caught a faint movement outside the door. She jumped round in alarm.

A light knock sounded on the door, and a woman's voice called softly, 'Marc? Are you there? He's busy, and I slipped away . . .'

Charlotte scrambled to her feet and went to open the door, calling out as she did so, 'No, I'm afraid Captain Forestier isn't here . . .' As she stretched out her hand to the door, there was a scurry of footsteps, and the unknown woman ran back towards the head of the staircase. By the time Charlotte had opened the door and looked out into the dimly-lit corridor, she had gone, and Charlotte was in time only to catch a glimpse of a woman's fur-trimmed pelisse whisking around the bend of the stairs.

She stood in thought for a moment, then shrugged. Captain Forestier's amorous adventures were no concern of hers. No doubt they were as disreputable as the man himself.

But a mystery is always puzzling, nagging at the brain.

In Forestier's case there were even two such mysteries. Charlotte slipped off her gown and shoes, and crept into bed in her stockings and petticoat. Even unanswered questions about the man who had given her his bed were not sufficient to keep her awake. As her head touched the pillow, waves of exhaustion broke over her, and she had barely time to turn and blow out the candle before falling fast asleep.

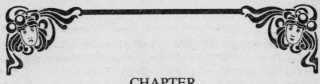

CHAPTER
FOUR

CHARLOTTE STIRRED. Daylight filtered through the slats of the wooden shutters, and voices calling from outside in the street told her it was morning. She could hear the bells tinkling on the harness of the pack-mules. She opened her eyes fully, staring up at the ceiling. It must be quite late.

Furniture creaked, and there was a muffled snort from the further side of the room. She gave a gasp, her heart leaping up in alarm, and sat bolt upright, clutching at the feather quilt.

Marc Forestier was asleep, sprawled out uncomfortably on the rickety sofa on the other side of the room. All the clothing that had been scattered over it had been pushed onto the floor in a heap. He had pulled off his boots, which lay propped drunkenly against one another, and was slumbering with his head pillowed on his folded coat and his stockinged feet sticking out incongruously over the end of the sofa.

He must have returned in the early hours, but sleeping so soundly herself, she had not heard him. She slipped cautiously out of bed and stooped to pull on her shoes, her eyes fixed on the sleeper. He twitched his nose and moved awkwardly on his cramped couch. Reaching out, she gingerly took her gown from the back of the chair.

Alas, preoccupied in watching him, and ignorant of the masculine habit of turning out the pockets before retiring, she failed to notice that the contents of the Captain's pockets—small coins, a tinderbox, penknife and, inexplicably, two bent horseshoe nails—lay scattered across the little table. The gown, as she drew it towards her, knocked the tinderbox, which skidded across the tabletop and brought the whole miscellany of objects clattering onto the wooden floorboards.

Charlotte stood frozen to the spot, holding her breath, her gown clutched in both hands. Forestier snorted, grunted, muttered, opened his eyes, and sat up.

He stared at her as if she were a part of the furniture, swung his long legs to the floor, scratched his head of long black curls, and stooping, picked up his left boot and began to tug it on.

'Good morning,' he said casually and indistinctly.

'I didn't hear you come in,' Charlotte replied in an agitated tone.

'No more you did. You were curled up like a little squirrel, sound asleep with the quilt tucked round your ears.' He turned his attention to his other boot.

She took advantage of his distraction to step hastily into her gown and drag the sleeves up over her arms. 'It was kind of you to give me your bed—I won't take up your room any longer . . .' she stammered, fumbling unhappily with the hooks behind her back. Her nervous fingers refused to do the job required of them, and she wrestled in vain to connect hooks and eyes.

Forestier stood up and stamped his feet to settle them in the boots. 'Here,' he said, glancing up and seeing her struggles. 'Let me. Turn round.' He strolled across in his shirtsleeves, and with a suspicious ease suggesting some previous practice, hooked the gown neatly together.

'Thank you!' Charlotte muttered.

There was a clatter of boots outside the door, which flew open immediately and the plump, blond officer who had passed them at the head of the stairs the previous evening put his head and shoulders through the half-open door.

'Hey, Forestier, they're looking for you . . .' he began. He broke off in surprise and confusion at the sight of Charlotte and the Captain who, having solved the problem of the hooks, was obligingly tying her sash.

'I beg your pardon,' he said hastily. 'I thought you

alone . . . Excuse me . . .' A ray of glee shone through the embarrassment on his chubby pink face, which disappeared abruptly with a slam of the door.

'Knock, damn you!' yelled the Captain after him.

'Now, you see!' cried Charlotte in dismay. 'He'll run and tell everyone! He'll say I, I mean you and I, that is . . .' Her voice trailed away and she stared at him miserably.

'Let him say what he wants. Does it matter?' he shrugged his shoulders dismissively.

'Not to you, perhaps, but it matters to me!' she retorted strongly.

'Pah! Let poor Cresson spread his little bit of scandal. He does no harm.' He put his hands firmly on her shoulders and turned her towards him, looking down at her, his long hair falling untidily about his face and into his eyes.

'There are more important things than Cresson's tittle-tattle. I saw your coachman last night and told him you would be heading for home this morning. He's a sensible fellow—an old soldier, as I understand. He agrees with me that you're out of your mind to want to come here, and ought to be home, doing whatever young ladies do while they wait for someone to come along and marry them—preferably a wealthy man.'

'You are in a good humour this morning, Captain Forestier,' Charlotte said coldly.

He smiled slightly and went to wrench open the shutters. The clean mountain sunlight flooded into the room, and when he had opened the casement, the cold air struck Charlotte's face, and the sounds of wheels and voices rose from the street with a new clarity. She shivered in the draught, while he leaned on the window-rail in his shirtsleeves, apparently indifferent to the chill air. He stared down into the street, the wind tugging at his shirt linen.

Someone shouted up to him from below, and he called back, 'We're ready—just as soon as someone tells me to move out!'

'Do you think you'll do it?' Charlotte asked. Through the open window she could see the mountains, dredged with white and veiled in cloud. It seemed that nothing could pass through them.

The Captain looked back over his shoulder at her. 'We'll manage it. *You* would not!'

'You are very sure!' She replied crossly, stung by his low opinion of her abilities.

He turned and leaned back against the window-ledge, and folded his arms. The pale sunlight shone around his tall figure, lending a glossy blue sheen to his black curls. Charlotte thought he seemed younger, now that she saw him by daylight. The previous night the yellow candlelight had served to emphasize his dark complexion and the lines the weather had carved on his skin. Now she realised he was probably no more than in his late twenties.

'It only surprises me that you've managed to come as far as this,' he told her bluntly.

'I should have stayed in Châlons?' she snapped. 'I would have learned nothing there! What had I to lose?'

She turned aside and put up her hands to her hair in an attempt to tidy it, pushing in the loosened pins.

He watched the movement of her arms for a moment, then said, 'What of the reputation you were so worried about losing a few minutes ago?'

'That need not have happened!' Charlotte retorted sharply. 'If you hadn't returned, Cresson wouldn't have found us together.'

'I should have spent my two hours of sleep on a horse-blanket in the open, I suppose?' was the response to this. 'Thank you. It was bad enough on that sofa.' He rubbed the back of his neck to ease the crick in it. 'I gave you my bed. I didn't have to surrender my only shelter as well.'

He left the window and came back across the room to her. 'If you worry about a trifling misunderstanding like that,' he went on, 'you must surely realise the foolishness of coming here. After all, it would hardly increase your prospects of a good match if tales of your running around an army camp and being discovered in the bedroom, if not quite in the bed, of an artillery officer of questionable repute, *were* to reach Châlons—or anywhere else!'

'You mean, if Lucien were to hear of it? Perhaps that would embarrass us both, Captain! But I suspect you are trying to frighten me.'

Despite her calm tone, she was alarmed, because the idea was an uncomfortable one.

He knew it. 'I suspect that I'm succeeding,' he said immediately. 'I see it in your face, which is a mirror for your thoughts, *ma chère petite*. Come, now. What I suggest is that you go down to the kitchens for some breakfast, and tell them to put it on my bill with the rest. Then off you go, back to Châlons and safety.'

'I appreciate your concern for my welfare,' she told him expressionlessly.

'Well, I'm not totally insensitive,' he said unexpectedly. 'I understand this is very mortifying for you, and you're entitled to a fit of pique. If it relieves your feelings, I've no objection to your throwing a few hard words at my head. It's a pretty hard head, and it's suffered worse knocks.'

Suddenly Charlotte thought she understood the cause of his relatively good mood, such a contrast to the previous evening. He was on the move, ready to depart and only awaiting the order. Last night he had been cooped up in this overcrowded inn, penned in by the solid barrier of the Alps, restless and ill-tempered, fretting at the delay and the obstacle in his path. He had been like a trapped animal. But this morning someone had opened the door of the cage and set him free.

Aloud, she said, 'I assure you I don't intend to give way to an attack of nerves, or any unseemly demonstration.'

He looked relieved. 'I was sure you would listen to reason after a good night's rest. We're agreed, then? It's best for you to go home?'

'If you say so, Captain.'

'I'm glad to hear it, because I've more than enough to worry me today,' he added with a brutal frankness. 'I can't be bothered with you and your unfortunate love affairs.'

Gold sparks glittered briefly in the young lady's grey-green eyes. 'I wouldn't contemplate bothering you any further,' she said in dulcet tones.

'Good!' he said cheerfully. He pinched her cheek with an insolent familiarity. 'You're a pretty girl with plenty of spirit. Don't worry! Some fine fellow will come along and marry you one day soon.'

Charlotte picked up her cloak, bestowed a gracious smile on him, and left.

'Pascal!' she cried later, coming up to the coachman as he was busily harnessing the horses. 'You can stop doing that, for we shan't need the carriage.'

'How so, not need it?' he demanded, peering up from a trace-buckle.

'It won't get over the pass. We shall have to leave it behind.'

Pascal straightened up slowly and stared at his young employer. 'The Captain was here last night,' he said doggedly, 'and said you'd agreed to go home.'

'What nonsense! I fear the Captain is given to imagining things!' said Charlotte serenely. 'We shall see if I am to be scolded and sent home!' she thought rebelliously.

'He seemed a level-headed fellow to me,' said Pascal, tipping his felt hat to the back of his head. 'Spoke sense, too. We've come as far as we can go, and that's that.'

'That is quite untrue. The carriage won't make the pass, but the horses will. We'll ride.'

The coachman raised a spade-like hand. 'Now wait a minute, mam'zelle. First,' he held up a sausage of a finger, 'what happens when we get to the other side, *if* we get to the other side? There we'll be—with no provisions, no bedding, nothing. Then, what about

Captain Forestier? That's a man used to having his orders obeyed.'

'*I* do not obey his orders. He is a graceless oaf whom the Revolution has turned into an officer, but *not* a gentleman. He will find that not everyone takes instructions from him!'

'You're wrong,' said Pascal bluntly. 'You can always tell a man who's born to give orders, from one who's learned it late in life. That one's always had people run to do his bidding, from the cradle. A gentleman, he is. He'll have been in a few tight corners, and got out of them with his wits and his fists, most likely. But a gentleman still, for all that.'

Taken aback by the solid conviction of his tone, Charlotte said, 'Even if you are right, Pascal, it makes no difference to me. Now, I've worked it all out. We'll take out essentials from the luggage and anything which may prove of use. Everything else we'll sell, including the carriage, to buy saddles—one will have to be a side-saddle—and tarpaulins to make tents, and a mule to carry it all.'

He wriggled a finger in one ear and shook his head violently. 'I'm not hearing properly!'

'Yes, you are. So just go along and see to it.'

'Mam'zelle,' said the coachman, planting his burly figure obstinately before her. 'Twenty years I followed the colours, along with your father, God rest his soul— and fifteen years I've served your family in capacity of coachman. A little thing not up to my knee, you were, and I used to lift you up and let you ride the horses round the stable-yard.'

Charlotte sighed. 'This is no time for reminiscences, Pascal.'

'Lord save us, you can't go traipsing across the mountains on horseback!' he howled in despair. 'The Colonel would turn in his grave.'

'How will all those other women do it, then?'

'You won't get a mule. Army's took the lot!' said Pascal artfully.

'You know farmers as well as I do. For sufficient money, there will be mules to be had.'

'It's the mountain air,' growled Pascal. 'It's turned your head!' He stomped away morosely, muttering to himself.

Charlotte went back into the inn, hoping to find a quiet corner where she might wait in the warmth. But the large public room was as busy as the night before with men hastily snatching a meal or warming themselves at the fire. One or two turned and eyed her with interest. Clearly she could not wait here, and it occurred to her that the room upstairs would now be empty. She made her way up the narrow stairs, seeking the colder privacy of the cramped little bedroom.

But though the upper floor of the inn was by now largely deserted, as she approached the room she had shared the previous night with Marc Forestier, she heard voices, a man's and a woman's, issuing through a crack in the imperfectly closed door. Charlotte would have retreated at once, but one of the voices was undeniably that of the Captain himself—whom she supposed had left earlier—and some instinct told her that his conversation somehow concerned her. She withdrew into the shadows of the gloomy corridor, and listened unashamedly.

'Well, then, what did you tell her?' the woman's voice demanded impatiently.

'Sufficient,' was his laconic answer.

There was a pause, and the woman said petulantly, 'You are playing some game! I don't know whether it is with her or with me, but I don't care to be made a fool. You might at least *pretend* to be true to me!'

'*I* am not your husband!' came the cool reply, a faint note of warning in it. 'I've made you no vows.'

'My husband? That wastrel!' the woman exclaimed in disgust. Then her voice changed, the tone becoming more dulcet and wheedling. 'I wanted you so, last night. It was a golden opportunity! And what did I find but you gone, and some little jade in your room who hardly sounded above sixteen from her voice!'

'She says she's eighteen—though, I grant you, she looks little more than sixteen. And formidably virtuous, *ma foi!* So I behaved in a quite exemplary fashion, and you have not the slightest cause for jealousy. I quite surprised myself. No man ever had a better opportunity, and I let it go! What do you think of that, eh?' He laughed aloud, and Charlotte, in the corridor, flushed crimson.

'I think it is when you have nothing else to do that you amuse yourself with *me!*' Resentment broke into the woman's voice, but it was quickly controlled. 'Marc, *chéri*, I accept your explanation for that little chit being in your room! How many women would do that? Any other woman would believe you deceived her! But I,' the voice grew playful. 'I trust you!'

'How very foolish that would be of you, if it were true,' he replied softly, with a chuckle which sent a quiver running along the listening girl's spine. 'Almost as foolish as I should be if I trusted you, my sweet! Which I do not. You are very beautiful, very clever, and very dangerous. But you lie with such panache that it is a pleasure to listen to all your untruths, delivered with such style and conviction!'

'How callous you are, Marc Forestier!' the woman accused him, anger in her voice. 'You have no heart at all. You care for nothing and for nobody!'

'Then that makes two of us, my dear.'

'And am I nothing to you?' the woman asked in an altered tone. 'After all this time? Everything I ever had to offer, you have enjoyed. I have denied you nothing.'

'And your other lovers, eh?' he returned brusquely. 'Don't pretend I am the only one to enjoy those favours! Come, Éloise, you are an exceptional woman, and you know I think so.'

'Am I not?' the woman asked in an odd, throaty voice. 'Yet I have run after you as abjectly as that lovesick child of yours last night was running after her soldier lover.' Her tone gained in passion, and Charlotte stirred uneasily, feeling it was time she left. 'Come, we have wasted time enough talking of *her*. Don't let us waste any more . . .'

'Alas, Éloise, my beautiful Fury, we have no time,' Forestier said patiently. 'They will be hunting high and low for me.'

'Then they do no more than I have done! We have time enough.' Her voice was now a hoarse, inviting whisper. 'I've waited so long to find you alone, *chéri*, and you cannot imagine with what impatience . . .'

'Show me,' he said softly.

Éloise laughed, and whispered something so quietly that it was unintelligible to Charlotte, who now feared to move lest they hear her in the silence which had fallen. Then the whispering stopped suddenly, and there was a rustling, as of clothing, and a creak from the wooden bedstead.

Charlotte, well punished for her eavesdropping, seized her petticoats in both hands and fled, with her face aflame, to await Pascal outside in the cold impartiality of the street.

When Pascal returned, it was with some satisfaction written on his homely countenance. For all his previous objections, he had managed remarkably well, considering the little time at his disposal and the depredations of the French army in the town. But he was an old hand. The side-saddle was old, discovered in the garret of a local notary's house, and the mule had but one eye and a propensity to kick out at anyone behind it, but it was strong and allowed itself to be loaded up without complaint.

However, although pleased at having got the better of the local inhabitants, Pascal had not changed his mind with regard to Charlotte's plan, and complained loudly and without pausing for breath, until told brusquely by his employer to hold his tongue, as she had heard enough for one day, thank you.

'And not only from Pascal!' she thought, blushing in

embarrassment at the recollection of the overheard conversation between Forestier and his mistress. She wished she could have seen the woman. She had sounded well educated, certainly no ordinary camp-follower.

The track up to the pass was steep and narrow, and it was not long before they reached the snowline. The artillery teams dragging the guns moved with agonising slowness. They had begun their task before dawn, as the mute witness of burned-out torches by the side of the track showed. The sledges had proved inadequate for such heavy loads over soft snow, so that eventually the men had dismounted the gun-barrels and laid them in treetrunks, hastily felled and hollowed out by the axes of the Pioneers. It was these strange, almost prehistoric, containers that were being hauled up the steep slopes.

Behind came the mass of men on foot, on horseback, on mule . . . and the inevitable throng of followers. Women had pinned up their skirts and struggled through the snowdrifts, and the *vivandières* found willing enough helpers to manhandle the precious cargo of brandy.

In places the narrow track was little more than eighteen inches wide, so that a laden mule could hardly find a foothold. Above rose the mountains, breathtaking in their beauty, yet menacing and cruel. The wind was icy chill. Charlotte rubbed the frozen tip of her nose with numb fingers and tried to wiggle her toes to keep the circulation going, but they were so cold they had even ceased to ache. It was all so different from the rolling, fertile countryside of her childhood. The wind threw icy particles into her face, and she looked up apprehensively at the blue glaciers and the vast expanses of snow beneath the cloud-veiled summits, remembering tales of avalanches, and buried travellers, and whole communities swept away by a roaring white death.

Still they plodded on, crawling up the slopes with ever more difficulty. The bright sun, which contrasted so oddly with the snow-decked landscape, had now disappeared and a clammy mist swirled about them. She realised that they had reached the fringes of the cloud. Her heart pounded, and to breathe was painful. It was as if her chest would burst, and there was a ringing in her ears.

At a bend in the track they were stopped by a senior officer who, standing in the stirrups, furiously cursed the women who encumbered the caterpillar progress of the caravan.

'Turn those women back! Are there no bawds to be found in Italy that every *fille de joie* in France must follow us?' His eye fell on Charlotte. 'Who are you?' he demanded fiercely.

'I travel with an officer of this regiment!' she returned promptly, though her frozen lips moved unwillingly to form the words.

'His name?' he demanded suspiciously.

'Captain Forestier.'

'Forestier? I know him. Go on, then, go on, keep moving!' He pointed irritably up the track.

'Mam'zelle,' came Pascal's voice gloomily from the rear. 'You shouldn't have done that.'

'I had to tell him something. He'd have turned us back!'

'What's the Captain going to say when he hears of it?'

'He won't. Why should he?' she returned optimistically. Just now she didn't care what he did. She was frozen to the marrow, and it was all she could do not to tumble from the saddle into the treacherous snowdrifts to either side.

At last, as the daylight began to fail, she suddenly realised to her amazement that they no longer climbed. The path had evened out and grown broader. Then, although still twisting and treacherous, it began slowly to slope downhill.

The Army of Reserve—men, guns, horses, mules and followers—had done the seemingly impossible! It had crossed the Great St Bernard Pass while the winter's snows still lay upon the ground. Charlotte's heart lightened, the painful struggles of the ascent forgotten.

She almost felt like singing out loud. They had done it! *She* had done it!

In her delight, she became careless. The horse stumbled, slipping on the ice, and pecked. She pitched forward over its neck and plunged into the snowdrifts. Down, down she fell. An eerie, luminous whiteness was all around her, a strange warmth, a silence, and a total isolation.

'I am buried,' she thought. 'I am buried alive!'

She tried to move, but everything was soft and intangible. There were no handholds. She had no longer any sense of direction, of which way was up and which down. She tried to move her feet, to kick, but, swaddled like a baby, she was held fast in this blue-white cocoon, this wet, caressing shroud. And it was so silent. It would be such a pleasant place to sleep . . .

'It's very beautiful,' she thought in a curiously detached way. 'Perhaps monks will come with dogs and dig out my frozen body.'

In the midst of this strange, peaceful, dreamlike sequence of disconnected thoughts, something suddenly grasped at her hair, and then at her shoulder. The blue whiteness became less opaque. She was moving, but through no effort of her own . . .

Suddenly she realised that someone *was* digging her out. She began to panic, where before she had been so calm. She became aware of the sheer weight of the snow pressing down on her, fearing that she would suffocate first, and her rescuers would be too slow, and too late.

Up, up she came, dragged roughly through the chill, white world. Up into daylight and fresh air and life . . . and a harsh, angry voice, which shouted,

'You stupid little idiot! I told you to go home!'

Charlotte sat in the snow, gasping and spitting out mouthfuls of ice.

'I did it!' she panted. 'I did it!'

'Did what? Nearly kill yourself? You did that!' Forestier hauled her to her feet and shook her furiously, and lumps of snow fell from the folds of her clothing. 'Why didn't you do as you promised me?'

'I didn't promise you!' she stuttered.

'Pascal, you blockhead, what do you mean by letting your lady come on this journey? Get a blanket or something to wrap her in!'

'Yes, sir!'

'You said I couldn't do it, but I did!' insisted Charlotte through the folds of the blanket. She poked out her head and stared at him triumphantly.

'Can you ride?' he demanded tightly.

'Yes, if you'll help me up onto the horse,' she claimed resolutely.

Without a word he swept her up effortlessly and dumped her in the saddle. 'Pascal, tie your lady on!'

'No!' Charlotte protested.

'Be quiet! Do you think I can afford to waste valuable time digging you out every time you fall off? Give me that rope. Sit still, do you hear?' he roared. 'Be thankful you're not a boy, or I'd put this rope to a very good use, here and now, and I don't mean just to tie you to the saddle!'

'I won't be strapped on like a piece of baggage!' she cried, more than half afraid he might change his mind and thrash her anyway.

'A piece of baggage is exactly what you are! A useless and unnecessary one! Right, that should do it. Keep your eye on the road!'

He stood back to survey his handiwork and then stooped to retrieve his hat, which had fallen into the snow. After slapping it against his leg to remove the crust of snow, he crammed it on his head. Then he put his fingers to his mouth and whistled.

In answer, a shadowy shape emerged from the gathering gloom, and a dapple-grey horse, with the fine head of the Arab, lustrous eyes and smoky-black pasterns which made it look as though it wore black stockings, walked across and stood by its master, drooping its head and flattening its ears before the wind.

'He's beautiful!' exclaimed Charlotte.

'He is also very intelligent, and certainly more so than some humans. Given a choice, *he* would not choose to be here!' the Captain snapped, pulling himself up into the saddle. 'Walk on, Kismet!' He clicked his tongue.

Kismet tossed his delicate head, and the horses moved off side by side. Despite the woollen blanket, Charlotte still felt very cold and, what was worse, damp. She had lost all contact with her feet. They might not have been there at all.

Patches of bare rock had begun to show in the snow layer. The men had lit pitch torches, and the flames flickered and hissed on the ice.

'You don't have to stay with me,' Charlotte said through chattering teeth.

'It is not by choice. The road is narrow here, and I can't get past that gun-carriage up ahead,' he said sourly.

'Oh,' she said flatly, and after a moment, asked, 'What brought you by, just at that moment?'

'I came to investigate a strange report I had received. Someone kindly informed me I need not worry, as the girl I'd brought along had safely crossed the pass. He then proceeded to congratulate me on my good fortune. As I had been unaware that I travelled encumbered with such a piece of impedimenta, I became curious, though I had more than a shrewd idea it would turn out to be you! I had to make sure. The road is better here, on our way down, so I took the opportunity to come back and see what object of feminine charm I'd acquired.'

'I told you Cresson would put that tale about,' Charlotte replied, disconcerted.

'Cresson may gossip a little, but in this case I think he had help. You wouldn't know anything about it, I suppose?'

'I had to say it,' she said defiantly. 'It is as you told me. I have to belong to someone. Yours is the only name I know.'

'So I am to be obliged to extend my protection to you? You are over-optimistic, *ma belle*. Do you think I have nothing to do but look after pig-headed young women, *and* for no reward?'

'I have very little money!' Charlotte's reply was scornful.

'I don't talk of money! Women generally pay in another way. You, however, would not stoop to that!'

'I dare say you dislike my having used your name,' Charlotte said angrily. 'But that does not entitle you to be impertinent! You have most certainly not "acquired" me! I am, of course, grateful that you dug me out of the snow, but if you expect favours in return, you will be disappointed!'

'You've a high opinion of your own desirability, Mademoiselle Lacoste! Why should I want a scrawny, spoiled, self-opinionated little miss with far too much to say, no sense, and a talent for getting in everyone's way?'

She set her mouth firmly, and stared stonily ahead of her.

Unexpectedly, he leaned across from the saddle and seized the bridle of her horse, bringing her to an abrupt halt. 'So listen to me, *mignonne*,' he said softly. She could not see his features clearly in the darkness, but the tone of his voice was sufficient. 'You have badly mistaken your man. I am not gallant or soft-hearted, nor do I need your company in other ways. If you attempt again to use me without my knowledge to further your idiotic plans, you will be sorry you ever left Châlons!'

Charlotte shivered, but not from the cold.

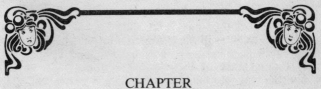

CHAPTER
FIVE

COLD, DAMP and exhausted, the Army of Reserve slithered and dragged itself down the icy track from the great pass, and finally came to a bedraggled halt just below the snowline.

Patches of unmelted snow were still plentiful enough in nooks and crannies where the sun could not find them out, and the wind was icy and relentless, carrying on it a disagreeable substance which was neither ice nor snow nor pure rain, but some kind of unpleasant mixture compounded of all three. Pascal pitched a tent in the lee of the wind behind an outcrop of rock, where there was a minuscule area of flat ground, and Charlotte crawled into it on her hands and knees and sat, huddled inside, completely exhausted and unable to do anything.

She ought to get out of her wet clothing, that was obvious, but to make the effort was just too much. She wanted to sleep also, but was too uncomfortable and miserable. The tarpaulin of the tent flapped and creaked as the driving sleet rattled against it. Worst of all, her feet were quite numb.

Charlotte roused herself sufficiently to scrabble at her sodden footwear with frozen fingers, and managed to drag off her shoes. Her once-white stockings were black with mud. As she was surveying them disconsolately, she was surprised to hear a familiar voice outside the tent.

'Where the devil has she got to?' it demanded.

'Over here, sir,' came Pascal's reply. Feet crunched on the ground outside. 'She'll be all right in there. I've set up a few tents and bivouacs in my time.'

The tent-flap opened, and Marc Forestier scrambled inside to join her in the cramped interior, and sat down heavily beside her. He was hatless, and clasped an unlabelled bottle of some colourless liquid.

'More over,' he said.

Charlotte moved silently to one side.

'Well,' he indicated the tent sides with a flick of his hand. 'Your man knows how to make you comfortable. I was going to send over Baptistin, my groom, to fix you up some shelter, but I see it isn't necessary. Here you are, quite living in luxury.'

'Yes,' said Charlotte dully.

'Where are your belongings? Get that wet dress off!'

She almost said, 'I can't, I'm too tired,' but managed to stop this fatal admission of weakness just in time. 'My fingers are too cold,' she conceded, adding quickly, 'I'll do it in a minute.'

'Look here,' he said sharply. 'I'm not a damn lady's maid! I can't be hooking you up and unhooking you night and morning. Rub your hands to warm them, and hurry up about it! You'll catch pneumonia.'

Charlotte obeyed unwillingly, managing with some difficulty to struggle out of the wet gown. It occurred to her, as she did so, that to get undressed in the close company of Captain Forestier was not the sort of behaviour she would have contemplated even twenty-four hours earlier, but here it scarcely seemed to matter any more, or perhaps she was past caring.

He was right about the pneumonia, of course. He had an irritating habit of being right, but not, she hoped, about her inability to complete her journey. She huddled in her petticoat while he rummaged in her baggage without the slightest embarrassment or troubling himself to ask permission, eventually dragging out a woollen gown, which he pushed into her arms.

'That will do. Put it on. Come on, look lively!' he ordered.

'There isn't very much room,' Charlotte said resentfully. 'Can't you go outside for a few minutes? Then I might be able to move my arms.'

'You can manage. *I'm* not sitting out there in the wind and slush, waiting for you.' He wrenched the cork from the mysterious bottle. 'Feet!' he said, inexplicably.

'Which feet?' she asked blankly.

'Your feet, you brainless woman! Whose feet should I mean? Take your stockings off. What's the matter with you? Has the cold frozen your brain?' He leaned forward and grasped her left ankle firmly.

'What are you doing? Leave it! I'll do it!' she protested, pulling her foot from his hand.

He waited impatiently as she dragged off the soaking stockings and dropped them, unrecognisable rags, on top of the wet gown.

'Right!' he said briskly. 'One at a time. Give me your foot, and don't start playing coy.'

'What are you going to do?' Charlotte demanded, stretching out her foot gingerly towards him. 'What's in that bottle?'

'Alcohol.' He tipped some of it into his palm, and seizing her frozen bare foot, began to rub it vigorously.

For a moment she could feel nothing, then a surging warmth ran through her foot, followed by the most excruciating throbbing pain as sensation returned. 'Stop, Captain, stop! My foot hurts!' she pleaded, trying to free herself.

'Good!' he retorted unkindly, refusing to release her. 'Better a little pain, which means returning circulation, than a frostbitten foot. Want me to fetch the surgeon to cut off a set of gangrenous toes?'

'No . . .' Charlotte whispered, appalled.

'So, give me your other foot. Come on, I haven't got all night! Do you think I've nothing else to do but play nursemaid to you?' He completed his task with rough efficiency, and then paused, his hand still resting on her ankle. 'You need a maid,' he said. 'Not some simpering lady's maid—I mean some woman who is used to this life, and can look after you.'

'I suppose,' she returned sarcastically, 'you mean to suggest one of your camp-following bawds as my personal attendant? Thank you, Captain, I'll manage by myself, with Pascal.'

'Pascal is going to need all his energies to keep your horses and mule alive and able to work. Do you think horses don't suffer as well as humans from cold and want? When we get to the next town, I'll find some decent woman, some soldier's wife—if you're still set on this crazy plan of yours, that is.' He changed the subject abruptly. 'If you have any food with you, eat it before you drop off to sleep. If you're hungry, you'll be cold.'

Charlotte contemplated him thoughtfully. Despite the rough exterior and sharp tongue, to say nothing of the frightening temper which, even dormant, teetered perilously on the verge of explosion like some fiery volcano, the Captain inspired an odd kind of confidence. Not trust, exactly—Charlotte would not have trusted him for one moment—more a sense of capability. He was a man who, if he set his mind to a thing, would see it through, with a mixture of ruthless practicality and unscrupulous unorthodoxy. She was not sure whether this made him a very reliable person, or an extremely dangerous one.

But it was very warm in the tent now from the combined heat of their bodies, and she wished he would let go of her ankle. Somewhat embarrassed, she said firmly, 'You can release my foot, Captain Forestier. Thank you for your help. I'm sure you have other duties. You can go now.'

He withdrew his hand, and rested his forearms on his bent knees. 'Don't dismiss *me* like that, *mignonne*,' he said evenly. 'I'm not a servant!'

'I'm very grateful you thought of me!' Charlotte said quickly. She had not meant to offend him. She remembered the mysterious woman who had sought him out twice at Villeneuve, and in an unwise attempt to lighten her ill-received dismissal of him, added, 'But I am sure there is another lady who would appreciate a visit from you!'

It had quite the reverse effect to that she had intended. The blue eyes, half obscured though they were by the untidy locks of black hair, narrowed sharply, and glittered as coldly as the glacier behind them. In that soft voice which made her heart leap in alarm, he said, 'You are mistaken, mademoiselle.'

She drew back. 'I—I didn't . . .' she faltered, unable to finish her sentence.

His gaze swept over her startled features. 'What's the matter?' he asked drily. 'Afraid of me? I'm not going to hurt you.' He picked up the bottle and drove the cork into the neck with a blow from the heel of his palm. 'Well,' he went on brusquely, 'I've work to do. If you need anything, send Pascal to find me. Get some sleep now.' He scrambled out through the tent-flap.

Left alone, Charlotte made a half-hearted attempt to eat some bread and sausage, before carefully pulling a second pair of stockings on over the first, mindful of the Captain's warning about gangrenous toes. Then she rolled herself up in her cloak and a blanket, and heedless of the wind tugging at the tarpaulin, the shouts of men or the neighing of horses all around her, fell fast asleep in pure exhaustion.

The next day they set off again. The sun was shining brightly, and as they descended the valley the green grass began to show and a few early mountain flowers peeped out from the shelter of rocks and stones. Behind them, the Alps towered, beautiful and fascinating, but no longer threatening. The Army of Reserve had accepted their challenge, and won.

Everyone seemed to feel the rise in spirits. The men were cheerful and jocular, and even the horses and mules pricked their ears and seemed to go forward more willingly. In such fine fettle, the army poured on down the valley and overran the ancient stronghold of Aosta, to the dismay of its inhabitants, who viewed their arrival much as their Roman forebears must have viewed the descent of barbarian Goths upon them.

Charlotte felt as though she had arrived in Paradise. The Captain had found her a lodging; she slept in a proper bed again, and best of all, she was able to take a bath, relaxing her stiff aching limbs in the warm water with an unimaginable sense of luxury. As a further surprise, he did prove himself as good as his word, and turned up that evening, leading by the hand a sturdy, cheerful woman in her early thirties, still attractive, though an outdoor life and many hardships had wrinkled her rosy cheeks like the peel of an over-ripe apple.

'This is Babette.' He introduced the woman. 'Her husband is one of our farriers. She's a good soul, and will look after you. I told you I'd get you a maid.'

'Thank you,' Charlotte said awkwardly.

'And now I've finished with you,' he went on unkindly. 'You know I think this a hare-brained scheme of yours, so don't expect me to play any further part in it. And in case you're thinking of mentioning the noble Lucien again, I'm being the best friend I can be to him, and to you, in telling you to turn back now. If you had more than a thimbleful of common-sense, you would!'

'You have been more than kind, Captain!' she retorted, with scarlet cheeks, her sharp tone belying her gracious words.

He threw her a sardonic look before prowling off down the narrow street, a tall, dark, lean figure like a predatory panther, every line announcing that he did not like this town with its cramped buildings and cluttered streets full of civilians. It got in his way. The civilians themselves, however, took good care not to get in the way of him, but the Savoyard housewives paused in their evening doorstep gossip to look after him as he passed, and then fell to whispering together.

'He's a handsome devil, the Captain,' said Babette dreamily, watching from the window.

'Devil, certainly,' muttered Charlotte, turning her back resolutely on the sight.

She explained to the maid as much as she deemed it

necessary for her to know of the purpose of her journey.

Babette listened dubiously. 'If your cousin is a gentleman, mademoiselle, he'll come back and marry you for sure. It's not as though you were a country girl, to whom soldiers promise anything! He'll be back.'

'I don't doubt my cousin!' Charlotte told her energetically.

'Bless you, mademoiselle, of course you don't!' Babette eyed the girl shrewdly. 'But this isn't a good idea of yours, this running after him. He'll perhaps not like it. And if you do go on, you'll need Captain Forestier's help.'

'I do not need *his* help! I have Pascal, and now I have you to help me. Speaking of which, Babette, we must discuss wages. Now, I cannot afford to pay you a great deal, I'm afraid . . .'

'You don't have to pay me anything for a bit,' she interrupted unexpectedly. 'The Captain's already given me some money on account of you.'

'He has done what?' Charlotte, surprised and not altogether pleased, stared at the maid incredulously.

'Well, you know,' replied Babette comfortably, 'he did say, when he paid me, that it was well worth it to him to be rid of you! But you know, my dear, that was just his way of doing it. He didn't mean that. He's a bit worried about you, I reckon.'

'I'm sure he isn't!'

'Now, don't go scorning his interest, mademoiselle.' Babette spoke severely. 'You *need* an officer to speak up for you, and better Captain Forestier than some of the others I could mention! And, mind you, I'm not a proper lady's maid. But when I was a girl, I was laundrymaid in a big house, so I know how things are done in good families!'

In fact, not only were Babette's laundry skills of immediate use, but she also proved a bottomless source of information, gossip and anecdote. For the first time, the grim realities of the life she had so optimistically embraced were brought home to Charlotte vividly in her frank and colourful accounts of regimental life. One of the women on their present journey, Charlotte was horrified to learn, had even given birth to a baby during the descent from the Great St Bernard.

'Bless you, mademoiselle,' the maid said when Charlotte expressed her concern. 'I've had three born to me, which died in the camp or on the march. So when my last boy was born, we sent him to my sister to rear. Now he's eight years old, and I've seen him only the once since the day I took him there. But I heard from my sister that he's really doing well, and learning his letters and everything!' she finished proudly.

Charlotte sighed. It was a cruel life which called for such sacrifices, and the commanders of the great armies gave little if any thought to the families which struggled to survive amid the hardships of the march, and the babies born amid the smoke of the cannon and the thunder of the great guns.

All that night she lay restless, occasionally dropping into fitful slumber, only to awake with a start from some all-too-real dream in which she was trapped amongst the guns or lost in the snowdrifts. She sat up at last in bed in the cold dawn light, clammy with perspiration, and asked herself seriously, for the first time, whether she was really attempting the impossible. Could she hope to go on, without someone like the Captain to guide her? Babette was right. She needed him.

They set out early into the streets to see what provisions might be had. But it was as if a plague of locusts had already ravaged the little town, and they counted themselves fortunate to obtain a bag of flour and some smoked bacon.

'Better than nothing,' said Babette philosophically. 'Pick up something else, very likely, as we go along.' She lowered her voice. 'Just turn your back, mademoiselle, and pull your shawl over your head. Make quick, now!'

'Why?' asked Charlotte, instead of doing as she was bid.

The answer came soon enough in the form of a

lascivious voice in her ear. 'Well, what have we here, eh? Pretty as a picture, and all alone!'

A pair of arms enfolded her, and held her fast in a familiar and unwanted embrace, as she gave a cry of alarm.

'Just you take your hands off my lady, and be on your way!' stormed Babette. She darted forward to pull Charlotte bodily from the arms of one of a pair of rakish young artillery lieutenants, evidently in search of diversion.

'Just you hold your tongue,' jeered the one who had seized Charlotte. 'Perhaps your lady wants to come with us! With a face and a figure like this, I'll wager she knows a trick or two to entertain us. What you do say, my pretty? You've a choice of two fine cavaliers—either, or both?'

He attempted to put his arm around her again, but Charlotte dodged aside, only to find herself roughly embraced by his companion, who held her tight, despite her struggles and kicks, and laughed heartily at her efforts to free herself. He grasped her hand and held it up. 'Well, now,' he said insolently. 'No wedding-ring— no jealous husband!' He grinned at his companion, and added, 'You won't have to go clambering out through the bedroom window in your shirt-tails, as you did last time!'

'Instead, Captain Forestier will very likely break your ignorant head!' said Babette sharply. 'I hope he does.'

The two young men exchanged glances, and the one holding Charlotte released her, but did not move away. 'This isn't Forestier's girl,' he said suspiciously. 'We all know with whom Forestier shares his bed!'

'Maybe you don't know so much as you fancy , then!' snapped Babette.

'Wait a moment,' the other remarked suddenly. 'I did hear a tale that Forestier had a girl with him. Not Madame, but another. Cresson said so.'

'Cresson says anything!' said his companion dismissively.

'Not about Forestier, he doesn't. And, come to that, I saw Forestier myself, sitting and talking in an inn with a girl who had fair curls very like hers.' He grasped a handful of Charlotte's hair to illustrate his words, and she tossed her head furiously to free herself.

'Well, you can ask the Captain yourself, for here he comes now.' The maid pointed down the narrow street.

'I'm not staying to ask him!' said the one who had first held Charlotte. 'You can cross his path if you want—I'm off! If Forestier is amusing himself with this little one, it's not to *us* he'll have to explain himself!'

Both young men set off in the opposite direction, and were rapidly lost from sight.

'You see how right I was?' demanded Babette. 'Without an officer to speak for you, you'll have nothing but trouble of that sort, or worse! And the name you need is Captain Forestier's.'

'Is he really coming?' asked Charlotte apprehensively.

'I'd spot him in any crowd; a big, tall fellow like that!'

Sure enough, there he came, easily distinguishable by his height and ramshackle good looks, moving slowly through the crowded street towards them. He seemed not to have seen them yet, because he was looking down at, and talking to, some unseen person beside him. As she watched, Charlotte saw him laugh.

Some instinct sent a prickle running up her spine. Charlotte seized Babette's arm, and dragged the startled maid into the shadowy concealment of a courtyard arch. They were just in time. Forestier and his companion passed by, so close that Charlotte could have reached out and touched the elbow of the woman who leaned on his arm. As it was, she had difficulty in restraining an audible gasp of surprise.

It was the woman whom she had seen briefly in Paris, at the Ministry of War, the woman in the fur-trimmed pelisse. She was smiling up tantalisingly, and Forestier lifted her hand, which rested on his sleeve, and kissed her gloved fingers, as the couple passed out of sight.

Charlotte stood rigid in her hiding-place, plunged into

thought, until Babette touched her arm. Then she asked, as carelessly as possible, 'Did you know that lady, Babette?'

'Oh, everyone knows *her*! It's Madame Thierry. Her husband is an officer on the Staff. *She* got him that job, you can be sure. She's a trollop, officer's lady or no. But *you* don't want to give any thought to her, mademoiselle. There's always a few of that sort about, mostly causing trouble. As for the Captain, well, you can't blame a man for accepting what's offered so freely!'

'That depends!' said Charlotte. She walked the rest of the way home in silence, with a great deal to occupy her thoughts.

All that day she tried to concentrate on the preparations for the next stage of her journey, but the image of Madame Thierry—and especially the image of Marc Forestier kissing Madame Thierry's hand—kept intruding in a most unwelcome manner. She had chosen to keep dissolute and dangerous company. The thought of travelling in it, unprotected, until she found Lucien was extremely disturbing. Some arrangement had to be made, and somehow it had to include the Captain.

A mood of grey depression gradually settled upon her. She did not belong among these people, they were a race apart. When evening came, she sat before the fire of crackling pine-logs in the stone hearth, and stared dejectedly into the leaping flames. Babette had packed up everything, and tomorrow they would be off. But Charlotte's former optimism had evaporated. To find Lucien seemed all at once an impossible task, or one impossible to undertake alone.

Babette came to put another piece of wood on the fire, and surveyed her young employer's forlorn figure shrewdly. 'What will you do about the Captain, mademoiselle?'

Charlotte jumped, so closely did the words echo her own thoughts. 'You heard for yourself what he said to me, Babette, and you know what he said to you,' she sighed. 'He won't help me any more.'

'Men say all manner of things they don't mean. He'd not abandon you, a young lady, among all these men, I'm sure!'

'Oh yes, he would. In fact, he has. I know what you're going to suggest, Babette. But I won't—I can't—go and ask him.'

'You said he was a friend of your cousin,' Babette pointed out.

'Much difference that makes!' said Charlotte sullenly. 'If I go to him again, I shall only be told I'm a nuisance, and stupid, and should go home. It's not as though he made any effort to be polite about it.'

'Did he or did he not come to see you were all right, coming down from the pass?' Babette demanded. 'Did he, or did he not, find you this billet, and seek *me* out? Officers and men alike, they all have a lot of respect for Captain Forestier. If you could persuade him to take you along with him, it would make a whole lot of difference. You're too young and pretty, my dear, to go travelling alone in this company! It's hard to bury your pride, but I don't think you've any choice. Why don't you put on your cloak now, and go and see him? I know where he lodges. He has an alarming way with him, and a wild temper, mademoiselle, but he's a good man for all that, if you can catch him in the right mood. Tomorrow will be too late.'

'He can only refuse again, I suppose,' Charlotte said, rising to her feet reluctantly. 'Very well, Babette, though I'm not at all sure this is a good idea. Let's go straight away, because if I think about it at all, I know I'll change my mind.'

Dusk had fallen when they reached the house where the Captain lodged. Charlotte told Babette to wait outside, and went up to the door alone. It stood ajar. She pushed it open and stepped into the stone-flagged hall. No one greeted her, and the reason appeared to be that some dispute had arisen between the owners of the house. From the kitchen, acrimonious words were being flung in Savoyard patois, accompanied by a few more solid missiles, signalled by the occasional crash of crockery.

Charlotte peeped into the other two rooms on the ground floor, immaculately swept and polished, but quite empty. Could he have left already? Ahead of her stretched a flight of stairs. She put her hand on the banister and ascended cautiously. She did not wish to be accused of being a house-thief, but it would take only a moment to look around upstairs and see if anyone was there who could give her some information.

A narrow corridor ran the width of the upper floor, with three or four doors in it. Charlotte listened at each, but it was not until she reached the one at the end that she thought she heard movement on the other side. She put out her hand to knock, but the door was only on the latch, and insecurely at that. As her hand touched it, it swung open to reveal the room and its occupants.

The woman saw her first. She pushed herself up in the bed, her loosened dark hair tumbled onto her magnificent naked shoulders, and stared boldly at Charlotte, not even troubling to pull the sheet across her full, ivory bosom.

Marc Forestier, who stood by the bed in his shirt and breeches, a glass of wine in his hand, swung round as he realised someone was there, and uttered a low oath.

'I—I'm so sorry,' Charlotte whispered, transfixed by the candle-light scene. How could she have been so stupid as to overlook the possibility that Madame Thierry might be with him?

For a moment, Charlotte stood before their eyes, feeling in her embarrassment as naked as Madame Thierry obviously was. Then the woman murmured, 'Why don't you see what your little friend wants, Marc?' She relaxed back onto the pillows, resting her head on one bare arm, and smiled in amusement.

Charlotte backed away from the door, into the corridor. She wanted to turn and run as fast as she could, but her feet seemed to be shod with lead, and before she could escape, the Captain thrust his way past the door, seized her wrists in a painful grip, and dragged her some distance down the corridor. She had never in her life seen anyone so angry, and the anger was directed fully at her. He shook her like a terrier with a rat in its jaws, so furiously that she felt as though her brain rattled, the world swirled about her, and she thought she would faint, or be sick, or both.

'What in damnation do you think you are doing here?' he snarled.

In her terror, she stammered, 'I didn't mean—I didn't know she was there! I only wanted to see you, and there was no one to ask. *Please* let go of me, you're making me feel *ill*!'

He pushed her against the wall so roughly that she gasped for breath, and held her pinned there, motionless. 'Have you no sense at all? You're not safe to be left for five minutes! Where's Babette? I told her to keep an eye on you!'

'She's downstairs,' Charlotte whispered. 'Captain, I only wanted . . .'

'Do get *rid* of the child, Marc,' Madame Thierry's voice called from the bedroom impatiently.

She had made a mistake. Charlotte saw him stiffen, and his expression freeze. 'It concerns me, Éloise, and *I'll* deal with it!' he called out coldly in reply. But his anger had been deflected from Charlotte, and he released her. When he spoke to her again, it was more quietly, and he seemed more in control of himself. 'You have no business to be out at this hour at all. The streets are full of our soldiers, and more than three-quarters of them will be drunk by now. Go straight home with Babette, do you hear? I'll come and see you tomorrow early. Whatever you want, you can tell me about it then.'

'Yes, yes, of course!'

'That lady,' he said threateningly. 'You didn't see her, you understand?'

'I'm not going to gossip!' Charlotte retorted, regaining some measure of confidence. 'It's of no interest to me what you do!'

As she hurried away downstairs to the waiting Babette, she heard the laughter of Madame Thierry floating down the staircase after her.

She was alone at breakfast the next morning when Marc Forestier strode in, without warning. He threw himself down into the chair across the table from her, and tossed his hat onto the cloth.

'Well?' he said coldly. 'You wanted to see me. Here I am.'

Charlotte set down her coffee-cup, trying not to let it rattle and betray her nervousness. 'I apologise for disturbing you last night,' she began.

'Never mind that!' he said irritably. 'Though you should have known better than just to come up, un-announced.'

'I could hardly have expected to find what I did!' Charlotte retaliated.

'Why not?' The blue eyes challenged her. 'I'm human. I like my pleasures. What did you think I'd be doing?'

'She's a married woman,' Charlotte said with dis-approval.

'How do you know?' he asked sharply.

'Because it was Madame Thierry. I saw her, at the War Ministry in Paris.'

He shrugged. 'Well, what should I have done? Asked *you*? That would have been a waste of time, wouldn't it? You're saving yourself for Saint-Laurent.'

'Don't jeer at me. I know the difference between right and wrong!'

'And I don't, eh? I shouldn't cuckold poor Thierry. Well, if I didn't, another would. Others have before me, and will do so after me!'

'That doesn't make it right for you to do it, and you know it!'

'You like to appeal to my finer feelings, don't you, *mignonne*? Unfortunately I haven't any, so you might as well save your breath.'

'Don't you have any feelings for her?' she demanded.

'Don't you—have any affection for—her?'

'Do I love her, is what you mean. No, I don't love her. Any man who let himself fall in love with Éloise Thierry would be better off in the lunatic asylum in which he belonged! But I like her. I admire her. I understand her, too—which *you* don't. She and I, we're two of a kind, and we know it. Nothing but our wits to recommend us and what physical abilities nature has given us. In my case, an aptitude for soldiering, and in her case a talent for—in other directions,' he finished, amending his final words just in time. 'That's what's kept us both alive,' he added after a moment.

'Well, it's no concern of mine,' Charlotte told him stiffly. 'Captain Forestier, I wanted to see you on my own account.'

A sudden grin broke the sternness of his expression. 'If I didn't know you better, *mignonne*, I'd feel almost encouraged by a statement like that! But, coming from you, I assume it to mean you want some favour.'

'Yes,' she said, quite calmly.

He leaned back, one arm slung loosely over the chairback, and eyed her thoughtfully. 'What puzzles me, Charlotte, is that you expect me to do—whatever it is—when there will be nothing in it for me but added and unnecessary trouble and inconvenience. Yet at the same time you don't hesitate to tell me what a worthless rogue I am. So why come to a scoundrel like me?'

'Because I believe that you are a ruthless, and extremely capable, man. That is why I've come to you, and not to another. *You* can take me to Lucien, if only you will. If you cannot, no one can. I want to find Lucien. I'm not stupid. Much as I dislike having to admit that you are right, I see now I cannot travel unescorted; I must appear to be under someone's protection. I don't ask you to look after me. All I want is to be able to give your name, and if anyone asks you about me, for you to say . . .'

She hesitated, and he completed her sentence for her.

'To say you are under my personal protection, and whoever it is, should keep away. It's a bright little idea, *mignonne*, and quite unscrupulous. I told you before that you were a perfect little hypocrite. You want to be thought my mistress, without earning the title, and you scorn poor Éloise Thierry, who could claim the title and has more than earned it!' He chuckled, possibly at some memory.

'If I were not obliged to ask this of you,' Charlotte flashed at him, 'I wouldn't!'

'You know what I think of your plan to travel on.' He unhooked himself from the chairback and leaned forward to peer into the coffee-pot.

'I know. That's why you chose Babette to be my maid, isn't it? And paid her? You knew what tales of horror she'd tell me.'

'You should listen to her. This coffee is cold. Is there any wine in this house?'

'No, there isn't, and if there were, it's too early in the day to be drinking.'

'One day you're going to lead some wretch a miserable life, *mignonne*. But not me! I won't do it. I won't take you with me.'

Charlotte swallowed. 'I understand that Madame Thierry might be suspicious, and not like it . . .'

'I don't take my instructions from women,' Forestier interrupted coolly. 'Neither from Éloise, indebted to her though I am—nor from you, to whom I owe nothing.'

'But you know how much I need your help,' she said quietly. 'Without it, I can't go on. Please . . .' She hated to beg him like this, to bury her pride and admit so openly her desperate need of his aid.

He shrugged. 'Why should I help you to do something I believe to be complete madness?' he answered indifferently. 'I have neither the time nor the desire to play knight-errant.' He caught sight of her subdued expression, and continued brutally, 'You brought yourself this far, so you can do the rest. I can't have you trailing after me. If you persist in going on, I cannot prevent you, but neither is it my responsibility. And now I bid you *adieu*.'

He pushed back his chair, picked up his hat, gave her a brief nod, and strode out of the room.

Charlotte's repressed and smouldering resentment burst into a flame of anger at this curt rebuff. She jumped up and ran after him, shouting furiously, 'Then I assure you, Captain, I am heartily glad to see the last of you! You're right. If anything were to put me off my journey, it would be the thought of having to spend it in the company of an ill-bred scoundrel, a disgrace to the uniform he wears! I am more than capable of looking after myself, and I certainly do not need *you*!'

He gave her a sardonic look, but no other reply, as he wrenched open the front door. Charlotte, quite beside herself with humiliation and anger, ran back into the dining-room, seized the coffee-pot from the table and hurled it out of the door after him as he went off down the street. Lucien had taught her how to throw properly when she was little, and it was a good throw now, which all but hit the Captain, crashing instead onto the cobbles at his heels, to the startled amazement of passers-by. She was immediately sorry, partly because now she would have to pay for the pot, but chiefly because she had missed him.

Marc Forestier did not even look round.

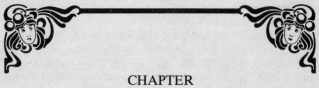

CHAPTER
SIX

LATER THAT morning, Charlotte helped Pascal to secure their luggage, resentment still burning strongly inside her.

'We'll see, Captain Forestier,' she muttered, struggling with a stiff harness-buckle. 'Trail after you, indeed! I shall get along a great deal better without you. Oh, no . . .' She released the buckle and studied the broken fingernail.

'Permit me, mademoiselle,' said a courteous voice behind her.

Charlotte jumped, and spun round to see a handsome young Hussar standing behind her, holding his horse by the bridle. With his gold-frogged and fur-trimmed Hungarian-style pelisse slung loosely across his shoulders, and his brown hair braided into thick stubby plaits in the quaint fashion of the Hussars, he contrived, against this chaotic backdrop of an army on the march, to look as though he stood, elegant and debonair, upon the polished floor of some Parisian ballroom.

He smiled at her now and leaned past her to fix the harness-buckle deftly.

'Thank you . . .' she stammered.

He bowed politely. 'A pleasure, mademoiselle. A Hussar, you see, does not leave a lady to hurt her dainty fingers on a common harness-buckle.' His dark eyes twinkled at her.

'You are very kind,' Charlotte replied awkwardly, thinking to herself, 'Unlike *some* . . . If I had to saddle up both these horses and the pack-mule all by myself, I dare say Captain Forestier would leave me to do it.'

The Hussar remounted his horse and saluting smilingly, trotted briskly away.

'Humph!' muttered Pascal, behind her. 'Fancies his chance, does he? Not while I'm around!'

'Don't be silly, Pascal. He was only being kind.'

'Was he?' growled the coachman mistrustfully. 'Well, I never met a Hussar who didn't spend his time chasing petticoats. Womanising dandies, the whole lot of them. I've got the measure of that one, though. I'll put paid to his little scheme.'

The morning passed uneventfully enough, though they made little progress, having to wait their turn to move off at the rear of the force, and finding the narrow road heavily encumbered with pack-animals.

They halted at midday to make their meal. Charlotte was busily and inelegantly kneeling on the ground, engaged in blowing energetically at the fire Pascal had kindled, when her eye fell on a pair of polished boots and gleaming spurs, and looking up, startled, she beheld her Hussar acquaintance again.

Hastily scrambling to her feet and pushing back her dishevelled hair, she exclaimed in confusion, 'I'm sorry, I didn't know anyone was there.'

'Forgive me,' he spread his hands deprecatingly. 'I didn't mean to alarm you. But as we meet again, perhaps I may present myself? Dufour . . .' He bowed again elegantly. 'I, ah, wondered how you were faring.'

'Well enough,' she replied cautiously.

'You travel alone, mademoiselle?' He raised an eyebrow interrogatively.

'I—Yes, with my servants.'

'You run some risk, *chère mademoiselle*, if you will permit me to say so. This company'—he gestured vaguely around them—'is hardly of the most respectable.'

'I know,' Charlotte said flatly. 'I've already found that out.'

'I hope you won't think me presumptuous, mademoiselle,' Dufour continued, 'but if I may be of assistance . . .'

'I don't know,' she interrupted him. 'I can really manage very well. I appreciate your kindness in offering. But, you see, I really am not free to . . .'

'*Chère mademoiselle*,' he protested, with a gleam in his dark eyes which belied his words, 'I assure you I have no dishonourable intentions.'

'Then something very odd has happened to the Hussars!' said a dry voice behind them.

'Captain!' Charlotte exclaimed, spinning round, an involuntary note of relief echoing in her voice.

He came closer, skirting the fire, a long, powerful, slightly hunched figure, moving slowly and deliberately, and resembling even more some feline hunter, lean and dangerous.

The Hussar took a step back. 'I beg your pardon, monsieur,' he said quickly. 'I wished only to know if the lady required any assistance.'

'She doesn't,' said Forestier curtly. 'And, if she did, she wouldn't need to go to the Hussars to find it. The artillery is well able to look after its own women.'

'I'm sure,' the Hussar said stiffly. 'Forgive me, I wrongly imagined the lady without protection.'

'Now you know better,' Forestier's tone was icy. 'She is with me.'

'So I see!' Dufour flushed. He turned to Charlotte, bowed correctly, and made off.

'Thank you, Captain,' she murmured. 'I am very grateful . . .'

'I don't need your gratitude!'

'No, of course not! You have, after all, washed your hands of me!' Charlotte snapped. 'So what are you doing here?'

'Preventing you from falling into the arms of the first smooth-tongued gallant to present himself, it seems,' he retaliated unkindly.

'*I* am not Madame Thierry,' Charlotte replied coldly. 'In any case, why should you care? You told me to look after myself.'

'Which it seems you are unable to do. Pascal came and

told me that pretty fellow had already found you out and was hanging round.' He jerked his head disdainfully towards the now distant figure of the Hussar.

'Pascal had no business to do any such thing!' she cried furiously. 'He'll hear about it from me.'

'Pascal has good sense, and you should be grateful for it. Anyway,' Marc hesitated. 'I've been thinking over what you said earlier, and I've changed my mind. All things considered, you had better come with me.'

Charlotte's heart leaped in relief, but pride spoke first. 'I have not the slightest wish to be a burden to you, Captain!' she flashed, her eyes sparkling dangerously.

'Don't worry, you won't be. You'll do as I say, and only what I say you may do. Is that quite clear?' he demanded brusquely.

'Very well. But it must also be clear that this is purely an arrangement of convenience. I am Lucien's fiancée. I trust you will conduct yourself, to the extent that you are able, in a suitable manner.'

'Have no fear. As you said just now, *you* are not Madame Thierry!'

'Éloise Thierry has to do with this!' Charlotte exclaimed suddenly. 'You've had time to talk to her since you saw me at breakfast, and something has led to this change of heart! Now, I wonder what it can be . . .'

'You're sharp, aren't you?' he said dourly. 'Éloise's husband is getting restive. Too many jokes are being made about him. He's finding it more and more difficult to pretend he can't hear them,' he added sarcastically.

'I understand. So it will suit your purpose as much as mine to have others believe me to be your mistress! It will cover your sordid affair with the wife of Captain Thierry!'

'All right, it suits me!' he snarled. 'So long as it *is* mutually convenient, then, we'll travel together. Are you agreed? Or shall I call back the Hussar?'

'We'll travel together!' she conceded hastily.

It was hardly the best of arrangements, she reflected, as they set off again, but for the time being, it was the best to be had. At least, they were on the move, and every step took her nearer to Lucien. Perhaps they would even find him sooner than expected, and she would be able to thank Captain Forestier for his kind protection and dismiss him into the arms of Madame Thierry. Charlotte rehearsed this scene several times in her mind's eye. The part dismissing the Captain was always satisfying. But the idea of Madame Thierry rankled annoyingly, and was undeniably disturbing. For the sight of that beautiful ivory body reclining on the pillows of his bed had made her realise how very little she herself understood of physical love. She was not ignorant of what was involved, but the realisation that a man might expect more than simple compliance from a woman was quite new to her. It was quite obvious, from what she had seen and heard, that Madame Thierry played an active, rather than a passive, rôle in proceedings. Charlotte mulled it all over, with mixed emotions. After a while, she took to rehearsing the scene of his dismissal without the person of Madame's figuring in it.

As for Forestier, being on the move agreed with him, too. As they descended into the warm sunshine, his manner relaxed visibly and he was almost pleasant company, although the sharpness always remained behind the pleasantries.

'It won't be long,' he said, leaning forward in the saddle to brush a few flies away from Kismet's ears. 'We'll be down on the plains of Italy, basking in the sun. You'll have to get yourself a straw hat, eh?'

'Kismet needs the hat,' Charlotte retorted.

'With a couple of holes cut out from his ears like a peasant's donkey? You wish me to look ridiculous, Mademoiselle Lacoste.' He glanced at her, a gleam in his blue eyes.

'You flatter yourself, Captain, that I give any thought to you at all.'

'Of course you do. Women have spiteful and vindictive natures! They are for ever fancying themselves slighted, and always wreak revenge if given half a chance.'

'You do have a very low opinion of women, don't you?' she said seriously. 'I suppose it's being with Madame Thierry so much.'

'Why do you have such a dislike for poor Éloise? What harm has she done you?' he demanded.

'She harms us all, behaving as she does!'

'You never feel lonely,' he asked mildly, 'isolated out there on your impregnable rock of virtue?'

'I can't imagine,' she retorted, 'how you ever came to be a friend of Lucien's. He is everything you are not. How long have you known him?'

'Oh, for years—since we were boys at military academy. He was my junior, of course,' the Captain replied in an off-hand way. 'He arrived the year I was graduating. I remember him well, then. He was a bright youngster. Always in trouble, mind you, more often than not led into it by others. But he was plucky, and not adverse to a scrap. We pupils of the military school had a running battle going with the boys of the town. Our uniforms made us recognisable, but not easy, targets. One day, just after Lucien came to join us, I turned a corner and found him in a fight with two town boys who had lain in wait for him. He was giving a good account of himself, although he was outnumbered. I lent a hand, and we soon settled our two assailants. After that, I suppose, I more or less took him under my wing.'

He fell silent, and Charlotte's brow puckered in thought as she turned over in her mind the significance of what he had told her.

The period to which he referred would have been before the Revolution. To gain entry to military academy at that time, a boy had needed to prove noble descent. Sometimes that nobility was a little precarious. Even the Bonapartes had managed to produce sufficient convincing proof to send their son to military school under the old régime. None the less, the Captain must be able to claim some distinguished forebears. It seemed that Pascal had been right. Her companion was a gentleman by birth and breeding, even though present appearances belied it.

'And your home?' she probed curiously. 'Where is that?'

He turned his head to look at her, a slow smile spreading across his lean, bronzed gipsy features. 'Anywhere,' he declared, sweeping his arm generously towards the chaotic caravan about them. 'Where the guns go, *mignonne*, that's where I go. Where they rest, I make my home.'

'But you must have some permanent place which means home to you. Some city or province in France. Where were you born?'

'Saint-Domingue,' he said calmly. 'Haiti.'

So he was of colonial family. It explained much: an air of rootlessness, and a certain defensiveness. European planters' families were notoriously proud of their pure descent from French stock and their links with French aristocracy. No wonder the Forestiers had sent their son, still only a child, on the long and dangerous voyage from the Caribbean to metropolitan France, to be educated there and find a niche in French society. Such families were also notoriously rich and equally notoriously arrogant and despotic. Revolution and war had probably destroyed the Forestiers' wealth. The arrogance had survived.

'You must have been very young when you left home. Have you never returned?' she asked in some sympathy.

'Never,' he said. 'Nor have I any wish to go back. I was twelve years old when they sent me off on board a leaking and rat-ridden sugar-trader. I arrived in France months later, half-dead from drinking bad water and eating mouldy bread, my clothes and hair infested with lice. The relative who had arrived at the docks to take charge of me was so horrified at the sight of his charge that he refused to allow me in his carriage. I had to follow behind in a hired chaise. On arrival at his house, all my clothes were burned, my hair was shaved off, and

I was repeatedly dunked in a bath which nearly scalded me, before being pronounced fit to rejoin society.'

'Poor little boy! What a terrible reception.' Charlotte said in genuine pity. 'You must have been very unhappy.'

'One has a choice. One can be unhappy and mope. Or one can hate, and fight. I hated everyone.' His voice was cold and bitter.

She did not reply, and glancing at her and seeing her concerned expression, he added in a change of tone, with a touch of humour, 'At least it decided me on entering the army and not the navy!'

Alas, neither their progress, the good weather nor Forestier's good humour were to last. The astonished Austrians, who at first had received reports of the advancing horde with disbelief and scorn, had recovered from their initial shock. From a fortress commanding the narrow road, they had blocked the descent from the mountains into the plains. Their way forward impassable, bottled up in the foothills, the army and its followers waited, inactive and frustrated, and grew hungry.

'The French army lives off the land,' the Captain explained moodily to Charlotte. 'We don't slow ourselves up with wagons of supplies. Move light, move fast—that's how we beat our opponents.' He sighed irritably. 'Only now, confound it, we're stuck in these foothills, held up by a bunch of sausage-guzzling Austrians in a toy fort, and very likely to starve!'

They were all short of temper now, fretting at the delay and existing on a diet of the local boiled maize porridge, polenta. Frustration and impatience led to an incident in which Forestier appeared at his worst. It arose because he fancied some neglect of Kismet by his groom Baptistin, a placid, shock-headed Norman farm-boy. Charlotte had already realised that if the Captain entertained affection for anything, it was for his favourite horse.

Nevertheless, she was unprepared for such a storm of

verbal abuse as now broke over poor Baptistin's head. She was at first struck dumb and almost paralysed, not only by the fluency of the curses which rained down on the unfortunate groom but by the virulence of them, and the sheer violence of their delivery. After a few minutes, however, her dislike of seeing an innocent person suffer, especially one unable to defend himself, overcame her dismay, and she attempted to intervene.

Her well-meaning attempt was brushed aside, and Babette, who was present, plucked at her sleeve and whispered in alarm, 'No, mademoiselle, don't interfere!'

Charlotte might have followed the maid's advice, however reluctantly, but then, to her shock and anger, she saw the Captain raise his arm as if to strike the luckless groom.

That was too much. She ran forward, and placing herself squarely between the furious man and his intended victim, stormed, 'No! I have been obliged to listen to your disgraceful reviling of him, but I shall not allow you to beat him! Stop it at once, do you hear?'

In the ensuing silence, one might have heard a leaf fall. Then he turned on her, his blue eyes blazing, and for one dreadful moment she thought he would strike her instead. But he let his hand drop, and only jerked his head to dismiss Baptistin, ordering, 'You, too, Babette!'

However, as the groom and the reluctant maid withdrew, he threw out his hand and gripped Charlotte's arm tightly.

'You will *never*,' he said in that quiet, dangerous voice, 'an attempt such a thing again, do you hear me?'

She was terrified, but clung doggedly to her convictions. 'I shall do what I think is right!'

'No. *I* shall do what *I* think is right, and you will hold your tongue and not interfere in my affairs!' was the uncompromising reply. 'How I treat my servants, like whom I take into my bed, is my concern alone. I need no advice from you. I told you, if you come with me, you will do as I say. So I trust you will remember and I shall not have to repeat myself again.'

'My father always said that to be in a position of authority was an honour which should not be abused, and a responsibility to oneself!' she retorted obstinately. 'He also said that a gentleman treats his servants with courtesy, not because he is obliged to, but because he *isn't*.'

'Don't moralise at me, mademoiselle!' he snarled at her. 'If you don't like my language, then stop your ears. You'll hear a lot more if you stay in this company!'

'People are afraid of you,' she said accusingly. 'Is that what you want, for them to fear you?'

'Perhaps they know me better than you do, and are less afraid of me than you think! They also know I'm no plaster saint, nor a Royalist colonel playing at *grand seigneur*!'

'No, but you are a gentleman born, and ought to know how to behave!'

For a moment, he stared at her, and then, with a surly grunt, turned his back and strode away, his hands thrust into his pockets, his broad shoulders hunched against the breeze, his long black hair fluttering about his head.

Charlotte, badly shaken by the encounter, set out to walk off the nervous tremor which had set in by way of reaction, and after a little while reached a mountain torrent which splashed its way, swollen by alpine snows, down the valley. She sat down on a grassy knoll to enjoy the clear mountain water racing past.

There was a horseman in the river, seated bareback. He waved to her, and she saw that it was Dufour. He was clad only in his shirt and breeches, rolled up to just below the knee, so that his bare feet hung either side of his mount's shining flanks. The horse was drinking, and Dufour, his brown hair freed from the usual Hussar plaits and hanging in loose locks round his face, looked no older than she was, rather like a good-natured schoolboy.

When she waved back, he hauled on the reins to bring

up the horse's head and rode slowly forward through the water. When he reached her, he leaned forward, his arms crossed on the horse's withers, and grinned.

'You should get rid of that brute of an artillery captain,' he said. 'He doesn't deserve such a charming and beautiful companion.'

Privately Charlotte more than agreed with him, but aloud she said, 'Not yet.'

He kicked at the horse's flanks with his bare heels and urged the animal up the sloping bank, halting by her. He seemed about to continue their conversation but suddenly looked past her, and his expression changed. A slightly obstinate look came over his face, and he rode on a few paces, as if, in some way, he protected her.

She turned hastily, expecting to see Forestier, but instead beheld a total stranger, who had ridden up unnoticed and now sat watching them. He was a sallow man in his mid-thirties, of somewhat morose appearance, but what caught her eye was a criss-cross of straight white scars which scored one side of his face— the hallmark of a duellist.

Ignoring her, the newcomer addressed Dufour. 'This is the girl you were telling me of? The one Forestier brought from Villeneuve?'

'This is the one,' Dufour said quietly. 'Leave her alone, it's nothing to do with her.'

Charlotte, who disliked the stranger's manner and tone, interposed sharply, 'Have you some objection to my travelling with Captain Forestier? Who are you, anyway?'

He transferred his sombre gaze to her. 'My name is Thierry. And no, I have no objection to your accompanying him. In fact, you render me a singular service, and relieve me of a tiresome chore.'

'In what way, may I ask?' she demanded, though the realisation that this was Éloise Thierry's husband was disconcerting.

A mirthless smile flitted across his face. 'Dufour there has been singing your praises and toasting your pretty

eyes with every glass. I see he didn't exaggerate! Good.
You should be more than able to keep Forestier happy,
and pleasantly occupied!' He leaned towards her. *'And
keep him away from my wife!'*

He jerked on the reins, and wheeled his horse to trot
briskly away.

'I'm sorry about that,' Dufour said apologetically.
'You must forgive him, and not pay too much attention.
Look, you shouldn't be wandering about out here on
your own. Let me take you back. You're not afraid to
ride with me?'

He reached down and lifted her onto the horse in front
of her, and they rode slowly back towards the guns. As
they drew near, they saw the gunners were busy about
them, binding straw around the wheels of the gun-
carriages.

'I've heard they mean to try and sneak past the
Austrians tonight, under cover of dark,' Dufour told
her. 'Come, I'll set you down here. Give me a kiss, and
I'll consider myself well rewarded!' he added impu-
dently, and when she hesitated, kissed her anyway.

'See here, Charlotte,' he said, before he rode away.
'Have a care with Forestier. I'm not seeking to further
my own cause, only to warn you. One hears all kinds of
reports about him, good and bad. He has some kind of a
demon inside him which takes control at times. I've seen
him myself in violent rages, and I fear even you would
not always be safe.'

'I'll remember,' she said soberly.

'And if you change your mind about him,' Dufour
added in his usual cheerful tone. 'Remember me—!'

That night, the most ferocious thunderstorm Charlotte
had ever encountered broke about them. The lightning
leapt from hilltop to hilltop in spectacular and terrifying
flashes of white and yellow. She could feel the heat of it
burning on her face, and mark the points where it
zig-zagged to earth in its fury.

Panic struck the horse lines, and Pascal, swearing and

cursing in the torrential rain which accompanied this onslaught from the heavens, tried to control the two horses and the pack-mule. Charlotte, fighting both the elements and the rising hysteria of fear, ankle-deep in mud, her wet hair plastered to her forehead and trickles of water running down her neck into her clothing, tried vainly to prevent all their possessions from being swamped.

'This is what we need!' Forestier yelled to her, above the storm's rage. He had cantered up to her on Kismet, his long hair whipping about his face in writhing black tendrils, like the snakes about the head of the Medusa. Kismet, his eyes white and rolling, threw up his head as the lightning cracked and crashed again, forking down onto the rain-lashed hills, and reared up, mane and tail flying, hoofs flailing the air. Horse and rider, lit by the weird light of the storm, appeared almost apocalyptic to Charlotte's terrified gaze: creatures of war, a devil's huntsman and his phantom steed, released from the bowels of some mountain by an unearthly force, a demon of the storm, as in an old legend. He was even laughing, and she could see how his teeth gleamed, though she could not hear the sound.

'You may need this dreadful rain, but I could well do without it!' she cried in reply, shrieking to make herself heard.

'The best cover in the world!' was the reply, half carried away on the wind. 'You should have seen the tropical storms we had on Saint-Domingue when I was a child! You could hear and see them coming a league away, twisting and roaring. They knocked trees flat, tore the roofs off the houses, and if a man or beast was caught in the path of one, it snatched him up in its teeth and shook him about like a child's rag toy!' He swung Kismet's head and rode away, etched in black against the dark blue sky.

Though Jove himself continued to hurl his thunder-bolts down on them to punish their temerity, the army inched forward under cover of the storm's rage. The gunners themselves strained to drag along their guns, for no one could risk an injured horse, falling in the traces, bringing the whole convoy to a halt.

Slowly, painstakingly and painfully, veiled by night, muffled beneath by straw and plundered mattresses from peasant homes, and above by the rolling thunder, the guns creaked forward, and in this manner passed wraithlike beneath the noses of the Austrians in their lofty stronghold.

The following morning, all sign of the storm had vanished. The spring sun shone down upon them, and the open, fertile plains of Northern Italy lay before them, unchallenged.

The carriage had been acquired in Aosta and was of local manufacture. As a result, it was more serviceable than elegant, but it was the most comfortable way to travel obtainable, and Éloise Thierry liked her comforts.

There were precious few of these left to her, she thought savagely, as the carriage rattled and bumped its way along the track which followed the river, winding from Piedmont into Lombardy. Even this confounded carriage—which she had almost had to beg Thierry to buy for her—shook every bone in her body. She was thirty-five, almost thirty-six, and she was sick of this life. What she wanted was a house in Paris, where she could receive her friends, and her *salons* might become fashionable.

As it was, she had a useless and penny-pinching husband, a bad marriage, and nothing ahead of her but miles and miles of dust and heat in the company of primitive barbarians. As for her lover—well, she had never fully held his attention, despite her best efforts and not inconsiderable experience in the arts of physical love. Now what little she still held was in danger of being lost, to a new threat. But perhaps it was the oldest threat any woman had ever faced: a younger rival.

The carriage had reached the appointed spot. It lurched to a halt, and Éloise descended to the springy turf with a sigh of relief and looked about her. The evening sun was glowing red and casting a rosy dust onto the smooth waters of the river. The scene was deceptively peaceful. It was also empty. He was late. It could be, of course, that he had been held up. It could also be that he was in no hurry—or even that he did not intend to come at all.

A cold finger of fear touched her heart. Once she had kept men waiting, impatient for the sight of her. Now they kept her waiting. She pulled a little mirror from her reticule, studied her reflection with dissatisfaction, and decided to apply a little carmine to her lips. She had only a few good years left. If she didn't get that Paris house soon, it would be out of her reach for ever. If she could be rid of her husband it would be something, but he had steadily refused to divorce her. She was still of use to him. He wanted promotion, and expected her to get it for him.

'Someone's coming, madame,' her coachman said.

Éloise's heart leapt up as the grey Arab horse and its rider appeared through the trees, walking slowly down towards the river. He had come. At least she had been spared that humiliation. She walked a little way to meet him, and laying one hand on the horse's neck, made a little *moue* of displeasure up at the rider.

'You are late!' she complained.

Marc jumped down from the saddle. 'It was difficult,' he said abruptly. No apology. He did not even kiss her hand until she almost pushed it under his nose. Éloise concealed her anger, and alarm, with difficulty, waiting until the coachman had led Kismet away.

She took Marc's arm and they walked a little way along the river bank until they were out of the man's sight. Marc took off his coat and spread it on the grass, and gave her his hand to help her down.

'Such rustic gallantry!' Éloise said archly, as she sank gracefully to the ground. She patted the grass beside her, and he sat down, resting his shirtsleeved arms on his knees. Picking up a handful of pebbles, he began to toss them one at a time into the rose-red river.

'Did you come here to do *that*?' she demanded, betraying her impatience despite herself. 'To play at ducks and drakes like a child, with stones?'

'I came here because you asked me to come, Éloise,' he replied evenly.

'*You* didn't want to come—to see me?'

'To see you is always a pleasure. But it's becoming an unnecessarily risky one. You're making a fool of Thierry too obviously. He doesn't like it.'

She had not intended to allow herself anger, but it bubbled up, born of resentment. 'Suddenly so scrupulous? You care nothing for my husband's bruised sensibilities, and you don't give a damn for the risk! I know you too well, Marc Forestier! You are tired of me. You want to be rid of me! Do you think I am such a fool that I can't see it? I've eyes in my head. Your attention is taken elsewhere these days, isn't it? Well, *she* won't . . .'

Éloise broke off in mid-speech as Marc turned his head, and his blue eyes rested warningly on her face. She thought better of what she had been about to blurt out. 'I won't be cast aside,' she went on sullenly instead. 'You never loved me.'

'I never told you that I did,' he replied quietly, and the words cut cruelly, for all they were true and not unexpected. 'I have never lied to you, Éloise, and don't pretend you ever loved *me*, because it's not in your nature to love.'

'There is lying,' she said spitefully, 'and there is "not telling the truth". You flatter yourself, no doubt, that you haven't lied to that little chit you take along with you on this campaign. But I'll swear you haven't told her the truth, either, have you?'

'Charlotte is no concern of yours, Éloise! Don't meddle in my affairs. I've warned you before!' He caught her chin in his fingers as in a steel trap, and forced her head round to face him. 'Keep away from Mademoiselle Lacoste, or you'll answer to me for it!'

She jerked her head free defiantly. 'What's the mat-

ter?' she taunted him. 'Are you afraid I'll corrupt her?
Such a little innocent, and a virgin, too, I shouldn't be
surprised. That sort of little prude guards her virtue like
a castle keep! Or have you managed to storm that
bastion yet?'

'Hold your tongue!' He raised his hand, and for a
moment she thought he was going to hit her, and she
ducked her head to avoid the blow.

When it didn't come, she regained her courage, and
said viciously, 'If she knew you as I know you, she
wouldn't be so anxious to have your protection!'

'Perhaps.' He turned away and tossed the last of the
pebbles into the river. It landed far out with a splash,
almost reaching the further bank.

Éloise nestled closer to him and put her hand on his
shoulder, idly running the tips of her fingers down the
length of his spine. 'You and I,' she whispered into his
ear, 'we have seen life as it really is. We don't pretend.
So we are not so stupid as to imagine ourselves *in
love*—but we still want one another. You know, you are
not like any other man, for me.' Her fingers picked at the
buttons of his shirt and slid inside it. 'You know it, don't
you, Marc?'

He drew a deep breath and caught at her exploring
hand, imprisoning it and halting its progress. 'Éloise, it's
finished . . .'

'No!' She twisted her free arm round his neck and
pulled him towards her. 'It can't finish! We are damned,
you and I, Marc Forestier, caught up in the toils of what
we are, shackled to our own selves, like a Greek tragedy.
You can't have her, Marc. There's no going back. But
you *can* have me . . .'

'Damn you,' he said softly.

He rolled over towards her, slipping his arms round
her and pushing her back onto the ground beneath him.
She gave a little moan of pleasure, because it was what
she had wanted, but she still felt that thrill of fear in her
heart she always knew when he took her.

Éloise Thierry's coachman sat watching the last of the

sun disappear over the horizon. It was of no interest to him how long Madame and her artillery lover took over it, but if it didn't occur to Madame to start back soon, they'd be making the journey back in the dark, and the coachman disliked this. There were brigands in these parts, and Madame had jewellery. He didn't want a stiletto in his ribs just because he had the misfortune to drive that high-class trollop to and from her assignations. As far as the coachman was concerned, the Terror had ended too soon. They should have guillotined the lot of them.

Two figures appeared in the distance, the man carrying his coat over his arm. The coachman muttered in relief. They were coming now. Madame looked like the cat which had been at the cream, but that officer looked out of sorts and ready to pick a quarrel with anyone. He'd driven Madame to meet that artillery captain before, and had always been wary of him. He was dangerous. Madame played with fire. The coachman sincerely hoped she'd burn her fingers.

In the jolting coach, alone and driving back to her husband, Éloise's expression of contentment faded from her beautiful ivory face. She hated all men. They took what they wanted, and left a woman feeling used and discarded. Well, Marc Forestier would find she was not so easily discarded. She contemplated her hand on which, in the dim light, the wedding-ring was just visible.

'And you, too!' she said viciously to the gold band. 'I'll be rid of you, too!'

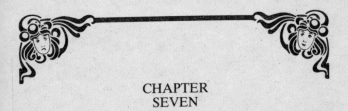

CHAPTER
SEVEN

As THEY progressed across the plains of Northern Italy,
Charlotte began to find that, instead of being surrounded by strangers, she felt part of an extended
family, a wandering tribe of familiar faces, among whom
she now began to be quite at home. She was acquiring a
variety of novel skills, such as improvising a whole new
cuisine over an open fire. The soldiers themselves
accorded her a kind of acceptance, making no comment
on her presence with them, and treating her
with a curious mixture of deference and good-natured
familiarity.

This was, Charlotte was only too well aware, only
because they believed her the Captain's mistress. His
gun-crew had even adopted her as a kind of mascot, and
the name *Charlotte* had been carefully painted along the
barrel of one of the eight-pounders. This ought to have
been reassuring, but it wasn't. It brought home to her
forcefully how much her future lay in the Captain's
hands, and the extent to which she depended on him.
She had been wrong, perhaps, to attach herself to such a
moody and impatient man. She feared he was more than
capable of discontinuing the charade and abandoning
her at any time, with all the unpleasant consequences
which could ensue.

Of the other officers, she knew best Jean-Luc
Cresson, to whom, she decided, there was more than
met the eye. She, Forestier and Cresson were seated
now at a table of a country inn, where they had together
disposed of a platter of spaghetti, and Cresson, who was
always at his best when well-fed, was regaling them with

tales of his misadventures. He seemed to have a talent for misfortune, extricating himself unharmed from each apparently hopeless and often hilarious situation with ingenuity and a certain bland ingenuousness. The unofficial motto of the French army—*Débrouille-toi*—seemed to apply to no one better than to this plump young officer, whose company Forestier evidently appreciated.

But as they sat laughing, a shadow suddenly fell over the table, and looking up, they saw the Hussar, Dufour, correctly uniformed, even immaculate, his hair neatly braided, and his ornate pelisse slung rakishly over his shoulder in the Hussar fashion. His handsome young face was unusually serious, even grave. Charlotte felt a chill premonition.

'Captain Forestier?' Dufour enquired politely.

'You know me,' was the even reply.

An odd silence had fallen around them, as people at other tables sensed the vibration of impending drama in the air. They had stopped talking, and were listening. In the silence, the clatter of a falling pewter pot shattered the tension like a pistol-shot.

Dufour glanced at Charlotte, and embarrassment momentarily clouded his face. 'I'm sincerely sorry, mademoiselle,' he said awkwardly to her. 'You understand, it is an affair of honour.'

A faint ripple ran around the room, like a communal sigh.

'I have the honour,' Dufour went on, turning back to Forestier, 'to represent Captain Thierry. Captain Thierry has been distressed by certain *unfounded* rumours concerning his wife.'

Dufour did not so much as flicker an eyelid as he spoke, but he surely knew the truth about Éloise Thierry, Charlotte thought angrily.

'If they are unfounded,' the Captain said indifferently, 'why come to me?' He turned his back on the Hussar with a contemptuous twitch of his broad shoulders.

'Your name, monsieur, has figured in these reports.'

Dufour cleared his throat. 'Captain Thierry is of the opinion that they originate with you, and you have slandered his wife's reputation.'

The Captain looked up sharply, his blue eyes alight with anger. 'Then tell Captain Thierry,' he replied in a low, hard voice, 'that he slanders *me*! I have nothing to state concerning the lady you mention. But I do have this to say: I would not publicly besmirch a woman's reputation, whoever she was, nor do I indulge in adolescent indiscretions, blabbing names into any ear which might be listening! Possibly Captain Thierry conducts his amorous affairs differently. That is how I conduct mine.'

Dufour flushed. 'I am obliged, monsieur, to ask you name your second.'

There was no reply, Forestier only glancing across the table at Cresson, and raising his eyebrows interrogatively.

'Yes,' said Cresson hastily. 'Of course I will, I'm honoured. Right, what's your name? Dufour, isn't it? While accepting Captain Thierry's challenge, I wish to make it clear, monsieur, that your principal has insulted Captain Forestier by this charge, which we deny.'

'No, he hasn't,' said Dufour angrily. 'Your man has insulted mine!'

'Rubbish,' maintained Cresson obstinately. 'Captain Thierry has questioned my principal's honour, and suggested he has not behaved in a manner expected of a French officer!'

'Your principal has seduced Captain Thierry's wife!' exclaimed the exasperated Hussar, more loudly than he had intended.

'Who hasn't?' commented an anonymous but clearly audible voice from a far corner.

Dufour whirled round angrily, but all the other tables were peopled by customers suddenly deep in their own conversations.

'I suggest, Monsieur Cresson,' Dufour said tightly,

'that you and I retire somewhere *private* and discuss the details.'

'I thought,' Charlotte interrupted vigorously, 'that these rumours were supposed to be unfounded!'

'Now, don't interfere, my dear,' said Cresson kindly to her. 'This is men's business. You don't understand.'

'Dear heaven, they are *serious*!' she thought incredulously.

'Your principal has no objection to sabres, I suppose?' Dufour asked casually, as he turned aside.

'Of course he has!' exploded Cresson. 'He's not some braggart of a cavalryman . . .'

'Do I take it, monsieur, that you mean *me*?' Dufour demanded, stiffening.

Before the seconds could pursue their increasingly acrimonious conversation any further, Forestier, who had been listening without any apparent emotion, said quietly, 'I have no objection to sabres.'

'Then, Monsieur Cresson, perhaps you and I . . . ?' Dufour glanced towards the door and then, with a polite bow to Charlotte, left the room.

Cresson, preparing to follow him, paused long enough to demand in a hoarse whisper, 'Are you crazy? Thierry's a cavalryman, and will decapitate you, most likely. Let me argue for pistols, Marc. Thierry's a rotten shot.'

'I know. That's why it has to be sabres.' He glanced up and a smile flickered faintly over his lean cheeks. 'So don't argue, Jean-Luc, there's a good fellow. It's enough that one of us fights a duel, without *you* taking on the entire cavalry as well! Stop antagonising that pretty popinjay, Dufour. Mademoiselle Lacoste here has a weakness for him!'

'I have not!' exclaimed Charlotte, incensed. 'I used to think him pleasant and polite. Now I think him as bad as the rest of you.'

'Sabres . . .' muttered Cresson disconsolately, following slowly after Dufour. 'Why you have to decide to be gallant *now*, for the first time in your life, I can't understand. You'd better make sure it's not the last!' He departed, his plump, amiable face creased in a ferocious scowl.

'Captain,' Charlotte began, seriously alarmed.

'It's nothing to worry *you*,' he said quietly. 'You should imitate the rest of the company here, and make as though you didn't hear our conversation.'

'Oh, what nonsense! The whole affair is ludicrous. Supposing you are badly injured?'

'Thank you for the expression of confidence!' The blue eyes rested on her face enigmatically. 'What do you care, eh?' He looked away.

'Don't be so foolish!' she burst out. 'I don't want you to be hurt! Certainly not to be hurt on account of her,' she added bitterly, flushing. 'Everybody knows what sort of a woman she is. This duel is quite unnecessary.'

'I thought you were anxious I should do the right thing?' he retorted, a slightly mocking note in his voice.

'*This* isn't the right thing! It's a childish piece of theatre, and will prove nothing. But it could end with both of you wounded.'

'I can't refuse,' he said in a low voice.

'Then you should have allowed Cresson to argue for pistols!' she declared mutinously.

He raised his black eyebrows. 'My, my, how those rigid moral standards are crumbling! It must be through association with me. We won't talk about it any more, *mignonne*.'

Charlotte fell into a turbulent silence, shared by Forestier, who now seemed to forget she was there. He sat with his shoulders hunched, staring moodily into his wine, as the candle-flame guttering in a bottle on the table played across his handsome features, set in a masklike impassivity.

Standing up, Charlotte threw her shawl over her head, knowing she was not wanted there, and set off slowly back to her lodging. She doubted that the Captain even noticed that she had gone.

Cresson and Dufour were talking, amicably enough

now, if formally, outside the door. She slipped into the shadows so that they shouldn't see her, and was just in time to hear Cresson say, 'Since it's to be sabres, we should agree that the point of the weapon shall not be used. We don't want any dead bodies!'

'I've bribed one of the surgeons to attend,' Dufour said reassuringly. 'It will be all right. I chose one who knows how to keep his mouth shut.'

Charlotte listened, transfixed by horror and incredulity, but Cresson and the Hussar shook hands and parted with every mark of civility.

The lodging she had taken was in a peasant's house, a tiny room dominated by a wide stone hearth, the bed tucked into an alcove veiled by a rough curtain. It was the sound of Babette dragging back this curtain on its wooden rings which awoke Charlotte the next morning, after a restless and anxious night.

She sat up, pushing back her damp hair, and wondered if she could possibly have dreamed the incredible events of the previous evening. By the light of day, surely all parties must see sense? They couldn't mean to go through with it . . .

The maid's words destroyed this faint hope. 'The sun is up,' she said, standing by the bedside with folded hands. 'It will all be over. They'll be on their way back.'

'What? Over?' Charlotte gasped, staring up at her disbelievingly. 'You mean the duel? You know about it? They've fought already?'

'Everyone knows. There's many who are angry about it. That woman Thierry has caused trouble before. They say it's got to the ear of the First Consul this time, and he's furious! They say—it's rumour, mind—he ordered Captain Thierry to send his wife back to France straight away, or resign.'

'But the duel?' Charlotte scrambled out of bed.

'I don't know, my dear. I heard they went off at dawn, while it was quiet and nobody was about to disturb them.

It's forbidden, you see, for officers to duel in time of war. Every man's needed, and you can't have the officers killing each other! That's why High Command is in such a temper about it. There will very likely be a court-martial out of it for someone!'

'That wretched, wicked woman!' Charlotte exploded. 'It wouldn't surprise me if she hadn't contrived this somehow on purpose!'

'Nor me, my love, but we mustn't say so,' Babette said warningly.

Charlotte scrambled into her clothes and ran out of the door. The ground was still damp with dew, and snatches of early morning mist lingered in gauzy shreds as she hastened down the road to the house where she knew Forestier lodged. There were tethered saddle-horses before the door, and one was Kismet.

'He's come back!' Charlotte whispered. Or been brought back?

As she entered the house, arguing voices struck her ear from above. She ran up the narrow staircase and into the room, where she drew a deep sigh of relief.

The Captain sat on the edge of the bed in his shirt-sleeves, while Cresson stood over him, protesting vigorously. 'No one will do anything, I tell you! The fellow brought it on himself! Everyone knows how it happened. No one—not Marmont, not even *le petit caporal* himself—will blame you! They'll smooth it over, sweep it under the carpet, you know how these things are done! Listen to me . . . She has the ear of Bonaparte's wife. What's the woman's name? Josceline, or Josephine, or something. Anyway, she has friends in high places. There'll be no court-martial! Someone on the Staff has *promised* me.'

He broke off as both of them became aware of Charlotte, standing rooted in the doorway. The two men stared at her.

She took a step forward. 'Capitaine? Are you all right?'

'I'm all right,' he said briefly.

'And—and Thierry? You didn't kill him?' she asked, horrified, and hardly daring to breathe.

'No.' He shook his head. 'But he's badly hurt, and in the hands of the surgeon. *He'll* very likely kill him.'

'Babette said it was against regulations, there will be trouble . . .'

'No, there won't!' Cresson said sharply. 'Don't worry, my dear. They can't afford to lose the services of a good artillery officer like Forestier here, not at a time like this! Besides, there are names to conjure with being bandied about in this matter. All anyone wants to do, is forget about it.' He turned back to the Captain. 'You'll be all right. Lie low today. I'll go and see what's happening.' He nodded to Charlotte and ran down the stairs.

'You're sure you're not hurt?' Charlotte asked anxiously.

He shook his head, hardly listening to her, staring frowningly in front of him. 'Poor devil,' he said. 'I knew he was a bad shot. I didn't know he was a pathetic swordsman as well. No wonder they put him on the Staff. I didn't mean to injure him badly, but the idiot came rushing at me like a madman, practically spitted himself on my weapon. The devil of it is, it makes it look as if I struck him down with a foul blow. It was agreed, no points of sabres . . .' He sighed, and unthinkingly put his right hand on his upper left arm.

'You *are* hurt!' Charlotte exclaimed. 'There's blood on your sleeve. Let me see.'

'Leave it, it's nothing, a scratch!' He attempted to push her aside.

'Scratches can fester. Take off your shirt and I'll wash the wound and bind it up. Oh,' Charlotte confessed suddenly, 'I was so worried last night—and then, this morning, Babette said it was all over, so quickly.'

Through the folds of his shirt, Forestier's voice came muffled. 'Had to be. Always a risk of someone on the Staff galloping up to interfere!' He threw the discarded garment down on the floor and examined his scored arm. 'Pah, nothing, drew a little blood, that's all.'

Perspiration gleamed on the bare skin of his powerful shoulders and trickled from the hollow of his collarbones down into the tangled black hair on his chest. Charlotte looked away, concentrating on her task of washing the cut. Never had she been so close to a man as naked as this. She swallowed, and tried to keep her hands steady as she bound his arm carefully with a strip of linen. She felt that his eyes were on her face, watching her closely.

'You look pale,' his voice said, close by her ear. 'Did it really give you such a fright?'

'Of course it did,' she muttered, tying the bandage.

'I'm not a fool,' he said brusquely, inspecting her handiwork with a glance. 'I could always deal with Thierry.'

'I suppose you could!' Charlotte moved away from him. She knew she sounded angry.

'For pity's sake!' he exploded suddenly, 'it's not my fault the idiot called me out!'

'You wronged that man, and now you may have killed him!'

'I was trying *not* to kill him!' he snarled at her. 'I didn't plan for him to throw himself on my sabre and have that dandy Dufour cry "Foul!"'

He got up from the bed and strode over to fling open the casement. After a brief pause he said, without turning round, 'I told you, I was never in love with her.' He waited for a moment, as if he wanted her to say something. But when she did not reply, he went on, in a brisk change of subject, 'In two days, we shall be in Milan.' His voice betrayed nothing.

'I know. I suppose,' Charlotte hesitated, 'you won't want to be bothered with me after this. You don't need me any more, to—to cover your affair with—with her.'

'Oh, that,' he shrugged his bare shoulders dismissively. 'I don't know why I told you that. It didn't fool Thierry, at any rate.' He came back and stood over her, looking down. 'You've come a long way from home, Charlotte,' he said seriously, 'and we've seen no action other than a few minor setbacks. It can't go on like this. Think about finishing your journey in Milan. It's a fine city. You can wait there and—and see what happens.'

'I won't give up,' she mumbled, her eyes fixed on his bare chest. 'It's true,' she thought, 'I must be abysmally ignorant. I didn't even know men grew so much hair on their bodies, like this.'

He stretched out a sunburned hand and raised her chin with his fingers, so that she was obliged to look up into his face.

'I'm not asking you to give up, Charlotte,' he said impatiently. 'I wouldn't insult you. You're a brave little soul and don't "give up". Just call it a change of plan. It's your decision. Think about it, at least. I'm advising you for the best.'

'Yes, I know you are.' Her voice trembled.

'You think,' he said quietly, 'that I'm every kind of rogue. Well, perhaps you're right, and I am. But in your case, Charlotte, whatever I've done, I've done for reasons which have seemed good to me.'

A perplexed wrinkle puckered her forehead. 'I don't understand you,' she faltered.

'No,' he said, 'you don't. You don't understand. Please God you never do . . .'

Unexpectedly, he stooped and lightly kissed her mouth. His lips lingered for just a little longer than was necessary, his long hair brushed her cheek and his damp skin had a curious warm, animal smell. Charlotte's heart lurched and almost seemed to stop beating for a moment.

'I don't want you to be hurt, Charlotte, believe me,' he said earnestly. He felt silent for a moment, looking down into her face. Then he ran his tongue over his upper lip, and said a little huskily, 'Run along back to Babette, now. There's a good girl.'

He walked quickly across to his shirt, stooped to retrieve it from the floor, pulling it on and tucking it into his breeches, his back to her.

Charlotte nodded, although he could not see her, and

went slowly out and down the creaking wooden staircase. She made her way back to her own lodging, relieved in her mind, but not at peace in her heart.

Babette blocked the entry to her room, her round face alive with the desire to impart some warning. The maid jerked her head slightly, and her mouth formed the words, '*She*'s here . . .' uttered in a low whisper.

But Charlotte had seen Éloise Thierry, wrapped in a hooded travelling-cloak, seated by the crude stone hearth. She rose to her feet, pushing back the hood so that Charlotte could see her face. It was quite impassive: not even a faint frown marked the smooth ivory skin. But the dark eyes glowed like the innermost embers of a furnace.

'What may I do for you, madame?' Charlotte asked coldly.

Éloise ran her fine eyes over the girl's slight figure, and shrugged. 'I came to see you, my dear, because I am leaving shortly. You know that, of course.'

'Yes, I know,' Charlotte said. 'And not before time.'

A flush darkened the ivory skin. 'You speak very freely, mademoiselle!'

'Perhaps not so freely as you behave, madame. It's far better that you'll be gone and can cause no more trouble to anyone here!' Charlotte did not care how rude her words were. They were the truth.

Sparks flashed in Madame Thierry's dark eyes. 'You stupid little prude! You imagine you have the right to despise me!'

A quiver of uncertainty ran through Charlotte, but she forced herself to ignore it. 'I don't suppose it would matter much to you, even if I said I did,' she replied firmly.

The impassive expression was wiped from the beautiful ivory features in an instant. Éloise Thierry darted forward and seized Charlotte's wrist tightly. She was extraordinarily strong, and although Charlotte tried to break free, she found herself held fast. Madame Thierry pushed her face into the girl's and hissed viciously,

'You are stupid, stupid! A silly little nobody! You know nothing, do you hear, nothing!'

'Let go of me,' Charlotte stammered, frightened by the wild look in her opponent's eyes. The beautiful face was so distorted as to look almost ugly.

Madame Thierry released her and half turned away. 'You think yourself clever—quite a little heroine, no doubt,' she said, more calmly.

'I'm not a heroine, and I may be wrong in what I'm doing. But I'm looking for the man I love.'

'Love?' Éloise Thierry laughed. 'Love, my dear, is a bright illusion. It's elusive, slippery, like trying to catch a goldfish in a fountain with your hands. Just when you have one, it slips through your fingers, so!' She snapped her delicate fingers with the pink, polished nails, and turned back to face Charlotte squarely. 'Do you know what it really is, my dear? Do you really know what it is all about?'

When Charlotte did not answer, she darted suddenly to the curtained alcove and flung aside the drapes to reveal the bed. '*There!*' She pointed vehemently down at the pillows. 'That is what it is all about!'

'There is more,' Charlotte said obstinately, trying not to show that the other woman had struck unerringly, sensing where she was uncertain and defenceless.

'You're so young,' Madame Thierry said. 'You were still a child during the Terror. I was a young woman, beautiful. Oh, I know I still have some looks. But I am not such a fool as to imagine I look as I did even then, what, six, seven years ago. It is this accursed army life. It dries a woman's face like a prune. I am starting to lose my teeth; soon I shall be using henna on my hair. But *then*, Mademoiselle Charlotte, then I was a beauty!'

'I'm sure . . .' Charlotte whispered. She felt as though she were mesmerised by her visitor, as before some glittering weaving snake, fascinating and deadly.

'And my beauty,' Éloise said in a low, harsh voice, 'was the coin I paid for my survival. Do you know,

Charlotte, what it is to pay with your body for the gracious permission to stay alive? Can you imagine what it is to obtain your name deleted from some list, to give yourself to a man you loathe and despise—some unwashed, sadistic commissar of the committee of Public Safety or debauched, middle-aged rake who holds a position of power in the Convention? To feel their bloodstained, foul, touch on your skin and to have to tell them,' her voice sank to a ferocious whisper, 'how you *love* them, Charlotte? Because that is what they all wanted to hear you say. That you loved them! *That* was their moment of triumph! Not to take your body, but to hear you thank them for it, and say you loved them, when they knew how you hated them, and felt how you shuddered beneath their caresses! They were all the same—they wanted to humble, and torment, to drag that woman down into the mud, with *them*!'

'I'm sorry,' Charlotte faltered. 'My own father was imprisoned during the Terror. Whatever you did, I understand that you had no choice—then.'

'But I have a choice now, you mean?' The woman's voice was lightly taunting.

'Yes,' Charlotte said. 'Now it is different.'

Éloise shrugged. 'It's never different. Men find a way to have what they want, either in love or in mastery, you'll see. But now *I* choose the men, that is all. I've earned that right, to please myself!' She threw a glance at Charlotte. 'There will be no trouble over this duel. I'll see to it. I know the First Consul's wife, Josephine. I knew her when she was vicomtesse de Beauharnais, before she trapped our General Bonaparte into marriage. When I knew her, we were all of us gambling our charms, trying to stay alive, even to eat! I had no nobility to bargain with. I couldn't catch a general, even one temporarily out of favour! I married poor Thierry.' She gave a ripple of laughter. 'Though he's a braggart and a wastrel, I despaired he'd ever call Forestier out!'

'Why,' Charlotte gasped, 'you did contrive this! You wanted someone to kill your husband for you!'

'You've a loose tongue in your head,' Éloise said coldly. 'If you speak so, you'll send Forestier to the guillotine! Neither of us, I fancy, wants that. Though I've often wished all the plagues of Egypt on his head, it's a handsome head, and it would be a pity to see it roll.' Her gaze grew absent. 'Forestier is a devil, but when you have once been in his arms, no other man . . .' She gave herself a little shake. 'But don't expect me to shed tears over a useless husband who will leave me nothing but his gaming debts!'

'Why did you marry him, if you despise him so much?'

'I had urgent need of a husband,' Madame Thierry said carelessly. 'I was in a certain condition.'

'The child was Captain Thierry's?'

'Good heavens, my dear, how charmingly naïve you are! *I* don't know. I told Thierry it was his, and he believed me. It might have been true.' Éloise spread her hands.

'Where is the child now?' Charlotte asked quietly.

'I miscarried,' Éloise said, 'after all . . .' A wry smile twisted her full, carmined lips.

'All the same,' Charlotte spoke firmly, 'Captain Thierry has stood by you, even to the extent of this duel. You owe him something! He has looked after you.'

'And I have looked after him!' Éloise retaliated swiftly. 'Who got him the Staff appointment he wanted? I did, Charlotte, and paid for it in that same old coin! He knows it. He was not so anxious to defend my honour then!'

Charlotte gave an exclamation of disgust, and turned her back. She heard the woman approach and knew she stood just behind her.

'And you think,' Madame Thierry said softly, 'you think you know what kind of men you move among? You do not know anything about men at all, and how they can treat a woman!'

Charlotte whirled round. 'I know you are a dangerous and treacherous woman! You've told so many lies in your life that I doubt you even know the difference between truth and fiction any longer. You are able to justify every misdeed, not just to me but to yourself! Don't you realise, *Marc* might have been killed in that duel?'

'Ah, Marc . . .' said Éloise. 'We come to him at last.'

'Yes, we do,' Charlotte's voice was icy. 'And perhaps we have also come to the reason which brought you here, madame.'

'Why should you care about Marc Forestier, whether he lives or dies?' Éloise said savagely. 'He isn't your lover. He isn't the man you seek. You're looking for Lucien Saint-Laurent, aren't you?'

Charlotte felt the blood drain from her face. 'Yes. Who told you? Was it Marc?'

'Perhaps.' Éloise had an oddly triumphant look in those fine eyes which seemed so full of secrets.

Charlotte felt as though turned to stone. 'Do *you* know Lucien?' she heard her voice whisper.

'Oh, quite well, my dear. He used to come to the house we had, before Thierry lost it gambling!' Real regret sounded in the woman's voice for the first time.

'I don't believe you!'

Madame Thierry shrugged elegantly again. 'You don't have to believe *me*. Ask Marc Forestier. Ask my poor husband, if the surgeon lets him live. They used to sit at the card-table all night, with others who liked to gamble. Marc Forestier was clever. When the cards ran against him, he'd throw in his hand, and leave—or come and see me.'

She glanced challengingly at Charlotte. 'You find it strange, perhaps, that I should deceive my husband with Marc, while poor Thierry was still in the same house, sitting downstairs at cards in the room below us?' Éloise laughed throatily. 'It was the danger, you see, *Mademoiselle Innocente*, the risk we might be discovered, which I enjoyed so much! Pah! How disgusted you look. Such a little innocent; or are you, I wonder, quite so innocent . . . ?' She put her head on one side and her beautiful eyes studied Charlotte shrewdly.

'And—Marc,' Charlotte asked awkwardly. 'Did he—enjoy the risk of discovery?'

'I don't think he cared,' Éloise answered frankly. 'And I don't delude myself he ever really cared for *me*. I amused him . . . then. I helped him to forget . . .' There was an imperceptible hesitation in her speech before she went on. 'Now he doesn't need me any longer.' A spark of hatred flickered briefly in the beautiful eyes, as they rested on the young girl's slim figure. 'Your Lucien!' she said spitefully. 'He was always greatly amused. He knew what was taking place just above his head as he sat at cards with my husband.'

Charlotte flushed.

'I often think,' Éloise's tone changed to scorn, 'that Thierry knew it too, but for him the cards were more important! And your Lucien, he was just like my stupid husband, when it came to the cards! He couldn't believe his luck wouldn't change. He'd sit at the table until he'd lost every last *sou*!'

Charlotte knew in her heart that there must be some truth in this, because her father had spoken of Lucien's gaming. It was that news of Lucien which had distressed him and turned him against the idea of their marriage. Aloud, she said, 'You tell me nothing new. But Lucien assured my father that all his debts had been paid. He gave my father his word. Father took it, and I take it.'

'But Lucien didn't tell you, or his uncle, how they were paid, did he, my dear?' The woman scented victory; there was a cool, cruel triumph in her eyes now.

Charlotte opened her mouth, but before she could speak, there was a movement from the door and Marc's voice broke in coolly. 'That's enough, Éloise!'

A scarlet flush spread up Madame Thierry's throat and over her face. Anger glittered in her beautiful eyes, but something else, too—fear.

'I'm speaking nothing but the truth!' she said viciously. 'If you don't want her to hear it from me, why don't you tell her yourself?'

'There is nothing to tell,' Marc said calmly. '*Nothing* to tell, Éloise, is there . . . ?' He moved slowly forward, and stood looking down at her.

Madame Thierry shrank back, and shook her head. 'N-no, nothing,' she muttered. She seemed almost to cower, glancing this way and that in a hunted fashion, like a trapped wild beast.

'That's right. Now, don't you think you had better go?' Marc's voice was deceptively mild.

She did not answer. She threw the hood of the cloak over her head so that Charlotte should not see her face, and pushing past her, hurried out of the room.

'She won't bother you again!' Marc said abruptly. He looked angrier than Charlotte had ever seen him, his face leaner than ever, and harsher.

'Did you gamble, together with Lucien, at the Thierry's house?' she asked quietly.

'A few times. Everyone gambles. Take no notice of anything Éloise told you. She's jealous.'

'Of me?' She stared at him incredulously. 'Because of *you*?'

'No, not because of me!' he shouted suddenly at her, and the words rang in the tiny room. 'Because you are young and fresh and unspoiled, and her looks fade and her figure spreads—and because every officer of this regiment knows either by reputation or from experience that she has the morals of a slut!'

'*You* should not say that of her,' Charlotte reproached him. 'Even if it's true, even if she was in your bed. *Because* you were her lover, you should not say it.'

'Ah? We defend our own sex, after all, do we?' He stared at her mockingly. His voice was brittle and his manner abrasive. 'Or perhaps we just like the opportunity to moralise at me again? Well, I followed you down here to say that Cresson came back, and we're to move out at once. Are you coming with me or not? Dufour would be willing to take you on, but you'd have to sleep with *him*. Pay, as Éloise has always paid!'

'I'll come with you,' she replied with difficulty, thinking, 'He was listening—How long was he standing there?'

'So, I'm useful after all. Ill-bred and immoral, but useful!' He gave her a sardonic glance, and walked out. 'Pack up quickly'—his voice floated back through the door dispassionately—'or I'll go without you!'

Thus, one fine morning, dirty, footsore, yet confident and victorious in spirit, though yet to prove it in battle, the French, Charlotte among them, entered the great city of Milan. The common populace cheered them, firmly believing them to have come to liberate Italy from the Austrian yoke. But there were carefully guarded scowls, too, from those who knew them better. The custodians of art collections and church plate, who during the previous campaign had had ample opportunity to make the acquaintance of these lawless, godless revolutionaries, and thus knew them best of all, hastily gathered up their valuables and hid them well away.

CHAPTER
EIGHT

MARC'S FIRST action upon their arrival was to secure
lodgings for them both in the large and comfortable
house of a wealthy Milanese grain merchant and his
family, who relinquished to them two fine, spacious
rooms on the first floor, with wrought-iron balconies
overlooking the street. Heavy wooden shutters filtered
out the sun and dust and kept the interiors cool and dim,
for Milan already stewed in early summer heat, herald-
ing the dog days to come in the following months.

The rooms were connected by a door, the further
room containing a large four-poster bed of patriarchal
appearance, hung about with red velvet curtains and
corded tassels. The other room was furnished principally
as a drawing-room, but contained in addition a comfortable divan.

Charlotte did not like this arrangement, which threw
them so close together under one roof. The truth was
that, since the duel and the departure of Éloise Thierry,
and more particularly since their conversation in Marc's
lodgings following the duel, she had become aware of a
subtle change in their relationship. It was nothing she
could name specifically. Outwardly, things were the
same. But inwardly there was a new element, at least for
her—a kind of physical awareness of him. She wondered
whether Marc knew of her changed feelings. It seemed
to her that he watched her in a way he had not done
before. Quite often she had looked up to see his blue
eyes resting on her, it had struck her, a little moodily.
Perhaps she imagined it, but it had seemed to her that,
whenever this had happened, he had avoided her gaze as

soon as he had seen it turned towards him. In manner and speech he was as direct as ever, and this—by contrast almost covert—observation of her made her doubly uneasy, as it seemed so out of character.

Standing now in the middle of the drawing-room amid their combined baggage, she felt she should make their relationship quite clear, lest any misunderstanding might be floating in the air. 'Before I let Babette unpack one thing of mine,' she said briskly, 'we should decide which one of us is going to sleep in here, on that divan.' She pointed to the piece of furniture in question.

'I suppose that is my cue to volunteer,' he said drily. 'It occurs to me, Mademoiselle Lacoste, that since meeting you I have done nothing but surrender comfortable beds in order to sleep uncomfortably on sofas and divans. I'm beginning to find it a very tiresome arrangement.'

'A better one would have been to have found us separate lodgings!'

'Listen to me, *mignonne*. Milan is overflowing with French troops. It was a stroke of luck I managed to find us this comfortable billet! If you want to go and try your luck at finding yourself alternative accommodation, then do so. I am staying here. You can have the bed. I relinquish it to you.' He swept his hand towards the door. 'Take it, or leave altogether, as you wish. It makes no difference to me.'

Charlotte betook herself and her belongings to the further room, reflecting that she had little choice, and she supposed they would manage somehow. Together with Babette, she unpacked her clothes, all sadly crumpled and creased.

'I'll go downstairs and see if I can't borrow a flat-iron.' The maid gathered up the garments and draped them over her arm. 'And when I've done that, if it's all the same to you, mademoiselle, I'll go and find my man. I'll come back tomorrow.'

'Of course, Babette, you must go and find your husband,' said Charlotte immediately. 'You don't have to worry about me. I shall be more than comfortable here.'

'It's a beautiful bed,' said Babette, fingering the red velvet hangings appreciatively. 'The quality of these curtains, now, that's something. I'll tell you what this is, mademoiselle, it's a marriage bed. It was made for someone's wedding, this was.'

She departed in search of the iron. Charlotte walked round the room, running her hand over the smooth-polished wooden columns supporting the canopy of the marriage bed, wondering for whom it had been made, and whether the marriage it represented had been one of love. She thought of Lucien, and sighed. The possibilities of her own marriage seemed as distant as ever, even though the miles between them were decreasing.

She was interrupted in her thoughts by the sound of voices in the other room. The groom, Baptistin, had arrived, and was either explaining some problem or had brought some message. Whatever it was, it had put Marc out of humour, and she could hear his voice growing louder and more aggressive. Because she liked Baptistin, and suspected that Marc, for all his autocratic way, liked him too, Charlotte stopped what she was doing to go to the doorway and enquire mildly, 'Is something wrong?'

Marc wheeled round. He seemed quite startled, as if he had forgotten she was within earshot. He hesitated perceptibly, before answering curtly, 'No, nothing at all. Go back to whatever you're doing!'

Charlotte's impulse was to reply to such rudeness by turning on her heel, but it struck her that he looked agitated and a little pale. 'Are you sure?'

'Of course I'm sure, confound it!' he shouted at her. Then he controlled himself with an effort, to add, 'It's a minor matter. Nothing to worry you. Something to do with the horses.'

He looked at the groom as if for support, and Baptistin corroborated hastily with a vigorous nod of his shock of spiky hair.

'That's right, mam'zelle!' he said in his country patois. 'I come to see the Captain and get it sorted out.'

To Charlotte, looking at master and man, it seemed that there was a faintly conspiratorial air about them, as if they had combined to tell her less than the truth. 'I see,' she said slowly.

'Look,' said Marc, 'I've to go out for a while. I'll be back in time for dinner.' He picked up his hat and hesitated as if he would add more, but then seemed to think better of it. 'Come along, boy,' he said to Baptistin, not unkindly, and tousled the groom's hair, whether to show his appreciation for his loyalty or to placate her, Charlotte was not sure.

She watched them go, and shrugged. Whatever it was, Marc was more than capable of dealing with it. She looked about the room, in which he had already had time to establish himself in his usual untidy fashion, clothes, books and equipment scattered about the floor, flung down on chairs and suspended from picture-frames. Some of his things had even strayed into her room, including a pistol of the kind designed to be carried on a saddle, which lay on a table by the door.

Charlotte sat down and studied her reflection in the oval dressing-table mirror. 'I'm as brown as a peasant girl!' she said to herself.

The long journey had certainly left its traces, but not entirely for the worse. Though the sun had burned her delicate skin unfashionably, her cheeks had a healthy, robust colour, and her eyes sparkled with health.

Marc had told her they were to dine with the merchant and his family, and suddenly an almost festive feeling came over her, as though the little family dinner were some kind of celebration, as in a way it was.

They had reached Milan almost without a shot being fired. 'A stroll in the sunshine', Marc had called their progress over the last week or two. With so few difficulties in their path, her search for Lucien must surely be rewarded soon. Her heart rose with an optimism she had not felt for some time, and she began to prepare for the evening almost with the kind of meticulous care she would have taken for a ball. She selected the best of her

gowns, a high-waisted dress of pink lawn with puffed
sleeves, now carefully pressed by Babette and looking
quite acceptable, and pinned up her hair and bound it
with a piece of pink velvet ribbon in the Grecian mode.
She was particularly pleased with this, and spent some
minutes admiring it. The neckline of the gown was cut
low, and she hesitated over whether to disguise the
décolleté with a muslin fichu, but then decided to leave it
as it was, so that she could display the gold chain round
her neck which was her only piece of jewellery.

Charlotte turned before the mirror with a feeling of
pleasurable satisfaction. For someone who had spent
some weeks sleeping in a tent by night, and travelling
dusty roads by day, her possessions crammed in a box
strapped to a pack-mule, she had achieved quite an
elegant effect.

It was well over an hour before she heard movement
in the further room, indicating that Marc had returned.
After some minutes, an impatient rap sounded on her
door.

'Aren't you ready yet?' his voice demanded irritably.
'What are you doing? If you don't come out directly, I'll
go down to dinner without you.'

'Wait, wait, I'm ready!' Charlotte patted her hair for
the last time and smoothed her dress before opening the
door, and presented herself for inspection with forgiv-
able pride.

'Ah,' he said in a barbed tone, running a swift glance
over her. 'So that's what you've been doing all this time.
Well, you look very fine. Is this for our host, or for me? I
can hardly believe it is for me—and our host, I should
remind you, is a respectable married man with two
remarkably pretty daughters.'

'Has he, indeed? Then, Captain Forestier, I'm sure
you will make the most of your opportunity!' Charlotte
retorted, annoyed at his lack of gallantry. She became
aware that she was the subject of some closer scrutiny,
from the blue eyes, and automatically raised a hand to
the bare neckline of the gown, wishing suddenly she had

been prudent and decided for the fichu, after all.

'They are closely guarded by their mama, but I shall do my best,' he returned, adding, 'Don't keep fluttering your hands over that pretty bosom, or are you trying to direct my attention to it?'

'No!' she said angrily.

'Women!' he exclaimed, almost savagely, so that she looked at him in surprise. 'They're the plague of a man's life. I've had less trouble from the Austrians than I've had from confounded women!'

Charlotte commented, 'I suppose this means that you were not able to solve the problem affecting the horses.'

He looked slightly taken aback, and asked, 'How do you mean?'

'Something has obviously upset you, and now you mean to be unpleasant to everyone, and especially to me, as a result,' she said bluntly.

'No,' he replied. 'Nothing's wrong with the horses—nothing I couldn't sort out.'

'Then perhaps you'd be so good as to try and act the part of a gentleman, and offer me your arm?'

Charlotte had expected a forthright answer, but after a moment's hesitation, he said suddenly, and in a much milder tone, 'I am a little out of sorts. But I had no intention of taking my ill humour out on you.' He shook himself, and added briskly—'Well then, mademoiselle?'—offering her his arm.

She realised that, in a roundabout way, he was apologising, and was making a determined effort, for her sake, to shake off his bad mood. She smiled at him, to show she appreciated it, and put her hand on his sleeve.

'*Allez*,' he said, almost kindly, and patted her hand. 'Let us go and show our Italian hosts what pretty girls we have in France!' And he smiled at her, so that, despite herself, her heart gave a little dance.

Their host greeted them as welcomingly as though they had not been foisted upon his home, and Charlotte appreciated his tactfulness, by which the little awkwardness which might have attended their entry was avoided. They all sat down to dine with every appearance of good humour.

The grain merchant was a pleasant, solid, middle-aged man, and Charlotte would have liked to talk to him, but they lacked a common language. Charlotte knew no Italian, the merchant spoke only that and a little German, a part of his business being, or so Charlotte understood him to say, to supply fodder to the Austrian cavalry.

'It must be embarrassing for him to have us here,' she whispered to Marc, 'and damage his business, too.'

'Why should it?' he retorted. 'Now he'll sell his grain to us, and probably make a handsome profit.'

Their hostess, a handsome woman with dark eyes like sloes, also spoke nothing but her own tongue. Though she smiled graciously at Charlotte, there was a marked reserve in her manner, which Charlotte initially put down to the unusual situation. She noticed, however, that the lady's sloe eyes gleamed appreciatively at Marc as he bowed and kissed her hand, but those same dark eyes assessed Charlotte sharply, and something very like disapproval showed in them. She whispered something to her husband, who shook his head, whereupon she stared very hard at Charlotte and then looked pointedly away.

Charlotte flushed, for it was clear that the lady's disapproval centred not upon their being billeted upon the family generally, but upon the presence of herself in particular.

As for the two daughters, they were, as Marc had said, as pretty as a pair of Colombines stepped down from the stage of the *commedia dell'arte*. Charlotte thought that they were aged fifteen and sixteen respectively. Their large brown velvet eyes regarded the world with all the unspoiled lustre of a fawn's, and they had teeth like white pearls, gleaming tantalisingly through cherry lips. They had seated themselves either side of Marc, and billed and cooed at him, for all the world, Charlotte thought a little crossly, like a pair of turtledoves, chattering to him in a charming, imperfect schoolroom French, which appeared to amuse him greatly.

She looked across the table at Marc himself, and thought, with a stir of unwilling admiration, that he looked tonight quite devastatingly handsome. She had never seen him in such high spirits, though it did strike her that the mood was a little forced, and the laughter not always reflected in his eyes. Still, he was laughing a great deal with his two enchanting little companions, and the combination of this extraordinary good humour, real or assumed, and the mellow candlelight had softened the harshness of his features. His bronzed, southern looks and long black hair seemed here in quite the right place. The light played on the colours of his uniform, so that the gold braid gleamed softly, the red glowed a deep crimson and the dark blue assumed a midnight hue.

He had definitely set himself to entertain his two pretty new friends and to let himself be entertained by them. He was trying to teach them some nursery tongue-twister in French. They, of course, could not say it, though he repeated it time after time. The more they tried and failed, the more they giggled and fixed their great fawn's eyes on his face, begging *le capitaine* to say the sentence just once more, please . . .

Charlotte, left to try and communicate monosyllabically with the parents as best she could, felt her good mood fade, and resentment take its place.

'It's no good!' Marc declared, when his two pupils failed yet again in the task he had set them. 'You try it, Charlotte.'

Unwillingly, Charlotte repeated the nonsensical little phrase, and, to her mortification, her tongue stumbled and she muffed it altogether.

'There!' he said consolingly to the two daughters, 'You see? Even Mademoiselle Lacoste cannot say it.'

The two girls turned their wide-eyed gaze on her, and stared at her exactly, she thought, as though she were some kind of curiosity on display in a fairground. Then the younger of them began to giggle, attempting vainly to stifle it behind her hand. Her mother leaned across the table and spoke to her sharply. The girl stopped giggling and exchanged surreptitious, knowing glances with her sister, then looked again at Charlotte, her brown eyes gleaming with suppressed merriment.

Fortunately the servant came in at that moment, bearing a great dish of saffron rice, from which rose a fragrant and savoury steam that whispered of chicken and wine and melted cheese.

But Charlotte had quite lost her appetite. She understood now, only too well, and with a humiliating clarity, the meaning of the signora's disapproval and her daughters' curiosity. The room was very hot and stuffy. She was unable, and now unwilling to talk to the merchant or his wife, and sat too far from Marc to talk conveniently to him. In any event, he was well occupied with his charming admirers. Charlotte pushed the risotto around her plate with her fork, and wished herself elsewhere, as far as possible, anywhere but here.

Her host was bending courteously towards her, pointing at her plate and asking her something.

'He's asking if you like the dinner,' Marc called across the table. 'You don't eat anything.'

Charlotte set down her fork. 'Tell him the food is excellent—but I'm rather tired. If they don't mind, I'll go upstairs.'

'You'll offend them,' he said sharply.

'I can't help that!' she retorted, pushing back her chair. 'You will have to make my excuses for me.' She stood up.

'Sit down, Charlotte!' he ordered, and she saw the flicker of anger in his eyes and heard the warning note in his voice.

'No.' Her tone was determined.

The Italian family had fallen silent, and sat watching them. The merchant drummed his fingers almost imperceptibly on the tabletop and eyed them appraisingly, as he might have done when negotiating some tricky piece of business. Otherwise a stillness hung over the room, in which the daughters looked down, and at each other, and their mother stared blandly in front of her. A feeling almost of claustrophobia closed in on Charlotte, and she backed away from the table towards the door.

Marc threw his napkin down on the table, and rising to his feet and moving with that almost feline ease and rapidity of which he was capable, blocked her exit from the room, seizing her wrist in a not very gentle grip. With a cool courtesy of tone, belied by the look in his eyes, he said smoothly, 'It is not necessary for you to leave. Come and sit down.'

'Let me go, Marc . . .' Charlotte's voice was shaking. She tried to free her wrist, but his grip tightened and it was all she could do not to cry out in pain. All the more angry, because she believed he must know he hurt her, she hissed, 'You're twisting my wrist! If you want to drag me back to the table struggling all the way and making a fine scene, you can do so! I'll let you break my wrist before I go willingly!'

He released her abruptly. 'You are making a scene already!'

'Then you had better go back and talk to your little friends!' she snapped. 'At the moment, we're entertaining them splendidly. Their mouths are hanging open and their eyes are starting out of their heads!'

'If you are going to talk so stupidly, then you had best leave us!' He jerked open the door so that she could go out.

He was obviously very angry, but something else, too, was indicated in his manner. Had it been any other man but Marc Forestier, Charlotte might even have thought he was embarrassed.

Her cheeks burning, she stepped through the door, and seizing her skirts in both hands, ran upstairs, miserably aware that she had succeeded in making herself look foolish before them all. She dragged the bedroom door closed behind her and leaned back against it, her eyes shut, and panting, her heart throbbing painfully in her breast.

After a while Charlotte felt calmer, but low in spirits. There was nothing now left to do, so she undressed slowly and miserably and put on her nightgown. Seating herself before the dressing-table, she untied the velvet ribbon and pulled it from her hair, so that it fell down in long curls. She sighed and picked up her hairbrush, only to sit with it in her hand, staring morosely into the mirror.

Unexpectedly, there came a tap at her door. The dinner-party was over, and he had come to pursue their quarrel. Charlotte was in no mood for a reckoning, but it could not be put off. If he had set his mind on it, to ask him to wait until the morning would be a waste of effort. She took a deep breath.

'Come in,' she called, in as level a voice as she could command.

He came in quietly, and stood behind her chair so that she could see him reflected over her shoulder. Their eyes met in the mirror, and although he said nothing, she could read the displeasure which still showed in them.

'You are angry, I suppose,' she said defensively. 'You think I should have stayed down there because *you* wished it.'

'No,' he said. 'I think you should have stayed down there because only a coward retreats without a fight, and you are not a coward, Charlotte.'

'You saw how those women looked at me!' she said emotionally. 'I was humiliated!'

'Only because you allowed yourself to be,' he told her brusquely. 'You should have carried the fight to them . . . made eyes at the husband, that would have spiked their guns nicely!' Suddenly, he smiled.

'That is the kind of solution only you would imagine!'

'How well you think you know me,' he said softly. 'Yet you cannot even distinguish between when I am angry with you and when I am only angry with others.'

'Go away!' Charlotte exclaimed vehemently.

She was not sure what she imagined he might do or say next. What he did was quite unexpected. He smiled slightly, and reaching past her, took the hairbrush from her hand. Gently, with smooth, even sweeps, he began to brush out her long blond hair. His touch was surprisingly soothing. Charlotte felt the tense muscles of her face, neck and shoulders relax. Her anger subsided, and a feeling of restfulness slowly replaced it.

Sensing the change in her mood, he set down the hairbrush and seated himself on a chair beside her, so that he faced her.

'So, they suppose you my mistress,' he said frankly. 'They are prosperous, but simple, people. Very moral and pious. Some might say bigoted. It shocks them that we lodge here together and are not married.'

'I don't need it explained to me, Marc,' Charlotte burst out resentfully. 'I know very well what they supposed me. They suppose me very little better than those wretched tawdry bawds who follow the army! And as for those stupid girls, sniggering and staring at me as though I were some kind of freak in a sideshow! They were quite eaten up with speculation, and probably hoped I'd dance on the table.'

He began to laugh, then, which did nothing to console her. 'Come, Charlotte,' he said indulgently, 'you can't allow yourself to be angered by those children.'

'Children, you call them?' she snapped '*Children!* A pair of very practised little flirts! And *you* encouraged them.'

'So it was all my fault, was it? And who wanted to come along with me and have others think her my mistress, because it suited her plans for a while?'

'Yes, I know,' Charlotte sighed. 'You don't have to remind me.'

'And if it were true,' he said in a different tone, 'would it be such a terrible thing?'

She looked up in alarm. The mocking banter had gone from the blue eyes, which regarded her with uncomfortable directness, as if they saw right into her mind and heart, waiting for an answer. She plucked at the neck of her nightgown nervously, wishing she were more modestly dressed.

'Don't fidget like that.' He put out his hand to take hers, and held it still. 'Well, Charlotte?'

'I don't know what you mean,' she muttered, avoiding that clear blue, demoralising gaze.

'Yes, you do,' Marc said. 'Why do you think I brought you along with me all this way, Charlotte?'

She pulled her hand free of his, so that he would not feel it trembled, and muttered, 'I don't know. Because of Éloise Thierry, because of Lucien, perhaps . . .'

'What do either of them matter?' he interrupted her impatiently. 'I'm talking of you, and of me . . . I didn't *have* to bring you along, Charlotte, any more than you had to come to *me* for help. I looked at you, and I liked what I saw. Perhaps it was the same for you, when you looked at me. Call it a lesson in human chemistry, if you like, call it what you will—You understand my meaning very well.'

Yes, she understood, and knew now that he had indeed sensed the change in her feelings towards him, knew that she was physically attracted to him, had felt the pull of that animal magnetism, perhaps from the beginning.

He ran his fingers lightly down her cheek and rested them on the pulse which beat nervously in her throat. 'Oh, I grant you,' he said, 'we both made any number of excuses for it. But the truth is, you wanted to come with *me* . . .'

'No . . .' Charlotte interrupted him desperately. 'Stop it, Marc. Stop it now, do you hear me? It isn't true. I'm here because I'm looking for Lucien, and I'm here with you because that is the only way I can find him!'

'You don't need Lucien,' he said quietly. 'Not any more.'

In the following tense silence his fingers continued their downward journey, across her neck and shoulder and tracing the soft contour of her breast. His touch, sensitive and warm through the thin cotton of the night-gown, aroused strange stirrings within her. He was aware of that, too, and smiled slightly.

'Forget him, Charlotte,' he whispered. 'He's a ghost in the past. We all have such ghosts in our pasts. Leave them there, where they belong.'

He caught at the gold chain round her throat, exerting a gentle pull on it which obliged her to move towards him to avoid it cutting into her neck.

'Please let go,' she whispered in reply. 'Please, Marc . . .'

'Those people downstairs,' he said softly, 'they think us lovers. Don't look so wild! Does the thought really frighten you so much? There's nothing to fear, let me show you . . .' His grip on the gold chain tightened, and his long hair brushed her face as his mouth sought hers.

'*No!*' Charlotte cried out again. She felt herself tremble, and knew, even as she heard her own voice, that her refusal was not just because of Lucien. It was because of something else, something which had to be destroyed, here and now, or it would destroy everything she had ever believed. It would destroy *her*.

She gathered her failing resolve, and pouring into her voice all the scorn of which she was capable, said in a clear and steady tone, 'You must be *mad*! What could ever attract me to a man like you? Go and find yourself a woman of the sort of Madame Thierry, who doesn't mind deceiving her husband and is not particular into whose bed she climbs! After all, you can always fight another duel!'

Marc's cheeks had paled beneath their tan. He looked shaken, as though her words had struck him physically, and in the blue eyes a familiar glint of anger sparkled, warning of danger.

'What are you talking about?' he demanded hoarsely. 'Do you think I compare you with Éloise? Good God, Charlotte, in all these weeks of travel between Ville-neuve and here, I've hardly ever touched you! I've never once asked you to come to my bed! Do you think, if I thought of you as I did of Éloise, that I would have been so damn patient? That I would have waited till now?' He was shouting at her, the blue eyes blazing, his words ringing on the air. 'But what do you think I am, a marionette? Do you think it's been easy for me to be near to a girl like you and never . . .'

'Be quiet!' Charlotte cried out. Her heart was throbbing in her breast, and every breath seemed an effort. 'You forget yourself, Captain,' she managed to gasp. 'And you forget Lucien!'

'Lucien!' he exploded. 'Confound Lucien! He can go to the devil and stay there! I'm sick of hearing you talk of him! Can you even remember his face, Charlotte? Well, can you?' He shook her. 'Answer me, damn you!'

'Of course I can,' she stuttered, terrified by so much savagery in his face. 'I love him.'

'You *lie*!' he interrupted her violently. 'Charlotte, you hadn't seen him for years when he suddenly came back to you for two or three weeks, since when you've heard nothing more of him. How can you talk of love or loyalty to him? You hardly know him!'

'I've known him all my life!' she cried out.

'You haven't! You knew a little boy who wanted to be a soldier. You never knew the man! This picture you carry of him in your mind, you've created it from girlish daydreams, not from real life! I've listened to you talk of Lucien Saint-Laurent, and you speak of a man who doesn't exist. I've known Lucien for years, a real Lucien, a real man, flesh and blood and human and fallible! The real Lucien and the man you speak of are not one and the same, Charlotte. Lucien Saint-Laurent is not as you imagine him!'

'Be quiet, I won't listen!' she cried out in agony, pressing her hands to her ears. 'You're lying! It's a sordid trick to make me agree to what you want!'

'You little fool!' he shouted. 'Do you think I need to trick you? Don't you think that at any time these past weeks I could just have taken what I wanted?'

As he spoke, the thin gold chain snapped in his

fingers, and with it snapped the last remnant of his self-control, the last frail barrier between her and his desire.

He swore violently, and seizing her shoulders, dragged her towards him and into his embrace. His mouth pressed fiercely against hers—she could feel his tongue against her teeth, probing, searching, demanding a response and a surrender.

Charlotte stumbled backwards. The chair crashed aside and she slipped, falling beneath his weight to the floor. She landed awkwardly, jarring the point of her shoulder, so that a jabbing pain shot through her back and made her cry out. Marc sprawled across her, pinning her down. His fingers grasped at her nightgown, tearing it away and bruising the soft white skin beneath with the imprint of his fingers.

'You do not understand what kind of men you move among'—Éloise Thierry's voice echoed in her memory. Charlotte had thought at the time the words had been spoken in revenge, but perhaps Éloise had wanted to warn her. To tell her that these were men who had existed in the world since the dawn of time, a warrior caste, superficially observing their own peculiar code of honour and discipline and duty, but beneath it all, violent, passionate and cruel. Was this what had drawn Éloise to Marc? Was he like one of those men of the Terror, whom she had hated and feared, but who were the only men she knew and understood?

These thoughts churned incoherently about Charlotte's brain as, hardly knowing any more what she did, she struggled desperately with someone she no longer recognised. Not Marc, but Marc transformed into some primitive and pitiless being. The noise of their battle must have been audible all over the house, and as she sobbed in pain and terror, it even flashed through her mind that someone might come to see what was amiss. At the same moment, she knew that no one would.

It was the French officer and his mistress, quarrelling

and fighting. The signora would be ushering her daughters away hastily out of earshot, and her husband, hearing the commotion, would probably do no more than chuckle and pour himself another glass of wine.

Charlotte could hear Marc panting and feel his breath on her cheek, and when she tried to push him off, he struck away her arm viciously. She had no weapon, and not sufficient strength to escape from her assailant. She resorted to the primitive, instinctive defences of a cornered animal, and as his hand came close to her mouth, she twisted her head and sank her teeth deep into his thumb.

He uttered an exclamation, perhaps more of surprise than of pain, and jerked his hand away, automatically recoiling from her.

Charlotte scrambled out from beneath him, half-naked, panting, tear-stained and dishevelled, stumbled to the table by the door, and seizing the horse-pistol, raised it in both hands to point it at him. It wavered slightly, but at that range she could not miss.

'Stay there,' she hissed at him. 'Stay there, or I swear I'll kill you if I can!'

Silence fell. The whole house seemed to hold its breath. Marc got slowly to his feet and dusted himself down deliberately, watching her all the while.

'Put that down,' he said at last, quietly. 'Don't be a stupid little fool.'

'Don't come near me!' Charlotte warned, as he took a step towards her. 'I do know how to fire this thing—my father showed me. At this range, I'll blow a hole right through you.'

He stood still. 'It's all right, Charlotte.' He spoke very softly now, and soothingly, as he might have spoken to a frightened horse. 'Look . . .' He spread out his hands as if to show he had no aggressive intentions. 'I won't touch you. I promise. There's nothing to be afraid of.'

'Get out of here!' she ordered, as she steadied the wavering muzzle of the pistol. 'Before I fire anyway!'

'Very well. Although I should point out that it's not

loaded!' Charlotte gasped, but he ignored her, and walked towards the door, where he paused briefly. 'I suppose I shall have to go and see what the ladies of Milan have to offer. Perhaps they won't fight so hard for their virtue!'

'Get out!' she flung at him.

He gave her a dry smile, and went out without another word.

Charlotte waited until she was satisfied that he had really gone, before letting the pistol sink down. She supposed he was telling the truth, and it wasn't loaded. She did not want to look. She set it down on the dressing-table with a trembling hand, and stumbled to the bed, to fall onto the pillows, shaking uncontrollably.

It was not just because an attempt had been made to violate her body. That had been unsuccessful. What had been violated, all too successfully, was her view of love between a man and a woman as a tender, gentle act. She had rejected Éloise's claim that 'it is never different' as the cynical view of a woman accustomed to barter herself for what she wanted. She had refused to believe that it could be true. She still did not believe it. Though her faith had been momentarily shaken, she clung obstinately to an instinctive knowledge that it did not have to be like this evening's experience. Even Marc must surely be capable of some tenderness, though he had shown little towards her. But if he did have gentler feelings, he kept them locked away, and she did not have the key.

Insistantly, a little voice echoed in her brain, saying, 'You *do* have the key, but you are afraid to use it!'

'Never,' Charlotte whispered into the crumpled pillows. 'Never with Marc Forestier . . .'

She lay for a long time until the one guttering candle burned itself out, and then, in the darkness, she pulled the sheet over herself and crouched huddled into a self-protecting ball like a small child. For a long time she listened for Marc's return, but there was no sound of movement in the further room, and eventually she fell asleep, knowing that he would not return that night.

CHAPTER
NINE

WHEN CHARLOTTE awoke, it was morning. Sunlight entered in yellow bars through the shutters, and the street noises rose from below. Church bells summoned worshippers to early Mass, and a solitary fly buzzed monotonously against the window-pane in the stuffy atmosphere of the room.

She moved and groaned. Her shoulder pained her, and her whole body ached as if she were bruised from head to toe. She did not want to get up and dress. To face the day seemed beyond any strength she could command, so she remained for most of the morning where she was, huddled in the untidy bed.

It was midday before she heard footsteps in the other room and knew Marc had returned at last. They paused outside her door, and his voice called softly, 'Charlotte?'

Charlotte did not reply.

He called her again, and still receiving no response, turned the handle and pushed the door open. She could see him clearly, his tall figure framed in the half-light in the doorway. He released the handle, and crossing the room quickly, dropped on one knee by the side of the bed.

'Are you all right?' His voice sounded concerned, as well it might, Charlotte thought bitterly.

She lacked even the energy or will to reply. She doubted that in her torn nightdress she was even decent. But a cold rancour was stirring within her. Let him see what he had done. Let him see the torn gown and, through the rents, the bruised flesh. If it stirred some flicker of remorse in him, then let him suffer it.

Very quietly, he said, 'I'm sorry. I didn't mean to hurt you.'

'But you did.'

He ran the tip of his tongue over his upper lip. 'Yes. I—I have a devil of a temper at times, I know. It gets the better of me.'

'It's not an excuse,' she replied. He clearly regretted what he had done, more than she would have expected him to do, but she was in no mood to forgive.

'I know it's not an excuse. I don't seek to excuse what I did. It happened, and I'm sorry, but you need not make such a drama out of it. You can hardly claim I ravished you.'

A note of defensiveness had entered his voice. Charlotte turned her head to look at him. 'You tried to!' she said vehemently.

Her ash-blonde hair fell across her face, and she picked it out of her eyes. His hand sketched the beginning of a gesture towards her, but then froze.

'And were you successful in your search, last night?' She could not resist asking him coldly, though she knew she twisted the knife in the wound of his contrition.

She wanted to hurt him. He had hurt her. Now, for the first time in years, perhaps ever, he found himself in the position of having to admit himself at fault. He did not know how to do it. The words were not in his vocabulary, and the attitude too alien for him to adopt. He floundered, seeking some means of conciliation. But she would not help him to salve his newly-awakened conscience, to escape with a brief apology and an even briefer remorse which already showed signs of turning to a more habitual truculence.

He avoided her gaze. 'I went to some place with Cresson,' he said. 'The wine was cheap, and the music agreeable.'

'And the girls pretty? *And* also agreeable?'

'Pretty enough. I drank too much. I can't remember. I didn't enquire as to whether they were agreeable. Cresson took me back to his lodgings, and I slept there.'

His eyes met hers evenly. 'I wasn't with a whore last night, if that's what you want to know.'

'I don't want to know!' Charlotte said stonily. 'I don't care.'

But she did—That was what caused anger to surge up in her again. It ought not to matter to her, she told herself. In fact, she should be content to be told his amorous inclinations were turned away from her. Yet she could not but be glad he had not come back to her here, now, straight from the still warm bed and painted embrace of some Milanese harlot.

The conflict in her emotions confused her. It had been the same when she had seen him with Madame Thierry. She had hated the possessive way that the woman had looked at him, the sight of her in Marc's bed, the thought of them together. Yet, at the same time, Charlotte feared the very thought that he might touch her.

'Babette is downstairs,' he said. 'I brought her with me. She's waiting to come up. I'll fetch her in a moment, but first,' he hesitated, then fished in his pocket and brought out a small packet wrapped in tissue-paper. 'I walked around this morning, clearing my head in the fresh air, and I bought this. I wanted to give it to you, if you will accept it. A peace-offering . . .'

He unwrapped the tissue and placed the object on the pillow beside her. It was an enamelled medallion on a chain.

'I broke your necklace last night,' he said awkwardly, in explanation.

Charlotte pushed herself up on one elbow, wincing at the pain it caused her. 'You cannot truly believe that I will accept that, and just forget!'

He flushed. 'No! But I—I would like you to have it. The girl in the medallion, I thought she looked a little like you. It took my fancy . . .'

Charlotte looked down at the medallion, lying on the crumpled pillow. It depicted the head of a girl, garlanded with roses. The workmanship was exquisite. He must have paid a lot of money for it, far more than he could afford.

'I can't undo what I did,' he said soberly. 'I can only try and made amends, and I don't know any other way.' His fingers touched the medallion. 'Please,' he said in a strained voice, as if it was truly a word strange to him.

He was vulnerable and human, after all. Charlotte felt a surge of shame at her churlish refusal to accept his own reluctant acceptance of his vulnerability. She drew a deep breath and picked up the medallion.

'Very well, Marc, I accept your gift, your peace-offering.' She saw the look of relief in his eyes, and added emphatically, 'But I swear, if *ever* you try to do such a thing again, I'll demand justice of the commander of the artillery, Marmont. I'll even lay my case before General Bonaparte himself!'

He stood up. 'That will not be necessary,' he told her evenly. 'You have nothing more to fear from me. I won't—I won't do it again.' He turned aside. 'I'll fetch Babette.'

Charlotte watched him walk out of the room, and lay back on the pillow, the medallion clasped in her palm. She had won a victory, but it seemed a sordid little victory to her now, and she knew it would cost her dear. She had probably done what no other woman had managed before; she had humbled his pride, and though it had only been for a moment, he would not forget it . . . and he would never forgive her.

He sent Babette upstairs as he had said he would. She bustled into the room and took charge of Charlotte with brisk efficiency.

'There, now, mademoiselle, I've got them heating water in the kitchen for you to have a bath. Let me help you out of bed. Whatever happened to your nightgown? You might as well take it off, my love, for it's not doing much good in that state.'

Charlotte swung her legs obediently over the side of the bed and allowed Babette to divest her of the ruined nightgown. At the sight of the bruises on her arms and shoulders, the maid clucked her tongue disapprovingly.

'There, I never would have believed it of the Captain. Though I knew he has a fierce temper, I would never have believed he'd hurt *you*. Whatever made him do such a thing? It's not like him at all.'

'Isn't it?'

'No, it isn't!' returned Babette vigorously. 'He's a strong-minded man and a hard one, but use violence towards a woman is something he'd never do, not in his right mind!'

The arrival of the bath-water at that juncture interrupted their conversation before Charlotte could reply. There was a lull while Babette organised the filling of the bath, and helped Charlotte into it. It was a small affair, like a deep armchair, in which the bather relaxed comfortably, half-immersed, with his or her feet sticking out of the end. She sighed as the warm water lapped around her, soothing her sore muscles.

Babette's mind was still working on the same problem. 'Something powerful pushed him to it, you mark my words. And very likely he was out of sorts anyway, on account of the bad news he had yesterday. It stands to reason, he couldn't have been himself.'

'What news?' Charlotte asked, not really wanting to discuss Marc.

'Why, did he not tell you, my dear? Very likely, he didn't want to upset you. But we heard yesterday that Captain Thierry was dying for sure of his wound, and was not expected to last the night.'

The bath-water splashed over the side as Charlotte sat up, grasping the rim. 'What? But he said nothing to me of it, nothing at all! I thought he was annoyed because of the horses.' She lay back again. 'Poor Marc,' she said in real commiseration, the events of the previous evening wiped from her mind for an instant. 'It will have hit him hard. Though he cares for nobody, yet I know he regretted injuring Captain Thierry so severely. Why didn't he tell me?'

'It's that woman!' said Babette fiercely, tipping the contents of a can of water over Charlotte's shoulders. 'No better than a murderess, that's my way of thinking! She wanted her husband out of the way, and plotted to make Captain Forestier strike the blow, which she couldn't do herself! It's a good thing for her sake she's away from here, for she'd not be popular!'

'Yes,' Charlotte agreed. 'She was a vengeful woman without a jot of conscience.' She was silent for a moment, then murmured, 'I wish I'd known. I wouldn't have said—some of the things I said.'

Perhaps, after all, he didn't mean to hurt me, perhaps it was Éloise, she thought. Éloise and I for a moment were one person to him.

'Well, you were bound to hear,' Babette was saying. 'If not from the Captain, then from someone else, for no one's talking of anything else. There's a few harsh words being spoken, mademoiselle, for the word has gone round that Captain Forestier struck a foul blow, with the point of the sabre, after points were barred.'

'It was an accident!' Charlotte exclaimed indignantly.

'You and I know that, my dear. It's convincing others.' The maid set down the can and picked up a towel. 'I did hear one other odd little tale, only rumour, mind, about Madame Thierry. It seems her journey home isn't proving too much of a pleasure for her. The carriage was stopped by local bandits, not twenty-four hours after she set out, and she was robbed of most of her jewels. It will leave her a poor woman, for Captain Thierry—God rest his soul if he's been taken—was a gambling man, and cash flowed through his fingers like grains of sand.'

'I can't say I'm sorry,' Charlotte admitted honestly, 'though it's hardly sufficient punishment for what she did. Help me out of this bath, Babette.'

Babette wrapped the towel around her mistress, and then paused. 'You know, my dear,' she said very soberly. 'I've seen all kinds of wounds, sabre, pistol, cannonball—The worst scars any man carries, he carries inside of himself, in his heart. The Captain carries some kind of a wound like that, inside of himself. I don't know how he came by it, or what it is, but I know what it would take to cure it, and that's a woman's love. Not some wicked jade like the Thierry woman, but someone like you, someone of his own, to love, and look after, and live up to. It's all any man needs. It's all any one of us needs, man or woman . . .'

'No,' Charlotte said quietly. 'Not me. He doesn't need me. I can't do it. Though you may be right. I still am not the one.'

The maid sighed regretfully, and there was a pause while she towelled Charlotte dry briskly, despite her protests.

'You're rubbing too hard, Babette!'

'Tones up the skin, my love. Stop wriggling about, and just step into this petticoat and let me tie up the strings.'

There was much fiddling with strings, hooks and eyes, and hairpins before Babette was satisfied, and stood back to survey the finished product of her ministrations.

'Are you going to wear this, my dear?' she asked, picking up the medallion.

'I don't know,' Charlotte said uncertainly, remembering. 'He may think it makes everything he did all right, and encourage him to think he can behave as he wishes.'

'You wear it! When a quarrel is over and done with, no good comes of raking over its half-dead ashes. Too many fires start that way, and we get burned in them!' Babette fastened the medallion around the girl's white throat. 'There, mademoiselle, you look as pretty as a picture again, just as you always do. The sight of you would melt anyone's heart, let alone the Captain's. Now, you're not to go grumbling at him any more over what he did last night, for the poor man has enough to worry him. He's finished, you know, if people believe this story of a foul blow.'

Marc was downstairs, sitting alone in the dining-room, one foot resting on the stretcher-bar of another chair, staring moodily at the plaster statuette of an obscure saint which held sway above the side-table.

Charlotte hesitated to disturb him, knowing full well that this relaxed attitude was deceptive, no more peaceful than a dozing leopard, ever ready to spring from his slumber and strike. She hesitated, too, because she did not know what to say. He had behaved badly towards her, and she could not brush the whole matter aside. At the same time, she felt an obscure desire to go and comfort him. Eventually she went and stood by his chair. Though he was aware of her presence, it seemed an interminable time before he looked up. His eyes were like blue ice. He said nothing.

'Babette told me about Captain Thierry,' she said awkwardly. 'I know what bad news that is for you. I'm sorry.'

'The surgeon couldn't stanch the blood,' Marc explained dully. 'I'd doubted he'd be able to save him, from the first.'

'Why didn't you tell me, Marc, yesterday?'

'Not your concern!' he replied brusquely. After a moment he added more mildly. 'You were all dressed up, and feeling pleased with yourself. There was no point in troubling you with my bad news.'

'There's going to be trouble now, for you, isn't there?' she asked quietly.

'What do you expect? A man who kills another in a duel with a foul blow is dishonoured in everyone's eyes—even his friends', if he has any.'

'But you didn't intend it!' Charlotte protested.

'Only Thierry himself could bear witness to that!' Marc said bitterly. 'And he's not likely to do anything to help me, even if he's still alive. I hope the poor devil was able to enjoy his revenge.'

'I see . . .' Charlotte said thoughtfully. She turned, and walked slowly out.

Babette had lingered in the doorway, eyeing the Captain shrewdly. 'Monsieur,' she said, 'it will do no good to brood on it.'

'I don't waste time brooding over dead men.'

'Come, monsieur, you know I don't mean that, though it's a sad business. I mean my lady.'

Marc stirred slightly, and the other chair scraped as his foot pushed it away. 'I don't give a damn for your lady,' he said, an almost vicious note in his voice. 'She can sulk from now till Doomsday for all I care. I've already told her that she can sleep soundly in her bed without fear of being disturbed there by me. I've no wish to be made a fool of twice!'

'Captain, the child hardly knows her own mind!' Babette entreated. 'She has her head full of nothing but finding this cousin of hers. Do you know him?'

'I know him,' he said softly, the same harsh note in his voice.

'And do you think she'll find him, monsieur?'

Marc's clear, cold gaze rested on the maid in a way which chilled her. 'It's very likely she'll find him,' he said quietly. 'But she would be better dead. Perhaps I should be, too,' he added, almost inaudibly.

'Babette!' Charlotte said urgently, as soon as the maid reappeared upstairs. 'Listen to me carefully. I want you to do something, and very quietly, so that Captain Forestier knows nothing of it! I want you to go and find a Hussar called Dufour.'

'I know the man. He was Captain Thierry's second in that dratted duel.'

'Ask Monsieur Dufour if Captain Thierry still lives, and if so, if he's conscious. If he answers "yes" to both those questions, then tell him I want him to take me to Captain Thierry. I must try and speak with him before it's too late. Tell Dufour not to come to this house; I'll meet him in the town. Hurry, and above all, Marc *mustn't* know!'

'He's sinking fast and will be gone by tonight,' Dufour said, 'but he's conscious.' His dark eyes rested on Charlotte. 'Did Forestier send you?'

'No, he knows nothing of it, and he mustn't!' Charlotte urged. 'He must never know I was here.'

'Be as quick as you can,' the Hussar said, pushing open the door. 'He's lucid, but he's weak.'

The room was in semi-darkness, and the dying man was propped on feather pillows. The indefinable atmosphere of death hung in the air. Another Hussar, whom Charlotte did not know, rose from the bedside as she entered with Dufour. Dufour looked at him enquiringly, and the other shook his head.

'Go on!' whispered Dufour to Charlotte, taking her elbow and pushing her towards the bedside.

Although she wanted desperately to speak to Éloise's husband, Charlotte felt a natural revulsion as she approached the man who lay dying from a blow Marc had struck. She had been with her father when he had died, but this man, still young, bleeding to death from a mortal wound received in error and for the sake of the so-called honour of a woman who had repeatedly betrayed him, filled her with horror, pity and despair.

The dying man's complexion was a horrid grey colour, as if he were already a corpse, and even the rapier scars on his face were faint in contrast. But the eyes were alive, and turned towards her, seemingly expressing some question.

'He wants you to bend your head closer,' Dufour whispered in her ear.

She leaned over Thierry, trying not to look at the reddened bandages into which the life-blood was slowly but surely seeping away. 'Captain Thierry, are you able to understand what I say?' she asked urgently.

'What do you want?' The whispered words were surprisingly clear.

'You remember me? Charlotte Lacoste. I—I travel with Marc Forestier.'

At the mention of Marc's name, a wry smile flitted across the dying man's features.

'Captain Thierry,' Charlotte pleaded. 'I know why you must hate Marc, but he didn't intend this! You must know, the foul blow was not struck intentionally. Please, please will you say so, before these gentlemen?' She indicated Dufour and the other Hussar behind her.

'You and he . . . ?' the dying man whispered.

'No, it's not as you imagine,' Charlotte said hastily. 'Captain Forestier is helping me to find my fiancé, Lucien Saint-Laurent. You challenged Marc over a question of honour. Please, Captain Thierry, it is a question of doing the honourable thing now.'

Thierry's gaze had clouded uncertainly as she spoke, but he nodded slightly and turned his head on the pillow to catch the eyes of the two Hussars, who moved closer to him in order to listen.

The dying man took a deep breath, gathering the last of his failing strength. 'You are witnesses,' he croaked. 'The blow was accidental. I was rash, too angry—my own stupidity—Captain Forestier is not to blame.'

'Thank you,' Charlotte whispered. 'Oh, thank you, Captain Thierry!' She took his hand and pressed it gratefully.

'It's better,' he said faintly, 'that he kill me, rather than I him. Forestier is a good man, and she was always a whore . . .' His fingers suddenly gripped hers. 'Saint-Laurent,' he whispered. 'Ask Forestier . . .'

His voice was transformed into an odd rasping noise. For a moment his eyes looked up at her, and then they clouded unseeingly and his hand slid from hers.

'He's gone,' Dufour said. He stretched past Charlotte to pull the sheet over the dead face. 'Come,' he touched her shoulder and led her outside.

'It will be all right,' he assured her. 'We'll make sure everyone knows, and that no one attaches blame to Forestier.'

'Remember!' Charlotte begged. 'No one must know I was here.'

Dufour nodded. 'Why Forestier ever bothered with her, when he has you with him, I'll never understand!' he exclaimed. He raised her hand to his lips, and kissed her fingers. 'I wish you were mine,' he said softly.

Charlotte walked back slowly. *Ask Forestier . . .* Well, she had already done that. She felt as though some great weight oppressed her, as if there were thunder in the air, despite the clear sky. She did not know what it was, only that it somehow threatened her.

CHAPTER
TEN

THEY LEFT Milan in subdued spirits. Not only Charlotte felt the change in the atmosphere—it affected the whole army. Everyone knew that the stroll in the sunshine was over, and the idyll was irrevocably shattered when news was brought to them that another part of their scattered forces had made contact with the Austrians and driven them back in disarray. With the Austrians fleeing before them, the French, like hounds which scent the stag's blood, pressed on towards the kill.

Marc's behaviour was scrupulously correct towards Charlotte. He addressed her with distant politeness, and only when necessary, and seemed to have withdrawn within himself and his world of guns, men and horses. Despite everything, she could not but regret the passing of the constant warfare which had been the hallmark of their tempestuous relationship. At least it had signified some human contact between them. Now they were as strangers. She would have liked to make some gesture of friendship, but perhaps he would not wish it.

The countryside through which they now passed was that of rolling farmland. Tiny villages clustered about a church, seen from a distance only as so many dots about a single straight campanile. Some even had no church, but were mere hamlets or clustered farm buildings. They struck camp in the neighbourhood of one of these. Charlotte asked a peasant-woman, who came selling fresh vegetables, what the place was called, and was given to understand that it had the name of Marengo.

Charlotte debated, and then went in search of Marc to

give him this information. She had seen him strolling off alone, his hands in his pockets, towards the river, and took the same direction. But when she reached the bank, she came first upon his clothes, piled in an untidy heap on the grass. A faint splash caught her attention, and shading her eyes against the bright sunlight, she saw that he was swimming, and some way down-river from where she stood. The sunspots sparkled like confetti on the rippling surface of the water, and Marc's lithe, brown body moved gracefully through it like an aquatic creature in its natural element.

Realising that he was quite naked, Charlotte's first instinct was to retreat hastily. But the sight was somehow both beautiful and fascinating, and she sat down on the grass, hugging her knees, and watched that lean, nude body dip and twist, now disappearing beneath the silver surface, to coast along the pebble-strewn river bed, the long black hair floating round his head like pond-weed, then suddenly, with a rush of water, rising up again to break the surface, the brown skin glittering with a silvery sheen.

Charlotte thought, He will have learnt to swim so well when he was a boy, on Haiti. She had an inner vision of him, splashing through the Caribbean surf under a bright blue sky, and she wondered if, despite his claim to the contrary, he did miss the sun-drenched island of his boyhood, from which he had been wrenched so young. How he must have hated it, up there amid the alpine snows and frozen winds of the Great St Bernard.

Lost for a moment in these thoughts, she had failed to see that he had turned and swum back towards the spot where she sat by his mound of clothing. The sound of his voice, so near at hand, made her jump.

'I'm coming out . . .' he said in laconic warning, and before she could do more than look down hastily, he did so, standing up and wading through the shallows to the bank.

Charlotte, scarlet-faced, fixed her eyes on her knees. She could hear him beside her, pulling on his clothes, and muttering curses under his breath because they clung to his damp skin.

'Well?' he said. 'You're looking for me, I suppose. What do you want?'

'Nothing, only to say this place is called Marengo, did you know? It's very quiet here, and peaceful . . . beautiful,' she finished lamely.

He had finished dressing and sat down beside her to pull on his boots. 'It's too quiet, and too near,' he said cryptically.

She ventured to raise her eyes from her fixed contemplation of her knees, and looked at him. His black hair clung to his head and neck in wet rat's tails. 'Too near to what?'

'To the Austrians. They're just over there,' he pointed. 'I swam down-stream just now, and nearly into a group of K. und K. Hussars, swimming as I was. Having no clothes, they took me for one of themselves, and I was able to give them a cheerful wave and swim off before they discovered—or I might have been a prisoner of Austria, even now.'

'But the Austrians are still retreating,' Charlotte protested. 'Everyone says they're running now, and won't stop till they reach Vienna.'

'Anyone who says that is a fool, and doesn't know the Austrians. Their officers are men of honour—the sort you admire so much. We thrashed them before, and for their honour's sake they must stand and fight now.'

'Your General Bonaparte is not a fool, and he believes they are retreating.'

Marc shrugged. 'Perhaps he's right. Even so, they'll do something to try and drive us off. Suppose you were chased by a snarling dog. Wouldn't you stop and turn to throw a stone at it?'

He threw himself back full-length on the grass, and placed his hand over his eyes to shield them from the sun. Completely unexpectedly, he went on, 'It was decent of poor Thierry to speak up for me at the end.'

'I'm sure,' Charlotte said carefully, 'He was an honourable man.'

'Not *that* honourable!' Marc arched his palm slightly so that he could look out at her from beneath it. 'Where did you get to that afternoon? You went scurrying out of the house. I asked Babette, but got no sense out of her.'

'I went for a walk. I wanted to see Milan.'

'View the cathedral and feed the pigeons, eh? I'm not a fool!'

She did not answer, and he rolled over on his side towards her, and pushed himself up on one elbow. 'You went and harangued Thierry on his death-bed, didn't you, Charlotte?'

'I *didn't* harangue him!' she said angrily. 'I only asked him to speak the truth before witnesses, and he did.'

'Did he say anything else?' There was no clue in Marc's voice to hint at whether this was an idle or a leading question.

'No. He—died. While I was there.' She glanced at him hesitantly. 'I think he wanted to talk about Lucien, but there wasn't time.'

At the mention of Lucien's name, he grunted. 'You want me to thank you, I suppose?

'No, I don't. It was not my intention you should find out.'

'Charlotte,' he said suddenly. 'About that evening in Milan . . .'

'Don't talk about that, Marc, please,' she protested, and he fell silent.

It was very quiet down on the sunny river bank. A lark was singing high above them in the clear sky. It seemed incredible that two great armies could be in the neighbourhood. It seemed there could be only the two of them. Charlotte looked at Marc. His wet hair was drying rapidly in the warm sun, and curling into black fronds at which the breeze tugged playfully. Despite the uniform, despite all she knew of him, he looked now no more than a young man of eight and twenty, untidy, serious, un-characteristically a little unsure, even a little lonely, and like no one else she had ever known.

Charlotte felt an irresistible and inexplicable urge to touch him. Almost without thinking, she stretched out her hand to smooth back that tangled, damp hair. But somehow, she did not know how, somewhere between the intention and the execution the action became transformed, and she found herself putting her arms round his neck. And then it all seemed to happen in one simple movement, his strong arms enfolded her, and she lay in his embrace on the warm turf and he was kissing her.

'No, Marc . . .' she gasped, and pushed him aside. 'It's no good, I haven't changed my mind!'

'Do you hate me?' he asked quietly, looking down into her face. His own was so very close, it was as if she could count the long dark lashes which fringed the blue eyes, and the little lines which sun and wind had written around his mouth.

'No, of course I don't hate you! You brought me all this way. I'm grateful for that,' Charlotte faltered.

He pushed himself away from her and sat up. 'And one good turn deserves another? That's why you went to Thierry?' That familiar, barbed, bitter note was back in his voice.

'No,' she said. 'It was a question of justice.'

'Oh, I see, Justice! If Justice had anything to do with life, Thierry would have killed *me*!'

'Thierry said that you were a good man. I think you're a good man, Marc, despite everything, deep down inside. I don't know why you sometimes behave as you do.'

'Don't you?' he asked enigmatically. He scrambled to his feet and held out his hand to help her up.

When she gripped it, there was an odd little hiatus as their palms touched, and she found herself looking up into his eyes. Then the moment passed. She was on her feet, he had released her, and walked off quickly without waiting for her.

Charlotte followed him in silence as far as the guns, and left him there, prowling restlessly around the eight-pounder which bore the legend *Charlotte* running along the barrel, passing his hand over the olive-painted muzzle and the rims of the wheels, patting the cold metal and murmuring to it, as though it were a living creature.

She felt sad, and dissatisfied, as if she yearned for something, but could not identify what it was. After some little while, during which she wandered about, exchanging brief greetings with people she knew, she came at last upon that incurable romantic, Jean-Luc Cresson, in whose mind, at least, the fiction of her intimate relationship with Marc would always be an established fact.

Charlotte had grown quite fond of this plump, garrulous and indiscreet young man, who scarcely troubled to disguise his lack of enthusiasm for the military profession. He was seated upon an old ammunition-box, eating a wing of roast chicken. He had removed his boots and stockings, and rested comfortably with his bare feet in a dented tin basin of warm water. He saluted her nonchalantly with the chicken wing.

'Look at them,' he said mournfully, removing one foot from the basin and presenting it for her inspection. 'It's my boots. I've only got one pair left to my name, and they don't fit. I bought them off a Milanese bootmaker, may he rot. He was no lover of the French, that's for sure, or he wouldn't have sold me these.'

'I do sympathise,' Charlotte said, smiling.

'You've a kind heart,' he assured her. He moved sociably along his ammunition-box to make room for her, and she squeezed in beside him. 'This is no life,' he said. He waved what remained of the chicken at the surrounding camp. 'I'm not like Forestier, who revels in all of this. Where I should really like to be now is in a nice little Parisian restaurant, facing up to an omelette, a dish of veal chops, a little cheese, matured *à point*, and a bottle of good wine. It's not the Austrian cannon that will do for me, it will be lack of good food.'

'I'm sorry. But you're right about Marc. If he loves anything, then he truly loves this life. Those horrible guns are like people to him. I really believe he thinks more of them than he does of people. He cares about no other life.'

'You've made a difference to him, you know,' Cresson said. 'I swear, he's been getting almost amiable under your charming influence. That is, what passes for amiable with Forestier. I should imagine that wretched groom of his, who's had the life half-bullied out of him till now, must think he's working for a different man. Not,' he added, 'that *I* don't like him, bad-tempered devil though he is! He's got the courage of a lion, you know, and a first-class brain. He'd have reached senior rank by now, if it weren't for his temper, and upsetting those higher up.' Cresson pointed up in the air with the chicken bone, as if superior authority floated in the atmosphere above their heads. 'I shall never understand how he survived in prison, being locked up all those months. They must have been glad to let him go! The wonder is that they didn't guillotine him!'

'He spoke to me once about being in prison,' Charlotte remembered suddenly. 'What happened, Jean-Luc? Why was he arrested?'

'Why was anyone arrested in those days?' Cresson returned blithely. 'The Committee of Public Safety ruled us then, and were worried about the loyalty of the officer corps. They scooped us up in handfuls and shook us through a sieve to see how many Royalists fell out onto the floor.'

'You too, Jean-Luc?'

'Ah, not me, my dear,' he said comfortably. 'A lady friend of mine, a woman of truly remarkable talent, put in a word for me in the right quarter. They "forgot" me. Of course,' he went on, 'Forestier was doubly unfortunate, because it was while he was in prison, that . . '

He broke off and gave way to a fit of coughing. 'Beg pardon, my dear,' he gasped. He was very red in the face, not, Charlotte suspected, from the coughing fit, but because he had belatedly realised that he had been on the point of some disastrous indiscretion.

But Cresson's embarrassment and her curiosity were both cut short by a sudden deafening explosion which caused the air about them to vibrate. A cloud of smoke rose on the horizon. Immediately the camp was in a hubbub, men running everywhere and shouting and giving orders. A group of Hussars, who had been playing dice near by, leapt to their feet and ran for the horse lines. One of them found time as he ran past to wave a brief salute to Charlotte, his teeth flashing in a grin. She recognised Dufour.

'Confound it, we've engaged the Austrians!' exclaimed Cresson, leaping to his feet, completely forgetting that these rested in the tin bowl. He plunged to the ground with a clatter and a yell.

'Never mind, my dear, never mind,' he exclaimed breathlessly, as Charlotte made to help him up. He sat on the ground and began to drag his stockings over his wet feet. 'Get yourself out of here! Just be so good as to pass me my boot over there, if you will, before you go.'

'But I don't know where Marc . . .' Charlotte began in dismay, retrieving the boot.

'You can't bother him now!' Cresson shouted over his shoulder, as he ran off towards his guns. 'He's busy! Get yourself to safety!'

'Mademoiselle!' shrilled Babette's voice. 'Where are you?'

The maid appeared, and seizing Charlotte's arm, began to drag her away. 'Come quickly! We must get out of the way, or the gun-carriages will run us down.'

Almost at once there was a shout, and a thunderous clattering and jingling, and one of the light horse batteries galloped past.

Charlotte leapt to safety and stumbled along in Babette's wake, having no idea where she was being taken. Without the maid to guide her, it was doubtful that she would have found shelter at all, for complete chaos reigned about them, and a deafening cacophony of noise. The Austrian guns ahead were firing again, and a sinister whine filled the air. A pall of acrid smoke was forming above them.

'Quickly, in here!' gasped Babette, pushing her into a small stone building, and dragging the door closed on them.

'Where is this?' gasped Charlotte, spluttering from the stench of the powder, and leaning back against the wall to clap her hand to an agonising stitch in her side.

'Bless us, I don't know,' Babette said. 'Bit of a storehouse, likely. Look, there's a lot of barrels over here, empty.' She peered into one or two.

Crash! From near at hand came an ear-splitting explosion and a sound of rendering wood and brick. Charlotte flinched, cowering down.

'That one missed us, anyway,' said Babette with satisfaction. 'You sit down here, mademoiselle, and don't you worry. Listen for our guns. They'll chase the Austrians off, never fear.'

It was very dark in their refuge, light entering only through one unglazed window and a small hole high up in one corner of the roof. Charlotte, half-paralysed with terror, sat down on a barrel and pressed her hands over her ears, as the noise of fighting continued unabated.

Babette kept up a running commentary, based on what her ears and experience told her. 'That's our guns. They've silenced that Austrian battery directly to the south—It's been quiet some while. That's a squadron of cavalry. Where did they spring from? If a shot lands among them, it'll send them scattering. Still, they're brave fellows.'

Charlotte had no idea how long they had been there, when they heard a new noise immediately outside. It was a strange, slithering sound, and something clattered against the door of their hiding-place.

Her heart leaped in alarm, as Babette motioned her to silence. They waited, listening intently. The scratching at the door continued, and the handle rattled. Someone was trying to come in!

As Charlotte held her breath, Babette went quietly to the window and peeped out. Then she gave a sudden exclamation, and ran to pull the door open. The figure of a man fell forward and sprawled onto the beaten earth floor at their feet, his features blackened by gun-smoke and his clothes ripped and stained in blood.

'Help me to get him inside, mademoiselle,' Babette gasped, seizing one of the wounded man's arms. 'He's one of ours.' They managed to drag the unfortunate inside, and propped him against the wall. 'A Hussar!' the maid commented. 'Hold up, young man! You're safe in here.' She wiped his face clean of blood with her kerchief.

The Hussar groaned, and muttered something beneath his breath.

'But I know this man!' Charlotte exclaimed. 'It is poor Dufour!' She leaned forward and shook his shoulder. 'Monsieur Dufour!'

Blood was gushing again from a wound on his head, and Charlotte, parting the clotted hair, saw that it stemmed from a great gash in the scalp, inflicted with such force that the skull beneath must have been at least fractured, if not split.

'Sabre-cut,' muttered Babette. She shook her head. 'There is nothing we can do for the poor boy. See, he's fainted. He will have lost too much blood. He took another slash across the forearm—he will have raised it to protect his face, and the blade caught him here, clean down to the bone. Wonder it didn't slice the arm clean off.'

'We can at least try and make him more comfortable,' Charlotte said. She pulled the fichu from her neck and bound it as best she could around the luckless Dufour's head. 'Help me settle him on the floor, Babette.' When this was done, Charlotte stared down at his waxen face. 'How pale he is,' she whispered, remembering how debonair he had looked before, and how he had laughed, only a little earlier, when summoned to fight. The fine uniform was now a ruin, no more than a collection of rags soiled with mud and blood.

As abruptly as it had begun, the noise ceased. The

thunder of the guns roared for the last time, and the cries of men and horses fell silent. An eerie stillness fell over it all. Babette pushed open the door and went outside.

'Stay here for a bit, mademoiselle,' she advised, putting her head back through the doorway. 'I'll go and see what's happened.'

Charlotte sat by the unconscious Dufour and waited as bid. She felt almost numb with shock. This had been no more than a skirmish. But what would be the horrors of a fully-fledged battle?

Babette was shouting outside, calling loudly to someone. There was a clatter of hoofs, as a rider galloped up and a dark shape filled the doorway.

'Marc!' Charlotte scrambled to her feet, and forgetting everything else, ran towards him and seized hold of his coat. Never in her life had she been so pleased to see anyone. Bursting into tears, she sobbed, 'It was horrible! I thought we'd all be killed!' She buried her head in his shirt linen, the hot tears of shock coursing down her cheeks.

Marc hesitated, his hand automatically touching the crown of her bent head briefly, in what might have been the start of a caress, but then his expression hardened, and taking hold of her shoulders and detaching her none too gently from his coat, he ordered, 'Stop that snivelling!' He pointed to the figure on the ground. 'Is he alive or dead?'

'I think he is still alive,' she gulped. 'Marc, it is poor Dufour.'

'Is it?' He stooped over the figure. 'So it is. Well, a few fair ladies will weep for him, I don't doubt. I'll get someone to take him to the field hospital, though it looks to me to be a waste of time.'

He pushed her out of his way and went outside. She could hear him shouting instructions at someone, and two men appeared and lifted the dying Dufour and carried him away.

Charlotte stepped outside the hut, putting up a hand to shield her eyes from the strong light after the gloom of the interior. Marc and Babette stood talking together just outside the door.

'If it's all right with you, mademoiselle, I'll go now and look for my man,' the maid said, hovering impatiently.

'Yes, of course, Babette, you must go at once!' Charlotte exclaimed. She rubbed her hands over her cheeks to dry them, ashamed of her outburst of tears, and pushed back her tumbled hair.

'Are you all right?' Marc asked quietly, watching her.

'Yes, quite all right now,' she replied firmly. Looking up, she added, 'And you?'

He smiled slightly. 'Lost my hat.'

The breeze ruffled his hair. His face was streaked with grime, and his blue uniform was so powdered with a thick layer of white dust that it looked grey.

'You might have lost your life,' Charlotte said soberly.

He raised an eyebrow. 'That would be inconvenient for you, wouldn't it, mademoiselle? You'd have to find someone else, and the gallant Dufour has gone to meet his Maker. Never fear, only the good die young, they say. You'll have me at your disposal yet awhile. Come along.'

She followed him out to where his horse stood waiting. Silently, Marc lifted her up and sat her pillion-fashion on Kismet's rump. Then he pulled himself up into the saddle.

'All secure?' he asked over his shoulder.

Charlotte put her arms round his waist, and muttered, 'All secure.'

He nodded, and they moved off slowly to where the army gathered up its dead and wounded and organised itself resiliently back into normality. Charlotte leaned her head against his shoulder and closed her eyes. Neither of them spoke, until at last he reined up and asked, 'Can you walk from here? I have to go and give an account of myself.'

'Yes, of course. Let me down.'

He lifted her to the ground. 'You won't get lost?' He looked down at her.

'No, I can take my bearing from that little church over there.'

He nodded, satisfied, and shaking the reins, rode off at a brisk trot.

Charlotte walked slowly along the dusty country road. A sergeant of her acquaintance, who recognised her, called out as he passed, 'Well, we made them run again, mademoiselle. Now we'll see nothing more of them but their shirt-tails!'

Charlotte smiled at his cheerful enthusiasm, and called, 'Let us hope you are right, Sergeant Gros!'

'Depend upon it,' Gros said staunchly. 'They've no stomach to face us again. I know those fellows of old. You should see those Austrians drill—their infantry all marching in straight lines, just like toy soldiers, and all in step. It's a fine sight. And their Hussars, handsome fellows in blue breeches, breaking hearts wherever they go. But it takes more than drill and waxed moustaches to win battles!' Gros chuckled, and waved to her as their ways parted.

Was it then really to be over so simply? Charlotte wondered. A few cannon-shot, a charge or two, a handful of casualties? It seemed so.

Just ahead of her was a low-roofed peasant cottage. An officer's saddle-horse was tethered outside the door, and as she approached, the door itself flew open and the officer came out.

The smile froze on Charlotte's face. She stood, rooted to the spot, as the landscape whirled about her. The man was untying the reins. She opened her mouth, wanting to call out, but her throat was suddenly too dry. Not until he had untied his horse and was preparing to mount, did she find her voice, and cry out, 'Lucien! Wait! It's me, it's Charlotte!'

The horseman swung round with an exclamation, and Charlotte broke into a frenzied run. She flung her arms round him and pressed her face against his chest. 'Oh, Lucien, I thought I'd never find you!'

'Charlotte . . . ?' His voice was incredulous and

dismayed. Charlotte looked up into his face and saw it was ashen pale. 'But you—how did you get here?' he stammered.

'I'm sorry to give you such a shock, Lucien.' The words tumbled out. 'I came with the army, over the St Bernard. I've looked for you everywhere. They told me you were in Genoa.'

'No, no, that was a mistake . . . I wasn't one of those caught in that trap . . .' He stared at her, still disbelieving. 'You can't have travelled here alone, Charlotte, surely?'

'No, Marc Forestier brought me.'

'*Forestier* did? But that's impossible. He . . .' Lucien broke off.

Gradually Charlotte's initial euphoria was wearing off and she began to realise that all was not well. This was not as she had imagined their meeting. She had dreamed of a joyful reunion, but his chief emotion appeared to be one of consternation.

'What's wrong, Lucien?' she asked quietly.

As if to answer her question, the cottage door opened again, and a girl came out. She was very young, certainly no older than Charlotte. She was very pretty, in a doll-like way, though her face was puffy now and her skin blotchy, for she was in an advanced state of pregnancy. She moved awkwardly, her hand resting on her swollen abdomen, her round blue doll's eyes fixed on Charlotte, who still held tightly to Lucien's arm, with an interrogative and suspicious look.

'*Chérie*,' Lucien said quickly to the girl, and a cold hand closed on Charlotte's heart. 'A surprise! This is my cousin, Charlotte Lacoste. Charlotte . . .' He turned to her. The expression in his eyes was such as she had never seen in his face before, or in any man's. Despair and pleading showed in them, as if he begged her to understand. 'This is Louise—my wife.'

The words hung in the air, as if every other sound was blotted out by them.

'Your wife,' Charlotte repeated flatly. 'I—didn't know.'

The girl was still suspicious. She frowned, and looked up at Lucien. 'What is your cousin doing here?'

'She . . .' Lucien's voice broke off helplessly.

Charlotte did not know what impelled her. Perhaps it was the dreadful expression on Lucien's face, like a whipped dog. She heard her own voice, loud and clear, declaring with assurance, 'I am with a friend, Captain Forestier.'

She turned away from Lucien, not wishing to see the gratitude which flooded into his eyes.

The girl's expression cleared and brightened. 'You mean Marc Forestier? Lucien, Marc is here! Mademoiselle Lacoste, I am so pleased to meet you. I have never met any of Lucien's family.'

She came forward and with a childlike impulsiveness, put her arms round Charlotte's neck and kissed her. 'Why,' Charlotte thought sadly, 'she is even younger than I first imagined. She is scarcely sixteen, if that.'

'Louise,' Lucien spoke in a constricted voice. He put his hand on his wife's shoulder. 'Louise, go inside. Go and sit down. I need to talk to my cousin for a moment. Please? It is a family matter.'

The girl smiled at him and then at Charlotte, and went back into the cottage, again with a docility childlike in its way.

'Thank you,' Lucien said in the same strained voice. 'Can we walk down here a little way? She might over-hear.'

Charlotte sighed, and they moved away a little from the cottage door.

'I cannot even ask you to forgive me,' he said in a wretched voice.

'How long have you been married to her?' she asked dully. 'Were you married to her already, when you—you came to Châlons the last time?'

'Yes,' he admitted miserably. 'Your father was

suspicious, I know. But I couldn't tell him. I couldn't tell *you*, Charlotte!'

'Yes, you could!' she cried in a sudden burst of anger. 'It was despicable of you to deceive me so, Lucien! You should have told me. You could at least have written, if you couldn't *face* me with the words. You could have put them down on paper!'

'Charlotte, I swear, I wanted to tell you!' he burst out. 'I tried to write, but the words just wouldn't come. I swear I never meant to deceive you, or my uncle, or anyone. But I was in a desperate situation. I had been gambling, and I kept losing. I owed money everywhere, to my fellow officers. A man must pay his gaming debts, and I could not pay mine. A scandal threatened.'

Charlotte stood there numbly.

'I—I was billeted on Louise's family at the time. Her father is a wine merchant, a worthy fellow and very wealthy. I—I had flirted with her a little. It meant nothing. I was bored. But she had taken me seriously. Then her father told me he had a fancy to see her married into what he called a "good" family, such as mine. I could hardly tell him that, Revolution or not, my family would instantly disown such a misalliance. He was willing to settle a generous dowry on her, even pay my gaming debts as part of our marriage settlement. So I agreed.' He fell silent.

'You don't love her?' Charlotte asked him incredulously. 'You married her, got her with child, and dragged her along with you all this way in her condition, and you don't even love her?'

'I do love her,' he said awkwardly, but with a real sincerity in his voice. 'I admit that at first I didn't, but I have grown to love her.' Urgency entered his voice. 'Charlotte, she carries my child. You can see how very near her time she is. She mustn't be distressed. She's a gentle, innocent, little soul and never did any harm to anyone in her life. Things are bad enough as they are. We've been in Italy for months, and nothing has gone right. The Austrians harried us from pillar to post while we waited for this new Army of Reserve to come and reinforce us. When our forces were finally split in two, it was only a miracle that I was not trapped in Genoa. Louise would have died there. Our soldiers ate the rats to stay alive. I beg you not to . . .'

'Don't worry, Lucien,' Charlotte said wearily. 'I won't give you away. Tell her I'm with Forestier.'

'Thank you,' he said with emotion. Then a frown crinkled his forehead. 'What I can't understand is that Marc didn't tell you about my marriage himself.'

Charlotte had not thought it possible that her heart could feel any heavier. But now it sank like a stone. 'He knew?' she whispered.

'But of course he knew. He was a witness at our wedding.'

She closed her eyes briefly. 'I see.'

'Well, I don't,' he returned frankly. 'What the devil is Marc playing at?' He paused, and stared at her searchingly. 'It's not like Marc to spend his time looking after a lady in distress. Forgive me, Charlotte, but it's incredible that he should have troubled himself with you at all. Marc's interest in women was always brief and practical!' He broke off, then asked slowly, 'Charlotte, is he your—lover?'

'You ask *that* of *me*?' she replied quietly, and saw the red flush spread across his face. 'When I have come all this way to look for *you*! No, Lucien, he is not my lover.'

'I'm sorry,' he muttered. 'It's just that I can't understand why he brought you. He's a good man, especially if one finds oneself in a tight corner. But he's not, well, what I'd call the ideal lady's escort! I just can't understand what's in his mind.' He leaned forward earnestly. 'He's looked after you all right? He's not—not been difficult in any way? There has been no unpleasantness? I mean, I know him. I know what he can do. I can't say I'm happy at the thought of your being in his charge all this time. He doesn't have much—respect—for women.'

'You needn't worry,' Charlotte said sharply. 'He's looked after me very well. Perhaps he's hardly a man for idle compliments, but at least he doesn't speak of love where there is no love. Perhaps he is simply honest with women, Lucien. More to be trusted in his way, even than you?'

'I deserve your anger,' he said.

'Oh, I'm not angry with you, Lucien,' Charlotte exclaimed in exasperation. 'At least, not in the petty way you mean. I just wish you had behaved better. And I hope you'll treat that poor girl better than you've treated me!'

'I love her. She's my wife and carries my child!' he returned angrily. 'Anyway, what of your so trustworthy friend, Forestier? Did he tell you about *his* wife, eh? Did he tell you what happened to her, and what a model husband he was?'

Charlotte felt the colour drain from her cheeks. 'No,' she whispered. 'He's never mentioned his wife.' *The rings*, the gold rings, they were *his* wedding-rings!

'Then I suggest you ask him!' he said spitefully. 'If he's as honest as you believe him, perhaps he'll tell you, and then you won't be so quick to criticise *me*!'

Though her brain churned chaotically, Charlotte managed to pull herself together and say calmly, 'You had better go back and reassure Louise. She must be wondering what keeps us so long.'

'Yes,' he glanced back at the cottage. 'I *am* sorry, Charlotte. About everything. It's the truth, I swear. Tell Forestier that I'm obliged to him for his good care of you.'

Charlotte nodded silently. Lucien hesitated, and then walked slowly back towards the cottage.

Louise must have been watching them from the window, because she came out to meet him. 'I didn't know Marc Forestier had a liaison with your cousin!' Charlotte heard her say excitedly, in what the poor child probably imagined was a whisper. 'Why didn't you tell me?'

And Lucien's reply, as he put his arm about his wife's shoulders and led her inside, '*Ma chère*, in good families, such things are simply not mentioned.'

CHAPTER
ELEVEN

CHARLOTTE RETURNED to where they had bivouacked, moving as in a kind of unreal dream, her feet taking her automatically in the right direction. In many ways she felt numb. She was aware of only one sensation, an aching void of desolation, defeat and deception. They had lied to her. They had deceived her. They had treated her with a callous and unfeeling cruelty almost beyond comprehension.

She had trusted them, both of them, for it was Marc's betrayal which, perhaps of the two, had been the more cynical and the more cowardly. He had deliberately concealed the truth, even silencing Éloise Thierry when she had been about to reveal it. Charlotte put her hands over her face to blot out everything for the moment. She could have wished herself dead. Not even when her father had died had she experienced so great a sense of loss, because then she had still believed in Lucien. Now there was nothing. Nothing behind her but illusion, nothing before her but a terrible empty blackness, as if she walked into a dense fog, from which there was no exit.

Marc was already waiting for her when she got back, sitting on a box by the fire. He rose to greet her. But then he saw her face, and whatever he had intended to say died on his lips.

'You've seen him,' he said simply instead.

'I've seen him,' Charlotte confirmed in a voice that hardly sounded like her own. 'I've seen them *both*.'

He expelled his breath in a long-drawn-out sigh, but made no attempt to make any other reply.

'You had no *right*!' Charlotte cried out suddenly, all her despair, humiliation and anger vibrating in the agony of her voice. 'You had no right to let me continue, not knowing, believing in him. You let me believe! Yet you *knew*. How could you be so cruel? What did I ever do to you, in heaven's name, that you could do this to me?'

'I told you,' he said harshly, his face deathly pale beneath the bronze. 'I told you to go back. You cannot say I didn't try to persuade you to go back.'

'If you had told me the truth, I would have gone back! But what you did was worse than a lie. You knew what had happened, and told me nothing.'

'Would you have believed me?' he countered. A familiar aggressiveness was entering his voice now. 'You thought him perfect! He could do no wrong—and I have never been able to do anything right in your eyes. Why should I think you would believe me? You would have accused me of attempting some trick to induce you to turn back.'

'You could have *tried*, Marc. At least, you could have done that. In the name of human decency, if you have any left in you, you could have tried!'

'It was not for me to tell you,' he rasped. 'If *he* hadn't told you, why should I? Why should I deal with all the screams and tears and hysteria? It was none of my business, and I've no time for weeping women!'

'Screams and hysteria,' Charlotte said quietly. 'Is that what you see when you look at me? A hysterical woman, making a nuisance of herself. Is that it?'

He looked away from her. 'Shriek your head off, for all I care. It's nothing to do with me. You probably imagine yourself some kind of martyr. It's a rôle women play well. But you'll have to go and sob on someone else's shoulder!'

'So, you wash your hands of it all, do you?' Her voice cut through the air, cold and scornful. 'You are never at fault, Captain! If there is ever any little unpleasantness, then a few words of apology and the gift of a trinket can settle it. You see, Marc, you see here?' She put her hand to her throat and touched the medallion he had given her in Milan. 'I'm wearing your last peace-offering, accepted by me in good faith because I believed it given in good faith. But you know nothing about such things, do you? You know nothing about keeping faith, or loyalty, or love, or of any kind of decent human emotion!'

'You are hysterical!' he said brusquely.

'Try throwing some water over me or slapping my face,' she suggested, tauntingly. 'Either of those actions would be well in character. You are not adverse to a little violence. In fact, you're a very bold fellow indeed, when it comes to forcing your amorous attentions on me, or fighting the Austrians and blowing fellow humans into eternity! But not when it comes to having the courage to tell me the truth!'

He took a step towards her. The blue eyes blazed with uncontrollable rage, and for a moment she almost believed he would kill her.

'Hold your tongue, you sanctimonious little fool!' he snarled. 'I've put up with your tantrums all the way from Switzerland to this godforsaken place, and very little I've got out of it for my pains! Now I've just about had enough of it! I didn't want to bring you along with me. *You* wanted that. Why should I care about your foolish love affairs and broken heart? You have never cared for me—why should I care for you? I am nothing to you, and you are nothing to me! You wanted to find Lucien. Well, you found him. You can sort the rest of it out for yourself. Though you find it hard to imagine, *ma belle*, there are a great many things in this world more important than you!'

Charlotte's anger had burned itself out for the moment. She felt indescribably weary, and sank down onto the box on which he had been sitting, in total dejection. An expression which was almost akin to a spasm of pain flickered briefly in his eyes as he looked down at her forlorn, dusty, bedraggled little figure. But then the eyes veiled themselves with their customary chillness.

'The girl, Louise,' Charlotte said quietly, without looking up. 'She's with child, and very near her time. The baby must be due any day now. So as not to distress her, we decided—Lucien and I—that she should be told I am here with you, and only with you. It's for her sake, and the unborn child's. Do you object?'

'It doesn't matter to me one way or the other,' he said coldly. 'Tell the girl what you like.'

'At least,' Charlotte went on, 'you won't be troubled with me any longer. There is nothing left for me now but to go back to Châlons. I would leave at once, but it's late in the day. First thing tomorrow morning, Pascal and I will set off back.'

'It would be best,' he said in a clipped tone. 'The passes will all be open now, and you will have no difficulty crossing the Alps.'

'I shall be all right.' She sighed. 'I am more concerned for Louise, Lucien's wife. She's so young. How can she have her baby here? How could he oblige her to travel like this in her condition? She is totally dependent on him. I would like to think he'll care for her, for them both, mother and child, but will he?'

'Charlotte . . .' Marc hesitated, and then came towards her and dropped down in front of her, balanced on his heels. 'I know he behaved badly by you.' His voice was quieter now, as if his anger too had burned itself out. 'But that doesn't mean the boy is bad at heart. He's only weak. He's been foolish. You condemn him too harshly, Charlotte. We are none of us perfect. He is not. I am not. You are not. But he has a wife now, and will have a child. New responsibilities. They will give him the encouragement he needs to make something of himself. He won't abandon her. Believe me, I wouldn't tell you this if I didn't believe it to be true, I swear.'

She looked up into his eyes, watching her earnestly. 'I don't condemn him, Marc. I expected too much of him. I know you are right—I did believe him perfect. That was wrong of me, and unfair to him. I don't hate him for what he did. I'm just so sorry, *so* sorry, it had to happen at all. Perhaps I was obstinate and foolish, but I believed he loved me.' Her voice, she knew, sounded very young, and betrayed a naked vulnerability; she looked down quickly at her hands, twisted together in her lap.

'It hurts,' he said softly. 'It hurts to love someone who does not love you. I know.'

Charlotte looked up again in astonishment. She had never heard him speak in such a tone of voice before, gentle, understanding, and a little sad. A gentleness had suffused his features, rendering them quite altered. Any lingering resentment she harboured against him melted away, and she felt again that impulse to reach out and touch him.

'Marc,' she whispered. 'Lucien said you had been married. What happened to your wife?'

The softer expression which had transformed his features was wiped from them instantly, and he flinched as if she touched on an old long-unhealed wound.

'My wife is dead,' he said quietly. 'She has been dead these six years.'

'I'm sorry,' she faltered. 'Forgive me. I had no right to ask.'

'I'm surprised you haven't asked before. Women are usually curious to know all about these things. I've been expecting you to refer to it, some time or other, ever since you found the wedding-rings in my box.'

Charlotte's cheeks burned. 'How—How did you know?'

'Because, *mignonne*, you retied the string of the bag in such a pretty little bow. You should have left it in a simple knot, as I had done.'

'I see.' She bit her dry lips. 'It was unforgivable of me,' she said contritely.

'Don't fret about it. I don't talk about my marriage much, but I don't mind telling you.'

He sat down on the floor beside her, and rested his arms on his bent knees. 'It wasn't a very happy marriage. But then, I wasn't a very good husband.' He glanced at her. '*You* will believe that.'

'Did you love her?' Charlotte asked gently.

He shrugged. 'I thought I did at the time I married her. I had not long come out of military school, a conceited young puppy thinking I knew all about the world and what went on in it. It goes without saying that I thought I knew all about love, when I had not the slightest idea what loving a person means, the sacrifices it demands. In due course I soon fancied myself "in love", and I married. We were both very young. Mireille was little more than a child, only fifteen. Had her parents not had other daughters to marry off, I doubt they would have consented to our union. But I supposed they imagined, as did I, that I had a fine career ahead of me. As for myself, I was very little older. I blush now to think of it. My God, I was what—eighteen? I truly believe, if ever I had a son who behaved at that age as I did, I'd box his ears and lock him up! That was one good thing about the Old Régime, which has been discontinued, the *lettre de cachet*. If one didn't care for the way one's heir behaved, one could literally have him imprisoned until he saw sense. But my father was in Saint-Domingue, and by the time he had received news of what I was about and was prepared to take steps to prevent me forcibly, it was too late. In due course I ended up in prison anyway, but not for that reason, nor at his doing! My father never communicated with me after my marriage. In his Will he left me five hundred *louis* . . . and paternal curses. Thanks to the Revolution, I didn't even get the five hundred *louis*. Wherever my father was by then, in heaven or the other place, he was probably laughing over it.'

Marc did not himself laugh on telling this, but fell into a moody silence for a few minutes. 'Anyhow,' he said at last, 'we were far too young to set our ship on such a hazardous course as marriage. Little wonder it soon foundered. Mireille was of a delicate constitution, and had always lived a sheltered life at home. I dragged her after me from one garrison town to another, from one set of dingy lodgings to another. Love soon took flight. We were chronically poor, not helped by the fact that, being a young blade, I liked to gamble. I was always a bad gambler! She fell sick, her prettiness faded. She grew querulous—always, as it seemed to me, complaining. We quarrelled. She cried. Poor soul, I grew almost to hate her—though I knew she still loved me, in a despairing sort of way, because she knew she had lost me. I took to spending as little time with her as possible, which meant I spent most of it in dissolute and unsuitable company.'

Marc was uneasy and silent again, seeming to relive in his mind a hundred petty squabbles and harsh words and disappointments. Eventually he continued. 'The Terror was upon us. There was a madness loose in France. People disappeared on all sides, and there was not a sleepy country town buried in the provinces where the cobblestones did not run red with blood from the blade of the guillotine. One evening, I was going to join some gaming friends. Mireille was ill, and begged me not to leave her alone, but I only became angry and set off anyway. Just outside the door, even as I set foot in the street, a gang of ill-looking fellows stopped me and demanded to know if my name was Forestier. I had not the wit or presence of mind to deny it. When they learned that it was, they said I should go with them. When I not unreasonably objected, a few well-aimed blows from a musket butt soon convinced me of my folly.

'I found myself tossed into prison with a score of others, and there we were left. You know how it was. The last thing anyone wanted to do was to make a fuss, draw attention to oneself. I laid low, kept quiet, did not even dare to send a message to my wife, that I was still alive, for fear they should remember me and I'd find myself on the next tumbril. Eventually, after three months of dirt and hunger and the stench of death, listening to the shrieks of those wretches who read their names posted up for execution that day, a rumour reached us, that we hardly dared to believe, of the fall of

Robespierre and the others with him. We knew it to be true, when one morning they came and simply let us go free—all who still lived. 'Go home,' they told us. 'The Republic brings no charges against you.'

'I walked out of that place, emaciated, dirty, lice-infested—but alive. There is no sensation like that of knowing oneself simply to be alive, when, by all events, one ought not to be. I went back to the lodgings where I'd lived with Mireille.

'The people there told me she was dead. She'd died two weeks previously, not even knowing, poor soul, whether she was a wife or a widow. It struck me so strangely; it was almost as if she had died instead of me. The people in the house were kind and sympathetic. I hardly heard what they said to me. I kept thinking that it was as if I'd killed her. I'd clung on to life, somehow, those past three months, although Death had my name on his roll-call. So he had taken her instead.' Marc gave a short, bleak laugh.

'So there I was,' he added in a more matter-of-fact tone. 'I'd no wife, no family, no money, no job. Fortunately, the Republic had sore need of qualified artillerymen. Though I'd been struck off the list of commissions, I was reinstated, and found myself back in uniform again. I made myself a life among the guns. It's not a bad life. It suits me—I'm suited to it.' He caught her eye. 'I've glad I've been able to tell you this,' he said quietly. 'You should know. Now you know I wasn't the man to escort you, as I told you I wasn't. You picked the wrong man, back there in Switzerland, *mignonne*.'

'No,' Charlotte shook her head. 'It was long before that. It was in Châlons that I picked the wrong man. I picked the wrong man to give my heart to. When I think of how he spoke then, and of all the dreams I had . . .' Charlotte broke off. 'You carry your bitter memories with you, Marc, and I shall carry mine.'

She got to her feet and walked slowly away from the fire. There was no permanence in love. It was only a picture in a fire. She did not want Marc's company, or anyone's, only to be alone and nurse her hurt. He knew it, and watched her go without attempting to stop her.

In a daze, Charlotte wandered through the camp. She felt as though she had suffered some total moral and physical degradation. She was humiliated, rejected and discarded. Such things had happened to women before, but she had never imagined that anything remotely like it could ever happen to her. This was how Marc's child-wife, Mireille, must have felt, left quite alone and rejected by her handsome, headstrong young husband . . . who recalled her now with pity, but without love.

She came upon a deserted spot beneath the spreading branches of a tree and sank down, leaning back against the trunk. The setting sun had played its cerise glow over everything, and above her the birds twittered a last few sleepy chirps. It was growing darker, and she was glad of the veil the night drew over everything.

Hidden by its kindly blackness, she wept. Wept for all the lost dreams and broken promises, wept for the last vestiges of a girlhood innocence which had been so eager to believe, so loath to admit that a man she loved could lie. She had been doubly betrayed. By Marc, perhaps, even more than by Lucien. Marc had let her go on, with such effort and despite so many obstacles. Marc, who had listened to her talk of her love for Lucien, and her fidelity, and had said nothing to ease the pain and humiliation of that dreadful confrontation which he had known must come. Only now was the full realisation of it coming home to her, with all the force a delayed shock brings to the mind and body. In her mind's eye she could see the girl Louise, her wide blue eyes and pretty doll-like face, and the hand with the gold wedding-ring, resting on her unborn child.

'How could you do this to me, even you, Marc?' she whispered to the darkness. 'And if I had consented to let you take possession of my body, would you have told me then, afterwards, as I lay in your arms? Was that to have been my reward?'

She did not know how long she crouched there. The

night was split by the leaping flames of the camp-fires all around, scattered across the plain about Marengo. She did not even see them. She was exhausted. The weariness that she had never allowed to conquer her on her arduous journey overcame her now, and she fell into a fitful half-slumber.

She was dimly aware that someone approached and bent over her. Two strong but gentle arms took her in their firm embrace, slipping round her shoulders and knees, and lifting her as easily as a child. Silently he carried her back through the camp to her own tent, and put her down gently on her bed of blankets. Charlotte lay back and looked up to where his form was etched blackly against the canvas. He sat beside her, hunched because there was so little room, his head bowed under the sloping roof, and holding her hand. She closed her fingers round his, grateful for his unspoken comfort.

'You're still angry with me?' his voice came quietly in the darkness.

'No, Marc, I'm not angry with you, or Lucien, or anyone. Anger doesn't help.'

'There are plenty of other, good, men, *mignonne*.' His free hand stroked her cheek with that same gentle touch as when he had brushed her hair in Milan. 'Men who are not like me, or like your cousin. Some day you'll meet someone who will make you forget all the harm we did you. Don't weep for Saint-Laurent. He was never the right man for you.'

'I won't weep for him any more. Not ever again. I know now that I don't love him, and I don't suppose I ever really did love *him*. I was in love with a dream, an ideal, not a real person. Poor Lucien. I was like you, Marc, when you married. I thought I knew all about love, but I needed to be taught that I didn't. I can't deny it's been a painful lesson. You were right when you said we have more in common than it would appear.'

'You must not let it make you bitter, Charlotte,' he said earnestly. 'You must not let it kill your faith. You're a fine woman, courageous, honest, intelligent and beautiful. You'll meet someone, and marry him, and be happy, some day. Any man would be proud . . .' He broke off, and his fingers tightened on hers briefly. 'Only don't marry a soldier, *mignonne*. We're a shiftless lot, short-lived, too.'

'You're still thinking of the Austrians, aren't you?' she said soberly. 'You still think that was not their rearguard today.'

He was silent for a moment. 'If it was,' he said, 'they were going in the wrong direction. Go to sleep. I've told Pascal of your decision to start back tomorrow, and he'll be ready. He—knows what's happened. I'm glad you're going. You'll be best well away from here. Get a good early start, first thing tomorrow, and make as much speed as you can. This isn't a good place to be anywhere near. It's got a bad feeling about it, even if I'm the only one whose bones tell him so. None of our generals shares my gloom, I must confess. Kellermann and Desaix have already taken their men and left us. They think the Austrians have had enough. Maybe they are right.'

'And what do you think?' she asked.

'I think there are forty-five thousand Austrians out there somewhere, double our number. I'd just like to know what they're all doing. Don't worry yourself about it. We'll find out soon enough. Come on, now, go to sleep.'

It was as if he instructed a child. Charlotte needed little urging to follow his advice. She was physically and mentally exhausted, and was already drifting away on a sea of slumber. She felt calm. Somehow the pain and grief had been lost along the way. It was Marc's presence, perhaps, which calmed her, which was strange, because they had always been at odds. It was so much nicer to be at peace with one another.

In her drowsiness, she spoke her thoughts aloud, muttering, 'Why couldn't it always have been like this?'

'I don't know,' he said quietly. He lifted the hand he held in his and kissed it lightly. 'Farewell, Charlotte.' He released her, and silently left the tent.

But Charlotte was already asleep. She had neither heard his last words, nor felt the touch of his lips on her fingers.

It must have been towards six o'clock when she awoke the next morning. She dressed hurriedly, remembering that she had to begin a long and tiring return journey that day. Babette was outside, busy heating water over the fire.

'The Captain says you're going back to France, mademoiselle.' She looked sideways at Charlotte.

'Yes, Babette, I am. I shall be sorry to say goodbye to you.'

'If it weren't for my Pierre, I'd go along with you, mademoiselle,' she declared in honest distress. 'I don't like to think of you making that journey without me. That Pascal can look after your horses, but who's going to look after you?'

'I'll manage, Babette. Don't worry,' Charlotte said mechanically, splashing her face with the warm water. A strange stillness hung in the air. There was a curious absence of the bird-song normally to be heard at this hour of the day, and the camp was only just beginning to stir.

'Have you parted with the Captain for good, then?' the maid went on in her frank way. 'It's a pity. He's a fine man, and it always seemed to me you were right for each other. You were always fighting, I know, but that's only natural. That's the way love goes sometimes. It's because you both care. When we were first married, my Pierre and I, we fought like alley-cats, I can tell you! My, the fur did fly. It's making up afterwards that's nice. Why don't you and the Captain make it up now?' she added coaxingly. 'It's up to you, mademoiselle. He won't make the first move. Men are like that, and it's no use trying to change them. Worse than a lot of spoiled children, they are. But if you were to go now and just put your arms round his neck and give him a kiss or two and tell him you want to stay, it would work miracles. He'd do anything for you after that. *Mon Dieu*, the man would do anything for you now, but his pride wouldn't let him say it.'

'Captain Forestier and I are agreed that it's best I leave straight away,' Charlotte told her firmly, towelling her face briskly. 'We have parted friends, for which I'm glad, and I wouldn't wish anything to spoil that. It will be a great relief to him to know that I am out of the way and off his hands. I must have been a great nuisance to him all this time. I'm sorry it can't be the kind of ending you would like, Babette, but I've told you before that you misunderstand both the Captain's point of view and mine. Really, Babette, I must say, for a woman of such experience of life, you conceive the most fantastic romantic notions.'

'Oh, do I?' demanded Babette with some spirit. 'Well, I remember him coming to fetch me, that morning in Milan, after you and he had that fine quarrel and fight. People were scattering out of his way like sheep before a loose dog, for he'd an expression on his face as would have frightened Satan himself!'

'Well, I suppose he was still angry,' Charlotte said calmly.

'Angry? My dear, he was worried and upset . . . In all my days I never saw a man so miserable! And to think of you two parting now, it's enough to break my heart, and that's the truth!' She sniffed noisily.

'I've told you, Babette,' Charlotte said wearily, 'that I have no quarrel now with the Captain. I came to Italy to look for someone, and the Captain was good enough to bring me. He could have spared me my journey and a great deal of pain, and I still don't know why he didn't. But all I want to do now is to close the door on the whole sorry mess and forget it. My search is over. The man I came to find doesn't need me. Now I'm going home. I should have stayed there.'

'And you don't think the Captain needs you, mademoiselle?'

'He has his life, Babette, here, among the guns. That's

all he understands, or wants, or needs.'

They were to discuss it no more, for the early morning sky was suddenly lit by a ball of fire as a man-made sunrise glowed over them all, and the echoing crash of the cannon broke into the peace. It sent the birds, which had been so silent till now, flying up from the trees in a wheeling flurry of dark shapes, crying out wildly. Horses neighed shrilly, and cooking-pots overturned and fell unheeded and hissing into the fires, as the cooks, together with the rest of the camp, leaped to their feet in stupefaction, watching the searing comet of orange traverse the sky and plunge to earth in a shattering roar, leaving a trailing plume of black smoke to foul the morning air.

Others followed it, across the whole band of the horizon, and a sound like an approaching monster, many-headed and baring tooth and claw, roared sullenly on the air. The earth shook beneath their feet as if some earthquake threatened, pounded by approaching hoofs.

The two women rose to their feet and turned their faces towards the gigantic groundswell of noise.

'Dear God,' Charlotte whispered. 'Marc was right. That wasn't the Austrian rearguard yesterday. They were advancing, not retreating, and now they're on us!'

CHAPTER
TWELVE

THROUGH THE gathering haze of smoke marking the deafening barrage of the Austrian artillery and the surging waves of men and horses, Pascal's voice became audible from near at hand, bellowing, 'Mam'zelle! Where are you?'

'Here, Pascal!' Charlotte shrieked.

The coachman appeared, dragging along by the bridle Charlotte's horse and Babette's mule. 'Here we are!' he panted. 'Up you go, mam'zelle, and ride like the devil out of here! You too, woman!' he added to Babette. 'I've seen your man, and told him I'd get you safely away.'

'What about you, Pascal?' gasped Charlotte, as he pushed her up into the saddle with an energetic shove.

'I'll follow on with the other horse and our mule. Now don't stay about here, asking questions. Go on with you!'

Pascal slapped the horse heavily on the rump and it leaped forward at a smart canter, Babette's mule following close behind. Around them the units were forming and the horse-drawn batteries galloping up into position. More than once Charlotte was almost swept from the saddle as densely-packed men pushed past her going in the opposite direction. She tried to look for Marc, but among all this horde and confusion it was impossible to distinguish any one man.

At last they reached the road, and set off down it as fast as they could. Suddenly Charlotte reined up and cried out, 'Stop, Babette, wait!'

'We can't stop here, mademoiselle! What's the

matter?' she protested, kicking the mule's flanks energetically and coming alongside Charlotte.

'That cottage, over there!' Charlotte panted. 'My
cousin and his wife were lodging there yesterday, and my
cousin's wife is expecting her baby soon. I must go and
see if she's safely away. You go on, Babette, I'll catch up
with you.'

'I'll do no such thing!' said Babette forcefully. 'I'll
come along with you to take a look. But we must make
haste, mademoiselle.'

The two women slid from the saddle outside the
cottage, and while Babette held their mounts, Charlotte
pushed open the door and ran inside.

It led into a spacious country kitchen. The
whitewashed walls were decorated with crudely painted
pictures of the saints, and the domestic pots and pans,
hanging from hooks in neat rows. But the room was
quite deserted, though the remains of a breakfast meal
lay on the table, apparently hastily abandoned, and
someone had lit a fire in the primitive range that
morning.

'Louise?' Charlotte called loudly. 'Louise? It's
Charlotte Lacoste. Are you here?'

In answer came a faint cry from a further room.
Charlotte caught her breath and threw open the door
beyond which the cry originated. It was the bedroom,
untidy and cluttered with half-packed belongings. As
Charlotte entered, there was a movement from the
carved wooden bedstead, and Louise's voice came
tremulously.

'Charlotte? Is it really you?'

'Oh, Louise, my dear, what are you still doing
here? And why are you in bed?' Charlotte ran forward and grasped hold of the hands the girl held out
towards her. She lay in her nightgown, her hair sweat-
soaked and tangled, breathing heavily on the crushed
pillows.

'Charlotte—my baby is coming. It's coming soon now,
I know it is!' She clutched despairingly at Charlotte's

hand. 'Charlotte, I can't leave here, I can't move. Don't leave me, please!'

'But are you quite alone?' gasped Charlotte in horror.

'The woman whose cottage this is went for the midwife, and Lucien had to leave before she came back. But now she won't be able to get back, because of the action.' Louise began to sob in fear.

'It's all right, don't panic!' Charlotte urged her as reassuringly as she could, though panic was also overtaking her rapidly. She detached her hands with difficulty from the girl's frenzied grip. 'Just lie quietly, Louise, of course I won't leave you. My maid is outside. I'll just run and tell her I must stay. Don't worry, I'll be back immediately!'

She scrambled to her feet to go, but in the doorway collided with Babette, who was coming in to see what was taking her so long.

'Babette, it's her baby. She's about to give birth, I'm sure. What can we do?'

'Baby, is it?' said Babette, with such remarkable calm that Charlotte was shocked into quelling her own panic. 'Then I'd best take a look at your cousin's wife. Then we'll see if we can move the young lady or not.'

She went to the bed and bent over Louise in a capable and reassuring manner. 'Now, just you let me take a look, madame, for I know a thing or two about babies.' She ran her hand over the girl's stomach. 'Does it come like a gripping pain, madame? Every so often?'

'Yes,' Louise whispered, but already she seemed to have relaxed, inspired by Babette's calm and capable manner.

'Do the pains come quickly, my love, or is there a good gap between them?'

'At first they came only every once in a while, but now they come all the time.'

Babette pushed her gently back onto the pillow. 'Well, don't you fret, madame. That's all in order, and everything will be well. Babies have been coming safely into this world ever since our ancestors were driven out of Paradise for taking an interest in the matter, so don't you worry! Why, my poor mother had sixteen of us.'

Babette patted Louise's arm and came back to where Charlotte still waited stock still by the door. 'Now, mademoiselle,' she said in a brisk undertone. 'We can't move your cousin, for the little one is due to make its appearance in the world at any moment. We'll have to stay here and help her.'

'But the Austrian shells . . .' Charlotte protested, as the guns crashed again and the cottage trembled in its innermost foundations.

'Can't be helped, my dear. Babies come when they will, and that's that.'

'Oh, Babette! It's not fair that you should have to stay here too, in such a dangerous place.'

'Hush!' she ordered sternly. 'The little mother-to-be will hear you, and the poor child is frightened enough. What do you know about babies, eh? I'm the one who's needed here.'

Charlotte's mind was running on rapidly, trying to envisage the many possibilities which arose from this new situation. 'What shall I do?' she asked in a steady voice.

'You can go and see if you can get that fire burning in the kitchen range. I saw it was smouldering still, so put in some more wood and then get a kettle of water heating on the top of it. Make what haste you can, my dear, but take care.'

Charlotte hastened back into the kitchen. She now felt quite in command of herself, though she winced automatically each time the cannon roared. She managed to open the little iron door in the kitchen range with the aid of a cloth, at first burning her fingers on the hot metal. The embers still glowed red within, and a sufficient addition of kindling would get the fire burning again, but there was no wood in the basket by the stove. Charlotte pushed the little door closed and went outside to find the woodpile.

The air was heavy with the sound and smell of battle.

The sky was darkening, not from the storm-clouds but from the gathering pall of smoke. Her horse and the mule were tethered by the door, and they both stamped restlessly, flinging up their heads in fear, and tugging at the restraining reins. It was clear that both beasts would break free and be lost if nothing was done, and they would need the animals. There was a small barn near by. Charlotte unhitched first the horse, and then the mule, and dragging determinedly on the reins, led the animals into the barn, and then shut the heavy door on them, bolting it with the wooden spar provided for the purpose. She wiped her forehead and dusted her hands. That took care of the animals, anyway.

She found the woodpile, and to her relief there was a good supply of ready-chopped kindling, so she filled her skirt and returned to the kitchen. As she reached the door, a thunder of hoofs announced the passage of a squadron of French Hussars, who galloped past in a cloud of dust towards the sound of gunfire, forcing Charlotte to fling up her hand to protect her face from flying grit. They reminded her of the luckless Dufour, and she felt a momentary pang of sadness. But Marc had once mentioned casually to her that no Hussar reckoned on living much past his twenty-fifth birthday. They had chosen a short life, but a full one. But a great waste, too, of fine young lives, Charlotte thought, as she stumbled gratefully into the kitchen.

Having got the fire to burn satisfactorily, she now turned her attention to the problem of water. There was none in the kitchen, but there was a well outside. She did not care for the idea of venturing out again, but there was nothing for it. She made two exhausting trips, letting down the wooden bucket and hauling it up filled with brackish water, so that her back and shoulders ached, and her arms felt as though they were being pulled out of their sockets. She dragged the full buckets into the kitchen and filled the great metal kettle on the range. Having at last got these unaccustomed and time-consuming chores out of the way, she returned to the bedroom to see how matters progressed there.

Babette was talking soothingly and encouragingly to the girl in the bed.

'How does it go?' whispered Charlotte.

'All's well here, mademoiselle. What about outside?'

'I can't tell,' Charlotte confessed. 'The dust is coming up in clouds. I've tried to pinpoint the gun positions from the orange flashes, but there are too many.'

'Hum . . .' muttered Babette. 'Why don't you take a look in that box over there and see if there's any kind of cloth I can swaddle the baby in when it arrives.'

Charlotte hunted in the box and found a light woollen shawl, which she brought back to the bed. Louise lay bathed in perspiration, her wet nightgown stained with dark patches.

'I'll fetch some water, and bathe her face,' Charlotte whispered.

She tipped a little water from the great kettle into a soup basin, this being all she could find. The cannonade and the sounds of battle were now a constant background noise which she forced herself to ignore. She came back and settled down at the bedhead to swab the girl's forehead and cheeks.

'The noise . . .' Louise whispered, drawing deep, dragging breaths. 'Just now . . . horses . . . what happened?'

'It's all right, Louise. It was only some of our Hussars riding past. All will be well,' Charlotte replied soothingly.

The girl shuddered, and her hand reached out and grasped Charlotte's wrist. 'Lucien . . .' she muttered.

'Lucien will be fine, Louise. You must not worry about him. Just think, when he comes back, there will be the two of you to greet him.'

As she spoke, there was a deafening crash near at hand, and the sound of splintering wood as a shell struck a clump of trees just beyond the cottage.

Louise shrieked, and Charlotte threw her arms about her and her body protectively across her. Heralded by the commotion, there slipped into the world a mewing, kicking purple bundle, which lay squawling at them with such an insistent tone that all other sounds were as nothing, fading into insignificance.

When she had been a child, a pet cat had given birth to kittens in the bottom of the nursery cupboard, and eight-year-old Charlotte had sat and watched the process fascinated, wondering that the babies were such funny little things.

But this human baby, the first-born son of Louise and Lucien, was in his own way funnier and yet more beautiful than she could ever have imagined. His little face was puckered like an old man's, and his skin at the wrists and ankles seemed too big for him, and wrinkled into folds. The tiny fingers, opening and closing as if he sought to grip something, were perfect. He waved his little arms furiously, and kicked his puny legs, and wailed tempestuously and in a curious seagull fashion.

'A beautiful baby, a perfect baby, and a boy, madame!' cried Babette, tears of joy running down her cheeks as she quickly and efficiently wiped the tiny mouth and nose of mucus. 'And has got a fine spirit with him and will be a soldier for sure, like his Papa!'

Charlotte had always vaguely believed that midwives held the newborn on high by the heels and slapped them. But that, Babette said, was not necessary unless the baby was slow to breathe, and then to be attempted only by an expert, for clumsy handling by inefficient and untrained midwives had resulted in more than one ankle or hip injury after that sort of treatment. She watched Babette wrap the child into a rigid cocoon, and taking him from the maid, laid the little bundle in his mother's arms.

They were so busy after that with what remained to be done, and with peeping at the baby every two minutes, that they had incredibly almost forgotten the battle which raged on, its fringes not more than half a mile away. But when everything was done, and mother and child settled, Babette went outside the cottage and after an absence of some moments, returned with a grave face. The two women stood in the kitchen, conversing in low voices so as not to disturb Louise.

'Things are not going too well, mademoiselle, and that's a fact. It looks to me as though our men are pulling back. There's retreating infantry going past at this moment.' Babette jerked her head towards the sound of the hastening feet passing along the road outside.

'But what can we do, Babette? How can we move Louise? It's just not possible.'

'There's no kind of farm wagon or any kind of cart hid out there in that barn, mademoiselle?'

'No.' Charlotte shook her head. 'I've been in the barn. I shut our animals in there. It's no good. You must escape, Babette. I shall stay here with Madame Saint-Laurent. I cannot think the Austrians will not take pity on a woman lying in, and a new-born infant.'

'You know I won't leave you and the young mama,' Babette snapped. 'So don't go talking to me of such a thing again. I tell you what, I'll make us a bit of soup with these vegetables here, and we'll just have to sit it out. You go and stay with your cousin now, for she's best not left alone. She'll get to fretting.'

Charlotte went back into the other room and tiptoed to the bed. But Louise was asleep, despite the surrounding racket, exhausted, and Lucien-Charles slept too, his tiny face squeezed up into a determined slumber.

'We chose the names before,' Louise had confided to Charlotte. 'Lucien, for his father, and Charles, for Lucien's uncle—Why, that will be your father, Charlotte!'

She turned away from the bed, and went to the window. It gave onto the rear of the cottage, and though the murk of battle hung over the yard outside, it was empty of life, at least for the moment. She sank onto a chair, and turned her mind to the possible arrival of Austrian troops on the scene. If Babette was right, and Marengo was proving a French defeat, they could expect such visitors quite soon, and she, Charlotte, would have to negotiate what civil treatment might be had. She hoped there would be an officer with them. The Austro-Hungarian officers were gentlemen, many of distinguished family, would understand French, and might be expected to be courteous.

She was not sure about their men, many of them illiterate peasants from the wilder Slavic reaches of the Austro-Hungarian Empire, knowing no more German than the essential words of command. Some of them, the Croats especially, had a reputation for ruthless ferocity.

As she sat there, her head resting on the wooden frame of the window, staring out into the abandoned yard, she all at once underwent a most extraordinary experience, which she was never fully to explain in all the rest of her life. The yard was empty, quite empty, and she knew it was. Yet, without warning, she saw Marc, saw him quite clearly, standing by the barn and looking towards the house. He looked very dusty and begrimed, as if he had lain in the dirt, and was hatless. At the same time, she knew that it was not Marc, that there was no one there. Whether it was a figment of her imagination, some buried train of thought projecting itself into the air, she could not say. But as she watched, the figure faded, melting into the barn wall, and at the same time, just as it finally vanished, a physical pain shot through her as though she had been struck.

Charlotte gave a little cry, and springing up, stumbled out of the room and into Babette's arms.

'Why, my dear, what's wrong?' asked the maid. 'You're as pale as if you'd seen a ghost. Is the young mama not well?'

'She's asleep, and the baby too. Babette,' Charlotte stammered, 'Such a strange thing happened. Perhaps I fell asleep for a second or two, I don't know. But I thought I saw Captain Forestier standing by the barn . . . only it wasn't he, you understand. At the same time, I felt such a pain . . . It's all so stupid. The pain has gone now, but I feel so frightened.'

Babette's eyes were troubled. 'You sit down, my dear.

You've been worried about your cousin, and you're nearly exhausted. Sit down here, by the range.' She led Charlotte to a chair and sat her down, fussing over her solicitously.

'You're right, Babette, how foolish of me. I'm sorry to have given you such a start.' Charlotte smiled up at her apologetically.

She fell silent after this, listening to the noise from outside. Every so often hoofs clattered past, but now they were going away from the battlefield. The French retreat continued. She did not see Babette take a taper and light a stub of candle before one of the painted religious pictures on the wall, crossing herself devoutly as she did.

They sat there for a very long time. The afternoon wore on, but the noise of battle was unabated. In fact, shortly before three o'clock, there was a sudden resurgence of it, a new swell and a roar, followed by a veritable cacophony of crashing guns, which made Babette run to the door and look out.

Charlotte, roused from her lethargy, went to stand by the window. After some time, she turned round to Babette and said quietly, 'Have you noticed? No one's gone past these last twenty minutes or more. What does it mean?'

'I don't know, my love. But one thing's sure, we don't retreat any more.' She puckered her brow. 'Could we have got reinforcements, do you think? General Desaix, perhaps? He left us yesterday, but he'll have heard the guns, and couldn't have got that far from us.'

'If it were only possible . . .' whispered Charlotte. 'It's been so hard to reassure Louise. She's been awake for an hour, and keeps calling out to ask what's happening.'

'We'll have to wait and see, my love.'

Wait they did, until the late afternoon, when a silence had fallen over everything. The cannon no longer roared, and the cries of men and horses were muted and spasmodic.

Suddenly a wild thudding of hoofs approaching the

cottage caused them both to leap to their feet. The rider halted, the door burst open, and Lucien, begrimed from smoke and dust, ran into the room. He stopped short when he saw them.

'Charlotte? How did you get here?' He started forward wildly. 'My wife . . .'

'It's all right, Lucien. She's all right, they both are!' Charlotte cried, running to him, and embracing him. 'Oh, come and see, Lucien, you've a beautiful baby son.'

'Just you wait a minute, monsieur,' ordered Babette, as he started towards the bedroom door. 'Let me clean your face. You'll frighten the baby and his mama.'

'Yes, Lucien, you're hardly recognisable!' Charlotte said with a smile. 'Why, you look just like a chimney-sweep.'

'Sweeps bring luck,' he said, and laughed.

'Hold still, will you?' she told him severely, and taking the cloth from Babette, rubbed it over his dirt-streaked countenance.

But he was impatient, and pushed her hand aside, hastening into the bedroom to his wife and new child.

'Thank God he is alive and well,' Charlotte breathed. 'I was so afraid for Louise.'

And for yourself? asked a voice inside her. Is there not someone else of whom you would like to have news?

The bedroom door creaked and Lucien returned, crossing the floor quickly to take Charlotte's hands. He bent his head and kissed them. 'I cannot thank you enough for what you have done for us, Charlotte,' he said earnestly.

'It is not I who should be thanked, it is Babette, here.'

'Never mind the thanks!' cried Babette impatiently. 'Will you never tell us what's happened, monsieur? We saw nothing but men retreating. Is it lost?'

'Lost? No, a victory! Though it was the closest thing I ever took part in. The Austrians had us beaten, for they outnumbered us and took us unawares. General Bonaparte was forced to send an urgent message to General Desaix, begging him, in God's name, to return if he could, and save us. And so he did, arriving in the nick of time and turning the battle our way, though it cost him his life, poor Desaix.'

'Thank God!' cried Charlotte in heartfelt tones. 'Though I'm sorry for poor Desaix. But Lucien,' she added urgently, 'have you seen Marc?'

'Not since early this morning. I'm sorry, my dear. I can tell you no more than that. Most of our guns were put out of action. Marmont regrouped the survivors, and I don't know what became of the gun teams or the officers.'

'I must go.' Charlotte pulled her hands from his. 'I can't stay here any longer. I must go and see if I can find him!' Her voice rose frantically.

'Come to her senses at last,' muttered Babette. 'But left it precious late, poor lady.'

'Wait, Charlotte, before you go.' Lucien caught her arm. 'Go and see Louise. She wants to speak to you.'

Louise held out her arms towards Charlotte, as she bent over the bed, and embraced her. 'I wanted to thank you, Charlotte, before you left. I won't keep you. I know you want to go and look for Marc Forestier.'

'If I can find him,' Charlotte faltered.

'You'll find him, Charlotte dear, because you love him.'

How simple and evident the truth sounded on the lips of this girl, speaking it out so baldly and unadorned, speaking it as only those who are in ignorance of all its concealing trappings can speak it.

'Yes,' Charlotte whispered. 'I do . . . I do love him.'

Smoke drifted across the battlefield like shreds of mist. Wrecked guns, reduced by unbelievable force to ghastly skeletons, pointed their muzzles skywards, their shattered wheels at drunken angles. Among the dead, men and horses, the wounded writhed and groaned, or crawled along as best they could. Here and there ambulance-parties moved among the grisly litter, picking up those who still had life in them and throwing them into the open carts with scant ceremony. Few of those badly hurt would survive, and everyone knew it.

Charlotte rode from one gun position to another, but her search proved fruitless. She recognised no one about her whom she could ask. Large numbers of Austrian prisoners were being brought in, their white coats obscured by mud, the faces of their officers marked by despair and incredulity, as if they could not comprehend the magnitude of the disaster which had overtaken them, almost at the moment when victory had seemed within their grasp. Casting about among all these sad sights on her own quest, Charlotte's eyes fell at last on the one sight she had prayed she would not see.

It was Kismet, riderless, and trailing broken reins, wandering unattended through all the remnants of carnage, his neck and flanks dark with sweat. Charlotte rode cautiously towards him, calling his name. At first he threw up his head and shied away. But then he stood docilely, as if he were tired, and allowed her to reach out slowly and take hold of one of the trailing reins. The saddle-cloth was stained dark too, and the empty saddle. With frozen, set features, Charlotte leaned across and wiped her hand across the pommel. She brought her tightly-clenched fist back and held it to her breast for a moment, before opening it out flat, and staring down at her palm, scarlet with blood.

CHAPTER
THIRTEEN

FOR A MOMENT blackness swept over her and she almost fainted, but then Charlotte quelled her panic resolutely, attempting to assimilate this new situation. Marc had been hit and unhorsed, so much, at least, was clear. Charlotte even knew, with a deep inner conviction, when. It had been when she had seen her vision of him by the barn, and felt the pain in her own heart. She was not superstitious: she did not believe in ghosts or in the supernatural. But there is a telepathy which draws us to those to whom we are bound by our deepest and strongest emotions. She shook herself, and tried to force her fevered brain to think rationally. If he were wounded—please God, it was not badly!—as the blood indicated he had been, then the field hospital was the place to go.

It was not difficult to find her way to this living hell. She was guided there by the screams of men whose limbs were being amputated already, ruthlessly and without anaesthetics, by surgeons who knew no other means of dealing with shattered bones or the danger of infection. No one went near such a place unless forced to. The soldiers feared and avoided it. It was one of the most dreaded of punishments to be sent to be an orderly in the field hospital for the day.

The injured men lay scattered in long lines on blood-stained straw, while the orderlies and surgeons moved methodically down the ranks like the priests of some primitive cannibalistic ritual. Charlotte, searching desperately for Marc, stumbled over the mutilated bodies, avoiding the outstretched hands which clutched at her skirts as their owners shrieked for aid. None of the surgeons had time to look up from their gruesome butchery to answer her questions. Speed, and speed alone, kept a man from dying beneath the knife. Charlotte was forced to seek alone. The more she searched, the more her desperation grew, and she began to lose hope of even finding news. Then she heard her name called, and saw, propped against a tree-stump, the sergeant, Gros, nursing a shattered right arm. She ran over, and fell on her knees beside him.

'Sergeant Gros!' she panted. 'What happened to you?'

'You're looking for the Captain?' His voice came laboured, and shot through with pain.

'Yes, I found his horse. Do you know where he is?'

'I saw him fall, mam'zelle.' The man fell silent, and closed his eyes against his own pain for a moment.

'Would you like some water?' Charlotte whispered. 'I'll go and find some.'

'No, bless you, mam'zelle. Brandy, more like . . .' He essayed a crooked grin. 'Our guns were all disabled. An Austrian shell landed clear among us, put the guns out of action, killed a score of brave fellows and smashed my arm here.'

'Captain Forestier, he was hit then, too?'

'Not then, mam'zelle. It was after that.' Gros shook his head, his voice now a hoarse croak. She hated to urge him to use his ebbing strength to speak to her, but she had to know, and Gros was determined to tell her, reaching out his good arm to grip her sleeve. 'It was a strange business, mam'zelle. I said to him, "Captain, the guns have gone and I've lost my arm. We'll do no more good here. If the French are to beat the Austrians this time, it will be without our help." "Can you get yourself to the hospital, Gros?" he asked me, and when I said I could, he looked about him in an odd sort of way, and said, "Well, *adieu* then, Gros . . . my battle is fought, too."' Gros drew a deep shuddering breath and fell silent.

'He said what?' Charlotte demanded, thinking she had misheard.

'You think it odd, mam'zelle? What he did next was a whole lot stranger. He mounted up that grey Arab horse of his, and rode straight out, looking neither right nor left, straight out under the Austrian guns. I'd say he'd taken leave of his senses, as I've seen men do under fire before, were the Captain that kind of a fellow. But he was used to flying lead and shot, and not one to lose his head in any circumstances. You could see by the deliberate way he did it, that he knew what he was doing, and meant it. I swear, mam'zelle, it was as if he wanted to die.'

Charlotte shook her head in horror. 'No,' she whispered, 'it's impossible. He wouldn't do that. He had no reason . . .' She bit her lip nervously. 'And—next, sergeant?'

'Next thing, boom goes an Austrian gun, and the edge of the blast took him, and threw him and the horse down together. The horse got up, but he didn't.' Gros moved and groaned. 'See here,' he gasped. 'If he was brought in, the orderlies will know. He was a well-known fellow, the Captain. Good officer . . . gunners lived in mortal fear of him—would have done anything for him, though . . .'

He closed his eyes again and Charlotte thought he had fainted, but then he opened them and called with a hoarse croak, 'Hi, you there, orderly! Lady wants you.'

The orderly stopped in passing and came over to them. He was a shambling fellow with a dirty bloodstained apron, and one empty eye-socket, whose disability had presumably gained him his unenviable job.

'Lady looks for Captain Forestier,' Gros croaked. 'Seen him, have you?'

The orderly rubbed his nose on the back of his hand, and stared at Charlotte with his one eye. 'Forestier? Artilleryman, isn't he? Big, tall, bad-tempered devil.'

'Yes, yes!' Charlotte cried. 'Is he here? Where is he? Please tell me!'

'That's the one,' the sergeant growled, 'and I'll thank you to speak of him with more respect. Devil he might be, but one of the best officers I've ever served under.'

The orderly shrugged. 'Was,' he said laconically. 'You'll have to find yourself someone new, *ma belle*. Your man is dead.'

Charlotte's lips formed the outline of the word 'dead', but no sound came through them.

'What d'you mean?' snarled Gros. 'Speak up, you lanky, one-eyed half-wit!'

'Dead, I tell you,' maintained the orderly stubbornly. 'He was brought in here for wounded. But when we took a look at him, there was no life in him. Looked like the cavalry had ridden over him. Terrible mess, he was in.'

'Where—Where is . . . Where . . .' Charlotte's voice stuttered and was silent.

'The body?' supplied the orderly helpfully. He pointed. 'Laid out with the rest, over there, and waiting for the burial-party. If you want to go and identify it, you'll have to be quick.' He turned his attention from her to the sergeant. 'And if you want the surgeon to take that arm off, sergeant, you'd better come with me. Can you walk?'

'Far enough,' said Gros, and struggled to his feet with the orderly's help and stood there, swaying.

Charlotte, struck by his stoical acceptance of the dreadful ordeal he was to undergo, and unable to do anything to help him, put her arms round his neck on an impulse and kissed his weathered cheek.

'Well, now,' he said with a grin, though his face was grey from pain and loss of blood. 'If I'd known you'd be here, *ma belle*. I'd have come here the happier.'

'I'm sorry, Sergeant Gros,' Charlotte whispered. 'Thank you for telling me about the Captain.'

'Bless you, my dear, I'm sorry, too. He was a good man.' Gros lurched away unsteadily, propelled by the ungentle hand of the shambling orderly.

The bodies of those who had died beneath the surgeon's knife, or for whom the field hospital's dubious care had come too late, lay in two long rows, ready for the burial-party to come and fetch them away. Charlotte made her way slowly down the near row, pausing at each artillery uniform, to see if this was the one she sought.

She was not alone in her sad quest. Other women, too, were engaged as she was, stooping over the lifeless forms, seeking a loved one. One or two had even found those they had lost, and sat by the still bodies, weeping softly.

There were others, too, less noble. A tawdry slut with greasy ringlets was crouched over one officer's body, her nimble fingers rapidly and efficiently removing any article of value from the pockets or about the person, and tucking them into her low-cut bodice. She worked furtively and in haste, glancing up regularly to see if anyone approached who would drive her off. As Charlotte drew near, she could see that this human vulture was attempting to wrest a ring from the corpse's finger. Finding it stuck fast, the loathsome creature put the dead finger to her lips to suck off the ring.

Charlotte, appalled and sickened, snatched up a stone and flung it at the girl as she would have done at a carrion crow. It struck the thief on the arm, and she swore violently, dropping the dead hand, and scrambled to her feet.

'Get out of here!' Charlotte ordered, advancing on her with fury in her eyes. 'You despicable wretch, get away, do you hear? Or I'll see you are shot for your foul thievery!'

The girl glowered at Charlotte, but said nothing and slipped away, no doubt to resume her grisly business elsewhere on the field.

Charlotte wiped her trembling hand across her forehead and continued on down the line, turning at the end of it to work her way down the other row. She had not to go far. The body she sought lay at the beginning of the second row, sprawled face upwards on the earth where it had been thrown down. The eyes were closed, and the long black hair was spread across the face in curling tendrils like a mourning veil.

Charlotte sank down beside him, and gently lifted his head onto her knees. Now that she had found him, it was all over. The last faint hope that the report of his death had been a ghastly mistake was eliminated. It was too late now to speak of love and build a bridge of tenderness across the chasm which had divided them. Nothing now remained for her but to sit here, watching over him, until the burial-party came, to ensure that no one robbed this body, at least.

Don't marry a soldier, we're a shiftless lot, short-lived, too . . . His voice came echoing into her head, uttering an unconscious prophecy. Or had it been unconscious? Had he really sought death out there on the battlefield? If so, why?

Charlotte's fingers smoothed the hair back from the familiar features. A hard man, and one feared by many. Yet many had loved him too, in their own way, despite it all. Baptistin the groom, in his loyalty, Cresson and Lucien, his friends, Babette and her husband, the sergeant, Gros, and the gunners who had feared him, but 'would have done anything for him' . . .

'Perhaps they know me better than you do, and are less afraid of me than you think,' he had said to her an age ago, it seemed now.

Had she never really known him at all? She had never tried to know him, to understand. If he had treated her callously, perhaps it had not been his fault. Growing up in a childhood world lacking normal family affections, emerging scarred from the ruins of a failed and brief marriage after a horrifying imprisonment under the shadow of the guillotine, little wonder that he had built a wall about his own emotions, refusing to be swayed by sentiment or tenderness, even to admit such feelings could exist within him. She had met him at a time when such feelings had long been crushed in him, or so it had appeared. Only at the very last moment, yesterday, when he had carried her in his arms back to her tent, had some flicker of human pity stirred in him, a brief flame, kindled too late to burn and flourish.

Charlotte bowed her head and gently kissed his forehead. His skin was quite warm. She had thought, somehow, that he would be cold. But she did not know how long it took for a body, slain in the heat of battle, to grow cold and stiffen. Yet it seemed impossible that where there was warmth, there could be no life.

Her face close to his, she studied his features. Increasingly, it was impossible to believe he did anything but sleep. Then, very faintly, she discerned, or thought she did, a tiny movement beneath the black hair across his temple, as if—as if a pulse still throbbed, somewhere, in this apparently lifeless corpse. Her heart leapt into her mouth. Could it be? She pushed back the hair with trembling fingers. It was her imagination, perhaps, wanting so much for him to be alive, refusing to accept his death. And yet—there it was again!

There must be some way, Charlotte thought feverishly, there must be some test. Her shaking fingers tugged at the buttons of his coat, and she pushed her hand beneath his shirt, feeling for a heartbeat, but in vain. Her spirits sank again. Then she remembered that when her father had died, the doctor, before pronouncing him dead, had held a pocket mirror to his nostrils. 'If it mists, there is breath,' he had told her. Charlotte had no mirror, but she still wore round her neck the smoothly enamelled pendant Marc had bought her in Milan.

Her fingers clammy with perspiration, she fumbled at the clasp, dragging it undone. Carefully, making sure she did not touch the surface, she held the glass-like enamel close to his nose. How long did one wait? She had no idea. She waited until she could bear the delay no longer and then held up the pendant so that the evening sun struck its surface. A faint dampness clouded it. He breathed! He was *alive*!

Charlotte lifted his head from her lap and scrambled wildly to her feet. She had to inform someone, fetch help to get him away from this place of death. While she had been occupied with Marc, she had failed to hear the creak of wagon-wheels and observe the approach of a burial-party. The men were at the far end of the other row, lifting the bodies with little respect and tossing them like rag effigies onto the cart.

'No, no, wait . . .' Charlotte whispered in terror. Her frantic gaze, looking wildly for help, fell at that moment on a familiar form, approaching slowly. She seized her skirts and ran towards him, stumbling over the rough terrain, sobbing for breath, her heart pounding agonisingly, as if it would burst.

'Monsieur Cresson! Jean-Luc! Come quickly!'

He caught her in his arms as she ran up to him. 'Hold up, my dear. Calm yourself, now.' His voice rang reassuringly above her head.

'Oh, Jean-Luc! Marc is there . . .' Her voice choked in panic.

'I know, my dear, I know,' he said quietly. 'I was just coming to look for him myself, and pay my last respects. I saw him fall. God alone knows what he was doing out there by the Austrian lines.

'But you don't understand, Jean-Luc, he isn't *dead*!' she cried, tugging at his sleeve.

Cresson's honest, plump face was twisted in compassion. 'You have to accept it, my dear. I know it's hard. But the horse went down on top of him, and as if that wasn't enough, just after that, Kellermann's Hussars made their charge which broke the Austrian ranks and gave us victory. They galloped right over that spot.'

'But he's breathing, I tell you, Jean-Luc! Why don't you come and look? But, hurry! Oh, please hurry! They are already taking the bodies for burial. Jean-Luc, they'll bury him. They'll bury him *alive*! You know it's happened before, to others. Don't let it happen to him!'

'All right, my dear, calm yourself. Where is he?' Cresson said soothingly, patting her hand.

Charlotte turned to point, and froze in that attitude.

The burial-party had cleared the first row and started on the second. As she watched, horrified, a soldier stooped and seized hold of Marc's ankles to drag the body to the cart. She screamed. The sound pierced the air with such force and agony that it reached the burial-party, and the man holding Marc's feet dropped them and looked up, startled.

Cresson uttered a lurid oath, and drawing his sword with a rasp of steel, ran like the wind towards the scene, yelling and brandishing the naked blade with such ferocity that the burial-party scattered before him faster than they had done earlier in action against the advancing Austrians. He arrived panting, and sheathed his sword. Then he dropped on his knees by Marc's still form and gently prised open the closed eyelids before he pressed his ear to Marc's chest.

Charlotte stumbled up, and placing herself squarely between the kneeling Cresson and the soldiers, put out her hand and said with concentrated fury, 'No! You don't touch him, you don't lay one finger on that body, do you hear?'

The men glanced at one another, but made no answer.

Behind her, Cresson muttered something, then he scrambled to his feet, and rounding on the burial-party, roared, 'Confound you! Can't you tell a live man from a dead one? This officer lives!' The man who had been about to drag Marc away blanched, and wiped his hand across his mouth.

'Now, listen, my dear,' said Cresson firmly. 'He's alive, but only just. He's in a bad way, and may be dying, do you understand that?'

'Yes, I understand.'

'So we'll get him away from here, but don't build up your hopes too high. It's best I tell you this now, *ma petite.*'

'I do understand,' Charlotte repeated impatiently. 'But I won't let you take him back into that awful field hospital. It's little more than a charnel-house. They pronounced him dead there!'

'I agree. It's better we take him away ourselves, and fetch one of the physicians to look at him. Those surgeons are the dregs of their profession, half of them drunkards. A proper physician is what's needed.' He turned to the men who stood watching and waiting. 'Right, living before the dead! Two of you, lift the Captain, and *gently*!'

They carried him back on a blanket. Either the jolting motion of being carried over the rough ground, or the pain caused by this process, had the effect of rousing him slightly from his unconsciousness, and as they put him down, he moaned.

'I never thought that I'd been pleased to hear a man groan in pain,' Cresson said with relief.

'He's coming round,' Charlotte exclaimed. 'He is, Jean-Luc! Look!'

Before their anxious gaze, Marc's eyelids fluttered and his eyes opened slowly. They stared up, at first unseeingly, and then focused, despite being clouded with pain, on Charlotte's face, bent over him. His lips moved, and he muttered, 'Charlotte . . . ?' so faintly that it could scarcely be heard.

'Go and get the physician, Jean-Luc. Promise him anything, if only he'll come at once.'

Cresson touched her arm. 'He's trying to say something else.'

'Marc, you mustn't,' Charlotte put her hand on his forehead. 'Be quiet, my darling. Cresson is going for the physician.'

The injured man's face twitched in a spasm of pain, and his lips moved again.

'Better let him speak,' said honest Cresson in his well-meaning and tactless way. 'They may be his last w—' He broke off, and muttered, 'Sorry! I'll go for the doctor immediately.'

He scrambled out of the tent, and Charlotte bent her head so that her ear was close to Marc's lips. 'What is it you want to say?'

His breath brushed her ear, and his voice came as an

agonised whisper, halting and almost inaudible, every syllable suffused with pain.

'I . . . told you . . . to leave . . .' He drew a dragging, pain-wracked breath. 'Why can you . . . never do . . . anything . . . I ask . . . ?'

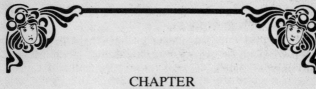

CHAPTER
FOURTEEN

THE PHYSICIAN emerged from the tent, and straightened up. He was a middle-aged man of respectable appearance. What, Charlotte wondered briefly, had brought him into army service? She watched him take off his spectacles and clean them carefully with his handkerchief. Then he set them tidily on his nose and surveyed her, and Cresson beside her, through them.

'Madame Forestier?' he enquired politely, inclining slightly in her direction.

'Never mind that,' said Cresson quickly, before she could reply. '*Allez*, doctor, you're not here to be sociable. Give us your opinion on your patient.'

The physician cleared his throat. 'My opinion is,' he said in a precise way, 'that a horse has rolled on him. To be exact, he has a broken collar-bone, a broken wrist, and broken ribs on both sides of the rib-cage. Whether there are internal injuries I have been unable to ascertain. Time will tell. He has also received a severe blow to the cranium, occasioned, no doubt, when he was brought down and struck the ground. Most skulls would have been fractured by it. Your husband, however, Madame Forestier, and I trust you will not be offended when I say this, has an extraordinarily hard head. From a medical viewpoint, of great interest.'

Cresson hissed with impatience, and Charlotte asked doubtfully, 'But the blood?'

'Ah, that, madame, stems largely from a wound in the thigh caused by a piece of flying metal. Although it has bled profusely, it is but a flesh wound, and as the metal fragment was still imbedded yet easily accessible, I took the liberty of removing it, although *I*, of course,' he added sternly, 'am not a *surgeon*!'

Disapproval echoed in his voice at the mention of this despised profession. He inserted his finger and thumb in his waistcoat pocket, and removed a lump of ragged metal the size of a plum-stone, which he dropped neatly into Charlotte's palm.

'There are, of course, extensive lacerations and bruises, both internal and external, to all areas of the body, caused possibly by kicks from horses' hoofs. Your husband was ridden down by cavalry, I understand?'

'Yes,' Charlotte said quietly.

'Then he is fortunate to be alive.'

'At the field hospital, he was said to be dead!' Charlotte remarked with some asperity.

'By a *surgeon*, no doubt, madame. It is wise to seek proper medical advice at such times. Although I have known cases where sudden heavy blows have induced a state of, let us say, suspended animation, often mistaken for death.'

'About his being ridden over by Kellermann's Hussars,' Cresson said, frowning. 'The only explanation for his survival I can think of is that a horse is a good-natured beast, and won't trample on a man if he can avoid him. He'll spring over him, or run round. Either that, or there were other fallen men in the vicinity, and their bodies served to shield Forestier.'

'It is possible,' the doctor said. 'I have known several other cases of men being ridden over and yet surviving to tell the tale. Well, madame, I must bid you goodbye. I am needed elsewhere, and there is nothing more I can do for your husband. Time and good nursing will save him—or not, as the case may be.'

He departed on this philosophical note, striding briskly away.

Though it was not possible to remove Marc at once, the eventual departure of the French forces and the lack of suitable medical skills—should these be needed—and accommodation in the area, together with the prospect of a lengthy convalescence, necessitated some longer term solution. Charlotte consulted with the indispensable Cresson, and it was decided after much discussion to take the injured man back to Milan. They travelled in stages in a hired coach, fitted out with mattresses to be a kind of ambulance. It was none the less a painful and difficult journey for the patient, but at last they found themselves back in Milan and established once more in the two first-floor rooms of the grain merchant.

The merchant and his family received them with great kindness, and sympathy. The two pretty daughters were in the greatest distress, lamenting loudly in their broken French and weeping quantities of tears over *le pauvre capitaine*. Not only did his two devoted admirers continually bombard the sickroom with flowers and fruit, but they also sent up so many religious medallions, little notes in appalling French, in which they expressed both their grief and promises to intercede with every saint in the calendar on his behalf, and ribbons of startling hue, woven into intricate loveknots, that Charlotte soon had a whole box of these mementoes. All this would no doubt have been very gratifying for Marc, had he been in a condition to appreciate it.

Charlotte was most struck, however, by the change in the attitude of the merchant's wife towards her. There was no sign now of the former suspicion and disapproval. Though the language-barrier made much conversation impossible, the woman's kindliness was evident and genuine. Charlotte was very grateful for all of this, for Cresson had to leave them almost immediately.

'You know, my dear,' he said with regret in his voice, 'the last thing I want to do is to abandon you here. I'd stay if I could, but the army has first call on me, and alas, I can't.'

'I know it.' She squeezed his hand. 'Bless you, Jean-Luc, and thank you for all you've done for us.'

He chewed his moustache unhappily. 'If you want to

go back to France, Charlotte, I'll be happy to escort you. Say the word.'

'Thank you again, but no. I must stay here with Marc. I won't leave him.'

He heaved a sigh. 'Well, I didn't expect to hear you say you would. He's in a bad way, there's no denying. But he's strong, and obstinate. He'll fight. Besides,' Cresson smiled. 'Forestier never did anything in his life to oblige anyone, and he won't start now by descending meekly to Hades without an argument.'

'I'm glad of it!'

'He'll get the best care, anyway,' Cresson said. 'I know that.' He hesitated. 'If, despite that, he should . . . If things should not go well . . .'

'If he dies,' Charlotte said evenly.

'Well, yes, my dear, it has to be said. If so, it will be up to you to inform the appropriate authorities. The army will want some kind of signed certificate of death, just to prove he's not simply deserted, eh?' Cresson smiled kindly at her.

'I understand, Jean-Luc. I'll see everything necessary is done. Is—Is there anyone in France to whom I should send his personal effects?' It was hard, but necessary, to talk like this. Charlotte heard her voice tremble.

'No. No family. You are all he has . . .' He glanced at her shrewdly. 'But you know that, don't you?'

'Perhaps,' she said a little dully. 'Though perhaps he would as soon be without me.'

Cresson scratched his nose in embarrassment. '*Should* you find yourself alone, Charlotte, you know I have the greatest admiration for you. You won't forget that I am your friend, and wherever I may be, you have but to seek me out and I shall do everything and anything in my power to help. I would consider it an honour.'

'Why, thank you, Jean-Luc,' she said, touched. 'I shan't forget.'

He cleared his throat awkwardly. 'Not that he's going to die or to abandon you,' he went on in his usual endearingly tactless manner, adding bluntly, 'But one thing I can promise you. He'll be a difficult invalid!'

Cresson probably never spoke a truer word. The invalid was not merely difficult. He was bad-tempered, ungracious and ungrateful, free in his language, and well-nigh impossible in every respect. Towards Charlotte he was cold, curt and frequently unkind, so that on several occasions she only just managed to leave the room before bursting into tears.

She had the help of Baptistin in caring for him. The groom had relinquished the care of all the horses to Pascal, and moved into the house in the capacity of manservant, to aid his disabled master. However discourteous Marc might be to Charlotte, his treatment of Baptistin was even more ungrateful. He grumbled at, criticised and cursed him at every turn. Despite this, she gained a little wry amusement, among all her worries, in observing that Baptistin had developed a method of his own for dealing with his master's moods. The complaints and abuse flowed unheeded over his head, and the boy would affect a sudden temporary deafness when ordered to do something he felt unsuitable for the invalid, which no amount of shouting could penetrate. Charlotte only wished she could adopt a similar attitude, but for her it was impossible. Every unkind word and impatient gesture cut like a knife, and she could only admire Baptistin's dogged devotion to his master, which never wavered, even on the worst of days. She was eventually moved to remark on it to him.

Baptistin looked surprised and pained. 'The Captain was always a good master, mam'zelle. If he's in a temper, you know about it, of course. But he's not one to go for a man without cause. It's always because he's worried over something, see? Like *now*—There's something eating at him, something on his mind.'

'You think he's in more pain than he admits, Baptistin?' she asked, concerned at this possibility.

He shrugged. 'Perhaps. But I reckon it's something

else. Something preys on him, and won't let him rest. It's in his mind, night and day. But otherwise, mam'zelle, he's the best I've ever worked for. He'd never come and take it out on a groom, just because he's held a bad hand of cards the night before—unlike many! He's always paid my wages regular—also unlike many. Excepting, of course, when he's got no money, and then he'll say, 'You'll have to wait, Baptistin.' And I always say, 'That's fine, m'sieu,' because I know it is, and he'll pay me when he can. He's not too much of a gambling man, but if he has a good win, he's always shared some of his fortune with me, and when I took the fever last year, he fetched and paid the doctor. He's a good man, see?'

'Yes, I see,' Charlotte said quietly.

She much missed Babette in all this time, for she had been obliged to take a tearful farewell of the maid, who remained with the army and her husband.

To make matters worse, Milan simmered in a sultry, sticky heat, detrimental to both the patient and those who cared for him. With the summer heat came summer fevers. Despite all precautions, Marc, in his weakened condition, fell sick, and Charlotte sat up night after night by his pillow, bathing his forehead and struggling to help him change his linen, wringing wet with perspiration. Any lingering prudery she might have entertained concerning male nakedness was quickly dismissed. There was just no time for that.

Several times, in his delirium, he called out her name, and she hastened to the bedside, to find him tossing restlessly. Although he was apparently unaware of her presence, she found that if she took his hand, it seemed to quieten him, and she sat for long periods by the bed, heedless of the risk of contagion, holding his hand and watching him.

By the end of August she was almost exhausted. The two daughters had been sent into the country to avoid the risk of taking the fever that was in the house, but the grain merchant remained, together with his wife. When she met Charlotte on the stairs, she took her hand and smoothed her pale cheek, and made long, incomprehensible speeches, the import of which obviously was that Charlotte should rest, or she too would fall sick. But there was no time for that, either. Marc occupied her twenty-four hours out of the twenty-four, and there was no time for herself.

But one afternoon she was seated by the bed, sponging his forehead to cool him, when he suddenly opened his eyes and put up a hand to push her away from him weakly. 'Go away . . .' he muttered. 'Get away from me—You'll take the sickness . . .'

It was the first sign of lucidity in many days. He fell into a restless slumber afterwards, and Charlotte dared at last to leave him and go and take a badly-needed nap herself. When she returned about an hour later, she sensed, as soon as she opened the bedroom door, that some change had taken place. He lay quite still in the bed, no sign of his previous restless tossing and turning, lying half on his face, one arm flung up across the pillow.

'No . . .' she whispered. 'Not *now*, not after so much . . .'

She hastened to the bed and leaned over him. He looked pale and very peaceful. She touched his forehead. It was warm, but not hot and sticky as it had been. He slept—he slept normally! The fever had broken. Charlotte sank down on the floor by the bed, and sobbed.

So the fever subsided and the broken bones mended, and Marc emerged from his sickroom, paler and thinner, but as abrasive as ever. His one aim now was to return to France, and although Charlotte begged him to delay until he was fully recovered, any suggestion that he should linger was bluntly rejected in his habitual impatient fashion.

'I'm a soldier, woman, not some aristocratic idler making the Italian tour. The army will write me off if I don't get back. I'll find myself struck off the list of commissions again, so I'll have no job. I could even get

arrested again. Besides, what about money? I haven't
drawn my pay in weeks.'

The arrangements were made, therefore, and they
prepared to depart. It had been an especially hot and
thundery day. That night Charlotte tossed on the sofa-
bed in the sitting-room, for Marc still slept in the four-
poster in the other room to which he had been brought
injured. Her hair was damp and sticky, and the bed hot
and uncomfortable. She pushed one foot out from under
the sheet to let it cool a little, and allowed her mind to
run on their proposed return to France.

It was not the thought of the journey which depressed
her. It was the thought of what would happen when they
arrived. Marc would go back to the army—and she? She
would have nothing to do but to go back to Châlons, to a
lonely and loveless existence.

From the other room came the sound of the bed
creaking, as Marc tossed equally sleeplessly. He stubbornly maintained that he was quite fit, but she was
doubtful. She could hear him muttering to himself. It
was possible that all the business of arranging their
departure had overtaxed him. She hoped he was not
suffering a recurrence of the fever. Automatically
reacting as the weeks of nursing him had trained her,
Charlotte swung her legs out of bed, and fumbling for
the candle and tinderbox in the darkness, managed at
length to strike a light. She took the flickering candle in
one hand and made her way to the connecting door
between the rooms. Pushing it open, she whispered,
'Marc?'

'What is it?' his voice said brusquely in the darkness.

She carried the candle across and set it down on the
table by the bed. The yellow glow illuminated the pillows and his face. She sat down on the edge of the bed.
Beyond the area of candle-light, the room was in a velvet
blackness, wrapping them in a cloak of intimacy.

'I heard you moving. Are you sick?'

'No,' he said irritably. 'I'm perfectly all right.'

Charlotte sighed at yet another rebuff. She had come

to expect it, but it always hurt, every time. Every harsh word was a blow to the heart.

Unexpectedly he said, in a more kindly tone than he had used in weeks, 'But you are not. You're tired. You've worn yourself out looking after me. You should have left more to Baptistin, and taken more rest yourself.'

She was so astonished at this first expressed acknowledgment of any of her devoted care that she was bereft of words.

'I'm a bad invalid,' he said wryly. 'I haven't been an easy patient.'

A heroic lie rose to Charlotte's lips, but then she thought resentfully, 'Why should *I* pretend? He doesn't.'

'Yes,' she said firmly. 'You are a dreadful patient—rude, ungrateful, unco-operative and thoroughly disagreeable.'

'So why have you stayed with me?' he demanded coolly.

Charlotte stared at him. In the flickering light, his eyes were as blue and fathomless as a mountain lake. It was impossible to read what lay in those depths. What should she say to him? *Because I love you?* How could she say those words? They would mean nothing to him. He had no time for her kind of love, a tender emotion which had no place in the world of hard reality and fleeting pleasures which he inhabited.

When she remained silent, he went on in a voice suddenly brusque again, 'Why didn't you get yourself back to France? It wouldn't have been so difficult. Cresson would have taken you.' He sounded almost resentful.

'I wouldn't have left you!' she cried, stung by this curt dismissal of her loyalty. 'Not when you were so ill.'

'Then you were a fool!' he burst out fiercely. 'An injured man is nothing but trouble to those who are obliged to care for him. A disabled man—and I might well have been left a cripple—is of no use or interest to the army, and of damn little use to anyone else!' Suddenly he pushed himself up in the bed and seized her arm. 'Sometimes a man is better dead, don't you understand me? And you should have left me for dead, there, at Marengo, Charlotte!' The words spilled out of him now in a kind of suppressed fury. 'You had no reason to come looking for me!'

'No *reason*?' Charlotte cried incredulously. 'They would have buried you alive. Would you have preferred me to leave you to suffocate in a heap of corpses?' She flung the words at him in angry retaliation, for it was as if he accused her of having done something wrong.

Marc shrugged and released her. 'I was going to say you did me no favour, but of course that wouldn't be true. Yes, I'm grateful. No man can contemplate being buried alive with equanimity, even if he knew nothing of it at the time. Cresson said you screeched like a Fury when they came to bury me, and would have fought them off with your bare hands.' He stared at her challengingly, as if he expected her to deny it.

'It was horrible,' Charlotte looked down at the bed, avoiding his eyes. 'I dream of it still.' She picked nervously at the sheet, until in an unexpected movement he stretched out his hand, laying it over hers, stilling the actions of her fingers. She shivered at his touch. It sent the blood pounding in her veins, echoing old memories and half-realised desires.

'I'm well aware I should have died afterwards, but for you.' He added, almost casually, 'Thank you.'

Every emotion Charlotte felt then—love, anger, longing, bitterness and despair—all bubbled up and burst forth in a torrent of words. 'Keep your thanks! I don't want gratitude! For pity's sake, for what kind of a person do you take me that you can even suggest I would have left you there on the battlefield?' She snatched her hand free from his.

'Most women I've ever met would have done so!'

'Then I am not one of what you would call "most women"!' she stormed at him.

'So, what led *you* to behave so differently?'

'What makes me act differently'—Charlotte shouted, before she could stop herself—'What is different is that I *care* for you! And if you mean to ask me *why* I do, then I can tell you straight away that I don't know, because *you* are only able to hurt anyone who comes near you! At times like this, I swear I wish I hated you, but I can't help caring, no matter how badly you behave!'

'Yes, I've made you weep,' Marc said quietly. 'I've heard you, these last nights and sometimes during the day, in the other room. I wanted—I wanted to call out to you, but I . . .' His voice stumbled and faltered. He leaned towards her, and the wall he had so tenaciously maintained about his feelings crumbled at last. His face was quite changed, the blue eyes glowing with passion and inner agony in the frame of long black hair that fell about his face in wild disorder. 'I couldn't, Charlotte, not because I didn't want to, but because I was afraid you wouldn't answer me . . .'

'I always came when you called!'

'No, you don't understand!' he interrupted her vehemently. 'I didn't want plumped pillows and glasses of water, I wanted *you*! I don't want or need anything else. It wasn't just that I wanted to say "don't cry"—it was that I wanted to say "I love you", because I do love you, Charlotte, but I didn't know how to say it, or how I could make you believe it after all I'd said and done to you.'

For a moment, Charlotte stared into his face quite wildly, hardly able to accept that the words she had longed so much to hear had actually been spoken. It even flashed briefly into her mind that the fever had returned, and he did not know what he said.

He saw the incredulity on her face, and an odd, bitter little smile crossed his. 'You do not believe me now,' he said, and there was a great sadness in his voice. 'Yet I began to love you at the very beginning, when you first walked into that wretched inn in Villeneuve. I couldn't tell you about Saint-Laurent, Charlotte. You had such faith in him, and I thought, wrongly, that you'd go back anyway, once you saw how difficult and dangerous a journey it would be. I didn't know you well enough then. I didn't know that you would go on and never give up. Later, by the time I realised it, it was too late. I was head over heels in love with you, and there was not a thing I could do about it. I couldn't tell you how much you meant to me. I thought you loved Saint-Laurent, and only despised me. I charged about in a blind, frustrated rage, like a wild boar trapped in a hunter's pit, wanting to destroy his prison, and destroying only himself.

'There were moments when I contemplated telling you about Saint-Laurent's marriage, even at that late stage, so that you would have gone back, and I would have been free of you, and free of all my torment. But I didn't want to be free of you. I wanted to see you, and talk to you, and watch you go about the camp. It wasn't a satisfactory arrangement, but it was all I could hope for, and if I could make it last another day by not telling you the truth, then that's what I did. It was cruel and selfish, and I'm sorry. I knew what would happen when you met him. Forgive me, Charlotte, I let that happen to you for my own selfish reasons,' he finished quietly.

'Don't blame yourself, Marc, I had to find out about him sooner or later,' she said gently. 'It could never have been a pleasant experience, however it came about. Perhaps I was selfish, too, thinking only about myself and my search, never asking why you let me stay, or thinking of you at all.'

'Why should you? You couldn't know how I felt.'

'Babette knew,' she murmured, remembering. 'She tried to tell me, over and over again. I just wouldn't listen. She understood me so much better than I understood myself.'

'Yes,' he agreed. 'Babette's a clever woman. She knew. She saw it in my face. I could hide it before you, but I let the mask slip before her. She knew all along.'

'But I do love you, Marc,' Charlotte whispered. 'I was so foolish, and so blind. You tried to die because of me, out there on the battlefield, but if you had died there, at Marengo, I should have died too.'

'Then let me show you that I love you,' Marc said softly. 'Show you in my way—perhaps the only way I know . . .'

Charlotte swallowed with difficulty. There seemed to be a great lump in her throat, and in her breast her heart began to throb painfully. It could only have been a matter of seconds, yet it seemed that an age went by before she slowly rose to her feet and drew back the sheet and slid, shivering with tension, into the warm bed beside him. She put out a trembling hand to extinguish the candle on the table, but he leaned across her and caught at her wrist.

'Leave it . . .' he said. 'There's no need to hide in the darkness, unless you are ashamed, or afraid . . . Are you afraid?' He spoke very quickly, as if he understood the tumult within her, sensing it from the rigidity of her body pressed against his.

'No, I'm not afraid,' she whispered.

He smiled, and firmly, but not ungently, pushed her back on the crumpled pillows. Charlotte felt much of the tension leave her and her muscles start to relax, though her body tingled with a different kind of awareness and expectation. Marc cupped his fingers around her face, and lowering his head, crushed her mouth in a long, lingering embrace during which his hand slid, at first lightly and then with increasing pressure, across her bosom and down the length of her body. She gave a little moan and felt herself respond, twisting her own arms round his neck and drawing him down onto her, wanting only to be as one with him.

If she had imagined this moment—and in all truth, she had done so often, lying awake at night on the sofa in the other room—then she had imagined it differently. It was not as she had played it over in her dreams, but something more, new and totally different. He led her into a world which was unknown and unexplored, full of revelations both wondrous and frightening, in which desires were aroused and needs were answered.

She had been afraid, perhaps, that he would be rough and hurt her. But her fears had been groundless, for he was very gentle and even, to her surprise, patient, not hurrying her, but waiting until he knew she was ready, helping her to understand her own body and its wants. There was one moment only, towards the end, when it seemed as if some force, more powerful than he, took possession of him. His grip about her grew more possessive, and he breathed awkwardly and heavily, murmuring words and broken phrases in her ear, which she was at a loss to follow.

But when it was over, and she lay in his arms, she knew that with no one but with Marc could it have been like this, that no one else could have made her feel as she did. Whether it was simple reaction, relief or fulfilment, or just because she felt so different, she did not know, but despite her best efforts, Charlotte could not prevent hot tears rolling silently down her face, and she turned and buried her head in the pillow, praying he would not see.

But he knew at once. 'Charlotte, did I hurt you?' she heard him whisper anxiously. His hand stroked the back of her head tenderly. 'I'm sorry . . .'

'No!' she muttered indistinctly from the pillows. 'You didn't—you didn't. I don't mean to weep. It's nothing. I'm *happy* . . .' She turned and pressed her face against his chest. 'I'm all right now, truly . . .'

'Yet, for all I love you so much, I did hurt you once, Charlotte, and in this very room,' he said wretchedly. 'God knows what came over me that night. I truly didn't intend to do it. It was a kind of madness. I couldn't stop myself. When you pointed that pistol at me, it brought me to my senses. The wretched thing wasn't loaded. You couldn't have killed me, only hit me over the head with it, perhaps! But that didn't matter. It made me realise, with a shock I couldn't describe to you, that I had actually been about to force you. I wanted you badly enough, but I wanted to take you in love, and not in fear and pain. I was horrified at what I'd been about to do.'

'Hush . . .' She stretched out her hand and put her fingers over his lips. 'It's all right. It doesn't matter now. Babette said it was a mistake to rake over the ashes of old quarrels. She was right about that, too.'

Marc caught at her hand and kissed the fingers which had touched his lips, then rolled over onto his back, one arm folded under his head. 'You know,' he said, looking up at the ceiling, 'When I left here that night, I was ready to go and put a bullet in my own brain. I might have done it, had I not fallen in with Cresson instead. He took one look at my face, and after that, stuck with me like a shadow all evening. He took me off to some place, as I told you at the time, with the idea, I suppose, of distracting me. It had quite the opposite effect. There were some girls there . . . It was the last thing I wanted. One of them kept coming and trying to put her arms round my neck. Cresson knew by then that I'd come from you, and he could see something was wrong, and that I didn't want that girl or any other woman. He kept trying to shoo her away. In the end he stood over me like a guard dog and swore at the girl, and told her to go and ply her custom somewhere else.'

'Jean-Luc is a good friend,' Charlotte said slowly.

'Yes, the best.' He glanced at her, and mischief suddenly gleamed in the blue eyes. 'And has always had a *tendresse* for you, you know.'

She had the grace to look confused, and muttered, 'He was very kind.'

'Offer to take you on, did he?' Marc asked pertinently, in his old disconcerting fashion.

'Not quite. Something like that,' she admitted. 'But very nicely.'

'Perhaps you should have accepted him. He's an honest fellow, and he'd have married you.'

'I wouldn't marry someone I didn't love,' Charlotte said quietly into the dusky blackness beyond the now guttering candle-light.

'And me?' Marc asked her, taking her chin and turning her face towards his. 'Would you marry me?'

'I don't think you want marriage, Marc,' she said softly, not knowing if he teased her or not.

'You're wrong.' His voice was very sober. 'I want everyone to know you're mine. I don't want to hide you away in discreet apartments, or tuck you away in the background. I want you to have *my* name . . . to be able to take you by the hand and say to anyone, *This is Charlotte, my wife* . . .'

'I always misjudged you,' she said softly, taking his hand and resting her cheek against it, unable to say more.

'Did you think that it didn't hurt *me* to see how those women looked at you, that evening, here in this house? I would have been so proud to have been able to bring you down to dinner with a ring on your finger *I* had placed there. I really hated poor Saint-Laurent that night. Had he walked in then, I think I should have killed him for all he had done to you.'

She understood then how much he must have suffered in all those weeks when he had loved her, and she had spoken of nothing but Lucien, obliging him to listen to her sing the praises of a man he knew to be unworthy of her, until he could bear it no longer, that evening here in Milan. He had hidden his love, and stifled it, and it had gnawed at him, increasing his bitterness and frustration until he had wanted to do nothing but hurt her, and in doing so, had hurt only himself.

As for her, betrayed by Lucien, she had vented on Marc her grief, her disappointment, disillusion and spite, little suspecting the effect of her words, and the dreadful decision to which they drove him.

'I'm sorry, Marc,' she whispered now, brokenly. 'I didn't understand. Forgive me, my dearest.'

He sighed. 'After Mireille died, I swore I'd never again ask any woman to share my life. I had no right to make another woman suffer in the way that Mireille had suffered with me, to destroy another being as I had destroyed her. I shall never want anyone but you, Charlotte, but a life with me is a life with the regiment. I can't change that. I know no other trade.'

'I know, but it doesn't matter.' Charlotte smiled at him, knowing that whatever the future held for them both, and wherever their wanderings would take them, it was right that they should be together. For a moment she seemed to hear again in her ears the clamour of battle, the neighing of horses, the thud of hoofs and crash of cannon. There was a Destiny in life which led them, blindfolded on hidden paths, until it drew aside the veil to reveal what was intended all along, that she and Marc should find one another, and tread together whatever path lay ahead.

She touched his shoulder. 'I want only you.'

Anne Mather's 100th Romance marks the sale of 100 million of her novels worldwide.

It's a special occasion. And to mark it, here's a special anniversary edition – Stolen Summer, a gripping love story. Beautifully presented, Stolen Summer costs just £1.25 and is published on 12th July.

Mills & Boon

The Rose of Romance

Mills & Boon
COMPETITION

How would you like a year's supply of Mills & Boon Romances ABSOLUTELY FREE?

Well, you can win them!

All you have to do is complete the word puzzle below and send it into us by 31st August 1985. The first five correct entries picked out of the bag after that date will each win a year's supply of Mills & Boon Romances (Ten books every month— worth over £100!). What could be easier?

```
M R E T T E L T W I N M
B I T T E R O O R E H A
N C L H A Y V N E E R R
O I G L R S E E E S O R
S T U O S E S S I K D I
O O H Q F A E R T A O A
R X M T E C N S Y N A G
E E N R N L U D A C I E
A F F A I R R M B R P E
L O M E T E O A L O G W
M O E H A W I S H A O E
R L N M D E S I R E S N
```

Mills and Boon   Letter   Envy   Hug
Harlequin   Love   Rage   Men
Romance   Rose   Exotic   Hero
Tears   Wish   Girls   Heart
Bitter   Hope   Vow   Win
Daydream   Trust   Woman   Desires
Affair   Kisses   Eros   Realm
Marriage   Fool   Woe

PLEASE TURN
OVER FOR
DETAILS
ON HOW
TO ENTER

How to enter

All the words listed overleaf, below the word puzzle, are hidden in the grid. You can find them by reading the letters forwards, backwards, up or down, or diagonally. When you find a word, circle it, or put a line through it. After you have found all the words, the left-over letters will spell a secret message that you can read from left to right, from the top of the puzzle through to the bottom.

Don't forget to fill in your name and address in the space provided and pop this page in an envelope (you don't need a stamp) and post it today. Hurry — competition ends 31st August 1985.

Mills & Boon Competition,
FREEPOST,
P.O. Box 236,
Croydon,
Surrey CR9 9EL.

Secret message ——————————————————

Name ————————————————————————

Address ————————————————————————

————————————————————————————

————————————————————————————

—————————————————— Postcode ————

COMP 1